miracle
visitors

COLLECTORS' EDITION
SF
GOLLANCZ   GOLLANCZ

Also by Ian Watson

The Embedding
The Jonah Kit
The Martian Inca

miracle visitors

IAN WATSON

GOLLANCZ
LONDON

Copyright © Ian Watson 1978
All rights reserved

The right of Ian Watson to be identified as the author
of this work has been asserted by him in accordance
with the Copyright, Designs and Patents Act 1988.

This edition published in Great Britain in 2003 by
Gollancz
an imprint of The Orion Publishing Group
Orion House, 5 Upper St Martin's Lane, London WC2H 9EA

Distributed in the United States of America
by Sterling Publishing Co., Inc.
387 Park Avenue South, New York, NY 10016-8810

A CIP catalogue record for this book
is available from the British Library

ISBN 0 575 07503 1

Printed and bound in Great Britain by
Clays Ltd, St Ives plc

Pour Bertrand Méheust, qui m'enthousiasma
pour le problème...

. . . aghast the Children of Men
Stood on the infinite Earth & saw these visions in the air . . .
But many stood silent, & busied in their families.
And many said, 'We see no Visions in the darksom air.
'Measure the course of that sulphur orb that lights the darksom day;
'Set stations on this breeding Earth & let us buy and sell.'

Mighty was the draught of Voidness to draw Existence in.

William Blake
Vala or The Four Zoas

PROLOGUE

STANDING UP ON the pedals, the schoolboy sprinted his bicycle over the cattle grid.

Ahead, the dusky rumples of Swale Moor spread out vaguely in the fast-failing light. The single-track road leading over and down into Goosedale was deserted. Rainclouds were clearing away fast to the east, unveiling a few glimmering stars, and Venus was already quietly bright, while the microwave relay tower silhouetted on the outcrop of Garth Rigg thrust two beady red warning lights up into the Yorkshire sky.

As a sheep blundered out of the furze and back, he squeezed his brakes then picked up speed again, whistling to himself. Ten minutes more and he would be back home at Neapstead in the dale.

His attention was caught by a bright violet light above the microwave tower—too intense to be a star or planet. The strange light swung from side to side like the bob of a sinking pendulum, then dodged sharply around the tower and began heading across the moor in his direction. The boy braked and watched, puzzled.

The light swelled, grew blue, incandescent. A blimp of burning gas, sinking down to the soil behind a rise a few hundred yards ahead.

It can't be; but it might be! he thought.

He raced his bicycle towards the rise.

Resting among the gorse sat a wingless metal ellipsoid as large as a milk tanker. It no longer glowed, but seemed to be pulsing as if breathing: a metallic lung, emitting a bee-like hum. As he watched, it steadied, firmed. Light streamed from a porthole.

An oval hatch opened, framing a beautiful woman with long white hair.

7

It was quite late when he reached home, but he had no idea what had delayed him.

The next day his eyes smarted and his skin itched. A pink flush coloured his whole body. When he passed water, he felt a burning irritation; but out of embarrassment said nothing about it—before long the peculiar symptoms went away.

For a while—he couldn't have said why—he caught the bus to school in Swale instead of cycling by the shorter route. Whenever he cycled over that moor afterwards, it always seemed as if something was missing—some dip in the road, or stretch of stone dyke that he thought should be there, but which wasn't.

PART ONE

ONE

" I RECOMMEND THE green chair." John Deacon waved his student into the room. A pretty boy, Michael Peacocke, a dark cherub with glossy eyes, thick eyelashes, a dainty nose. Who had scored an outstanding twelve on the Stanford Hypnotic Susceptibility Scale.

Michael sat. He crossed his legs then uncrossed them in a fidgety way. When Deacon had invited him to help his research towards the work in progress, *The Hypnotised Mind*, he'd appeared to be as pleased as if he'd won some prize; but now that the actual moment had come, he seemed nervous and on edge.

"All I want to do this afternoon," explained Deacon easily, "is to get you acquainted from the inside with the Extended North Carolina Scale. That's the scale for measuring the subjective depth level of the trance, remember? After I hypnotise you, I'll ask you to call out your 'state' at regular intervals. A number will pop into your head. We'll recap what they all stand for in a moment. Don't bother about how the number gets there. It'll be right. It always is—even if it takes both you and me by surprise."

Deacon ran a hand across his head. Now that his wispy, sandy hair was receding apace, his crown was speckled with freckles, and his head looked a bit like a hen's egg fringed with flaxen feathers as though from some hard delivery, the fluff advertising its supposedly free-range origin. His eyes were light blue, his lips humorous, if slightly sad.

His room was golden-crisp with early autumn sunshine: a freshly-baked loaf. The view south, from the University of

Granton, was of grazing land encroached on by a new industrial estate; distant smoke from burning stubble smearing the sky. One could hear the hum of a chain saw, taken to sick elms . . .

And where was he really? Originally he'd set out with a trust that he could chart all the altered states of mind, and with this chart enter his own soul, discover hidden treasure there. Now charts and arcane records seemed to be all there was—a mental filing cabinet of them to match the cabinets and card indexes in this room. He was an anthologist, lost at a crossroads beneath a hundred signposts.

Yet, on his desk lay review clippings of the symposium he'd edited the year before—*Consciousness: Ancient and Modern*—agreeing how insightful and stimulating it all was. And consciousness research was still in its infancy; no one even knew yet what consciousness *was* . . . Somehow the failure was elsewhere than in his work. It hovered offstage. The failure . . . beckoned, like a guide.

Deacon outlined the North Carolina Scale to Michael.

Zero represented the normal waking state. From numbers one to twelve a subject felt himself relaxing more and more. At twenty-plus he could expect to feel strong sensations of, say, numbness if suggested. After twenty-five, powerful dreamlike inner feelings. By thirty-plus a subject could regress into the past, experience false tastes and smells, completely blank out actual items such as chairs or even people from his awareness. By forty-plus, a fully convincing false reality could be induced . . .

"What's the limit?" asked Michael. "How far down can you go?"

"Oh, brief states have been reported as deep as a hundred and thirty. Around fifty to seventy is what I call the 'sense of joke' phase. Ego evaporates, there's a feeling that you needn't be this one person, but could equally be anyone or anything. A sort of detached Observer—some 'higher' aspect of the self—seems to be richly amused at the proceedings . . . And thereafter is a kind of passive Buddhist void. Pure awareness, of a sort of nothingness. That's a very intriguing state of mind indeed! To me it's the most fascinating aspect of the trance mind. The Void. But we shan't be going so deep yet-a-while. Today's is just a mapping session, to familiarise you. We'll need—oh, at least half-a-dozen, maybe a dozen sessions before that."

After disengaging the telephone, so that no incoming calls would disturb them, Deacon switched on the tape recorder and sat on the edge of the desk beside Michael to induce the trance.

He spoke routine words. He placed his hands upon Michael's eyes for a moment . . .

"State?"

"Thirteen," said Michael promptly, taking Deacon by surprise. Surely rather premature?

"Go just a little deeper . . . State?"

"Forty-five," came the flat, blank answer.

("You're joking!") But he didn't say it. This was a farce. The boy wasn't hypnotised at all . . . Yet he was, he could tell by the voice.

"Are you sure, Michael? Stay where you are. State, again!"

"Seventy." So automatic, dissociated.

"Go no deeper, do you hear?" ("Yes, I hear," the boy said promptly.) "I forbid you to. Return to forty-five *now*. To forty-five. Where are you? State, please!"

"Seventy-five."

"Return, dammit!" ordered Deacon.

"I can't. I'm on the moor. It's right there in front of me. It's stronger than you are."

What was? He'd lost control of the trance. It was as though some outside influence had elbowed him aside—some suggestion planted under deep hypnosis. Yet Michael had assured him he'd never been hypnotised before. Buried, repressed material, then? It couldn't happen!

"Where are you, Michael?"

"On Swale Moor near my home. I see the light in the sky. It comes down and lands. A metal egg with portholes. It can't be but it is! It's a flying saucer!"

"How old are you?"

"I'm sixteen. Eight days past my birthday." The pedantic precision of the hypnotised . . .

13

"A lovely woman with long blonde hair stands in the hatch. She beckons me. I hear a voice in my head encouraging me. Though she's not speaking words. She's . . . mooding me, can I say that?"

"Yes yes, you can say it." Allow it all to unwind. It must be some sex fantasy that had meant an enormous amount in private to the boy for years. Which he'd run through time and again till it became a tape-loop in his mind, lurking there unerased.

"She has two men with her. They're dressed in ski-suits, just like her, and they've got long blond hair too. One of them shouts that it's quite safe. Do I want to come aboard? Oh yes—she moods me on. I must jump through the hatch. I'm not to touch the earth and their craft at the same time. So I do. I jump into a semicircular cabin with a glowing ceiling. There's one padded couch in it, nothing more. I can see through to another room with proper seats and screens and controls—that must be the control room. One of the men shuts that door in a hurry—"

The speechless woman 'mooding' him must be some fantasy figure of pent-up libido—and the two men were the superego twins, Guilt and Anxiety, their voice the voice of conscience. And now they had shut the door on the 'controls' . . .

"He does most of the talking. His name is Tharmon, he says. I'm scared because—" (Michael started to sweat) "—I can't even see the outside hatch any more, there's only smooth hull. The other man hands me a glass of water. He says I'll feel better when I drink it. At least I think it's water. It has a queer metallic taste, it jars my teeth . . .

"It must have had something in it. I feel a lot happier now. The woman's name is Loova, Tharmon tells me—"

"You say they're blond?" interrupted Deacon. "Do you mean Nordic types, like Scandinavians?"

"No! Their skin's yellow. Their eyes are like Chinese eyes with hardly any eyelids. They're much longer than normal eyes. They go right round the corners of their cheeks, as though their eye sockets are a different shape from ours. What long fingers they've got! The fingernails are as smooth and pink as plastic . . .

14

And Loova just smiles and smiles. Maybe she can't mood me and talk at the same time."

(But Michael Peacocke isn't scared of women. He has a fine thing going with his girlfriend, buxom little Suzie Meade—or he seems to.)

"They've come from the stars, from the Pleiades. From a planet called Ulro, says Tharmon. The name means 'Earth' or 'World' in their own speech. He says that the human race is in danger because of our vile nuclear weapons. The people of Ulro want to save us. They can't reveal themselves, though. That's against their ethics.

"Luckily their biology's slightly different from ours. Their women can fertilise themselves, if their glands release a particular hormone. It makes the woman's egg capable of doubling the number of chromosomes in the germ-cell, so that the egg fertilises itself. Tharmon explains it all. The people of Ulro have found a hormone that will do the same thing for the sperm fertilising the egg. The egg will copy the chromosomes in the sperm and double those, contributing none itself. It will make a baby entirely from the male chromosomes. So you get a child that isn't really the mother's at all, even though she bears it. It's entirely the father's.

"They can use this hormone on an Ulran woman when she mates with a human male, and she'll bear babies of either sex that are fully human. Tharmon calls it the parthenogenesis of the male. A virgin birth—out of the loins of donors . . . like me! Young donors are best, he says."

A masturbation fantasy. Surely that's what it was. Its self-reference was amply underscored by the name of the 'alien' world actually being 'Earth'.

"If we do destroy ourselves, they can still save a small kernel of pure humans this way. They'll be born on Ulro and carry on our race. They've prepared a special community."

"So what happens now?"

"They leave me alone with Lover, I mean with Loova—"

Quite!

"And shut themselves up in the control room—"

The boy grinned, inanely, with excitement. "She runs a pink

fingernail down the front of her ski-suit. It just falls apart like a pea-pod. Her flesh is a creamy dusky yellow like an old ivory ornament, but there's no hair on it anywhere, not even—"

No, because you hadn't seen female pubic hair then, had you? You didn't know what to imagine.

"She has breasts like little puffballs you find in a field in the autumn. They're very rounded and . . . *new-looking*, as though they've just sprouted from the ground. When she touches me it's as though she's never seen a naked human male before—"

Inverted truth, indeed!

"She pulls me into her, on the couch. And it hurts me! Oh I'm enjoying it, but there's a cold pain in my balls as if they've been dipped in a bucket of ice. I never knew it hurt a man the first time! Now's the only time she makes any sound: like a softly growling dog, a growling bitch—"

Hatred of the fantasy figure; resentment.

"When it's done, she gets dressed without looking at me, then opens the door. Tharmon comes back in from the control room. She pats her belly. He grins. Then it's foggy, I feel sick and empty-headed. They open the outside hatch again, and there's the moor, black dark . . . And out I jump. As soon as my feet hit the ground I'm scared, I run away. A tingling follows me. My whole skin pricks with pins and needles. I'm too frightened to look back till I reach my bike. By then the craft is a bright red egg-shaped fog. Suddenly it rises up and skitters away across the moor—as though it's bouncing over waves. I can hear noises, like fast burbling morse on the short wave band, inside my head. I'm trying to think about what happened, what they told me. B-but . . . I'm just cycling home along the road. How has it got so late?"

"You can come back now, Michael. Return to forty-five." He hesitated. "State?"

"Forty-five."

He counted him down in big leaps through the thirties and twenties; Michael followed tamely. From twelve to zero Deacon counted backwards one by one.

Michael woke. He moaned, like some hot metal surface contracting, and held his forehead.

16

"Have we started? I've got a filthy headache."

Deacon hunted in the desk drawer for paracetamol. "In fact we've finished. How much do you remember?" he asked casually. He tapped out two tablets.

"Well, you said 'State?', then I said 'Thirteen' because that was what popped into my head, and then . . . you just counted me back to zero. Was I no good?"

He remembered nothing.

"Look at your watch; half an hour's gone by. You were fine. Sorry about the headache! You must have been sitting too stiffly . . . It won't happen again. I'll fetch some coffee to wash these down—"

Deacon came back with the coffee just as the recorder was winding up its last few inches of tape; it clicked off.

"Can I listen to myself?"

"Well, I've got a lecture soon . . . We'll have a longer session next Monday. I'll play you the tape before we start. All right?"

When Michael left, Deacon re-engaged the telephone, then pushed the rewind switch on the recorder. While the tape was spinning back, the telephone rang. He lifted the receiver, and heard a high-pitched scraping noise. The screech of a fingernail on slate. The teeth-jarring noise sounded like the squeak of tape racing through the machine, much magnified. He spoke into the receiver, but no one was calling. Puzzled, he cradled it, then halted the tape and pressed for play.

His own voice was asking, 'State?' 'Thirteen,' replied Michael. There was a pause. 'Go just a little deeper. State?' This was where it had gone really wrong.

The tape wound on—in complete silence. There was nothing more on it.

He flipped open the lid and ran the cassette forward, spot-checking.

Not a word.

But he'd seen the recording needle flicking about! Michael couldn't even have erased the tape during the couple of minutes he was out of the room—that would have taken as long to do as it took to record in the first place. Why should he have done it

17

anyway? Deacon sat staring, exasperated, at the mute recorder. Damn the machine.

Hurriedly he began making notes.

He had no evidence now.

TWO

DEACON PARKED IN the gravel drive of his burly Gothic-trimmed house, down a quiet road lined with horse chestnut trees shedding golden leaves.

Fourteen-year-old Rob was guiding the hover-mower on the back lawn. An Old English Sheepdog galloped around him, a curtain of hair in its eyes. Waving to Rob, he went in by the kitchen door, perfunctorily kissed Mary, poured a sherry for her, one for himself, and started telling her about the trance that had gone wrong.

He broke off. "Why is Rob leaving all those fungi?"

Mary laughed. "He says they're edible . . . Parasol mushrooms. I don't intend cooking them!"

"They look poisonous to me." He cracked the window open. "Rob," he called. Then louder; the mower was too noisy.

"Don't *fret*, John. I said I don't intend cooking them."

(He'd been overworking lately . . . She imagined cracks suddenly running across his crown like crazy paving. Funny if he was about to hatch at last! What would emerge?)

"You were telling me about this boy Michael?" she reminded.

"Oh yes, don't you see? It's such a strongly repressed fantasy there should have been a lot more abreaction—more of an emotional outburst, more *struggle* when I stumbled on it! But it just spilled right out, as though he was programmed to spill it. The whole thing was taken out of my hands. He went all the way to seventy-five."

18

"Didn't Freud say that flying's a sex symbol? Hence the flying saucer."

"Oh it's obviously sexual," he agreed. "I mean, the control room being shut off. That punishment by pinpricks afterwards. The Lover-woman's breasts sprouting like falsies—he'd never seen a girl's breasts before and was making them up. The hairlessness. The fact that she couldn't talk—because *he* wouldn't know what to say. I know he's from the countryside, but he's an only child, and his mother was Italian, so maybe they're a bit straitlaced."

"You have a funny concept of the country! Swains and milkmaids tumbling in the hay . . . Did you say that the spacewoman was called Luvah? And one of the men Tharmon?"

"It sounded like 'Loova'. But I know what he meant!"

"No you don't, John. You're being illiterate. I remember now. Those are both characters in Blake's Prophetic Poems. Luvah's a man, not a woman. He's a demi-God who nurses infant Mankind. Later on, he gets locked up in *Ulro*—which is a sort of deep-down Hell. Enitharmon, not plain 'Tharmon', is another demi-God, the enemy of Luvah."

"Are you sure?"

"Of course I am. I used to love Blake when I was at college. He seemed so . . . magical. Such an imagination!"

"So Luvah's really male? Michael was screwing a man in his fantasy. I suppose that explains the tacked-on breasts! The poor kid must be fairly knotted up inside. Repressed homosexuality—which he can't acknowledge . . . Damn. What should I do?"

"He probably just had some pederastic frolic when he was a schoolboy. That doesn't make him queer. He has a steady girlfriend, hasn't he? If you go digging into this, you'll just mess him up." Mary regarded homosexuality not as wicked, but as faintly absurd. It seemed so *restrictive*. She was a dark, lithe woman, growing stocky of late, who had handed on her strong bushy black hair to both the children, Rob and Celia. With her firm jaw, long nose, and brown-flecked eyes deepset close together, she recalled (to herself) the black and white collies of her youth in the Welsh sheep-farming hills: well-trained and

19

masterful, godlike bolts of energy to the bleating, scurrying flock; however, at heart, with a strong scent for the fold. They had an instinct for penning in securely, amidst the intoxicating wild. The playful beast gambolling round the garden was only a satire on that sort of sheepdog, more like a sheep and named accordingly.

"It's fascinating, a psychic structure as powerful as that. If only the damn recorder hadn't gone on the blink! Well, I'll just have to repeat the whole performance. I *must* know how a hypnosis could get so completely out of hand. I suspect, Mary, that I might just have stumbled on a new discrete state of consciousness distinct from the usual trance terrain. An independent subsystem. In a word, a new ASC—" Freudian interpretations, besides being out of fashion, were really far too simplistic.

"ASC?"

"An Altered State of Consciousness. One which can be explored *through* hypnosis, since it shares some of the same mental structures, but it can't be controlled *by* hypnosis. That's very strange. I can't pass this up. Besides, there's my responsibility to the boy . . . This thing's like an independent, alien ego within the mind: a parasite one with its own will and initiative which copies the 'shape' of a particular ASC—"

The kitchen door flew open. In bounded Shep, to thump his tail against their legs before subsiding, panting. Rob followed, a dark wiry youngster. Looking a little like a Romany boy, in school cap and blazer rather than rags and earrings, he stood waiting for his palm to be crossed with silver.

"You saw I left the mushrooms, Dad?"

("And did you hear me shouting?") "They're fungi," corrected Deacon.

The sound of the front door banging shut—Celia, at seventeen, asserting herself with a newly acquired doorkey—brought Shep to his feet again.

"We still aren't going to eat them," said Mary.

"Not eat what?" asked Celia—a dark girl with her mother's ebullient hair and the big oval face of her father; coming in, she wrestled Shep as the dog planted its polar bear paws on her shoulders.

"Our parasol mushrooms," said the boy.

"I don't *trust* fungi," explained Deacon.

"Maybe they're hallucinogens?" insinuated Celia. "Perhaps you could feed them to the Consciousness Research Group and find out?"

Deacon shrugged. "We've got a Ministry of Health contract to study the effects of cannabis—that's Bernie Jorden's line. And Rossiter and Sally Pringle do some work with the mental hospital. That's about all."

"Aha, the chemistry of madness," chuckled Celia. "Serotonin and LSD? It's so false, grooving away in your own heads on official time while kids are being busted on the street for doing research into *their* heads in their own way."

"Outside of any framework, Celia." It was an old argument.

"The framework called *life*, Dad. It's one big experiment from birth to death. And if you cross the road at the wrong time and die, even that's okay because you made the choice."

"That seems like an excellent reason for having a proper framework for crossing roads: roads in the head as much as roads in town."

"Really? What does 'proper' mean? You wrote in the intro to your own book that what's irrational nonsense for the everyday mind can be perfectly valid *and true* in another state, and it can tell us a damn sight more ("Celia!" Mary snapped) about what being alive and conscious are. I quote chapter and verse."

Celia was only making waves—paddling a little way from shore, the better to return. So he hoped; so Mary hoped.

"I doubt you'd drive a car better if you were high on berserker mushrooms," he said to her.

"Most people already drive as though they're stoned Vikings. Most people are crazy, Dad. They're stuck in a mad repetitive trance. You wrote that."

"I didn't say they're mad exactly. What I said is that there's a constant loading stabilization of 'brain chatter' that keeps us in an ordinary baseline state of consciousness most of the time."

"In a trance, like most of the teachers at school."

"You're not implying," enquired Mary, "that it would be a nice constructive idea if you took drugs?"

"Oh Mummy." Celia's face became spiritual. "I just can't stand hypocrisy. Dad has all these far-out ideas, but . . ." She gestured at the neatness of the garden; and Mary smiled faintly, in complicity.

Quite abruptly, Deacon felt grief-stricken.

THREE

LOITERING BY THE off-licence hatch of the Bunch of Grapes, Michael watched the glitter of upside-down spirits bottles reflected in cut-glass mirrors behind the brightly-lit bar, and listened to the grumble of talk and the clack of the fruit machine. A bar billiards cue rose high in the air as someone tried to bring it to bear on the ball without butting too many backs. He swayed slightly as he waited for Suzie, pleasantly tipsy. Tonight everything would be fine. He felt no urgency—no prematurity.

She came out of the toilet: bouncy, dressed in fray-bottomed blue jeans and a chunky-knit fisherman's sweater, her red hair descending in crinkly wedges like some rusty ziggurat. Draping one arm around her, he tucked his hand into the back pocket of her jeans, and they set off across the Common towards the distant lights of the highrise Halls of Residence, rocking slightly about a common centre of gravity located somewhere in her abdomen. Behind them wagged moon shadows, for the Moon was high and dazzling, only a shave off full, the rays from Tycho and Copernicus so bright that you couldn't make out any details.

A church clock struck ten as they reached the mid-way lake. Apart from the white boat of a swan sailing towards a fellow white hump on the small stone island, the whole Common seemed deserted.

"Mike, look up there! Look at the Moon!"

A bright violet orb—a halfpenny to the Moon's penny—floated beside the Moon. As they stood staring up, the mysterious object became a dazzling ultramarine, painting their hands and faces with ancient savage woad.

"It's so *cold*!" Suzie burrowed into him. His body felt frozen, as though the Common had suddenly been translocated beyond the Arctic Circle, and they were standing on a field of blue ice.

"It's like a great blue eye, watching us! Mike, I'm scared."

The false moon swelled, competing in cold brilliance with the real Moon. Bands of green and yellow swirled round rapidly, now, bearing a hot red blotch: the pupil of an eye, hunting.

Suddenly the glowing orb darted downwards and sideways in a Knight's move that clued them in to how close it really was—hovering before them now in a rocking, sloshing motion as if floating on a watery swell. The red spot swam counterclockwise through the swirling colour bands, coming to rest, staring at them. A white searchlight beam flashed out from it, catching them briefly, blindingly. Heat swept their bodies, though their clothes still felt as cold as ever.

When they looked again the thing was gone, was nowhere.

"Christ!" cried Michael. "This afternoon! The trance—I remember! John Deacon *knows*. And he didn't tell me!" He drew Suzie to him, stroked her hair. "It's all right, love. I know what that was. They promised they'd find me again. It's the Space People, Suzie! Isn't it wonderful? They've woken my memory up again."

Already in the distance they heard the *bee-baw* wail of a siren approaching; presently a fire engine halted on the far edge of the Common, its blue light whirling in tiny replica of the recent apparition. Helmeted figures spilled out and stared across the Common.

"Someone must have thought it was a fire . . . I'll take you back to your room. I must phone him."

"Shouldn't we tell them we saw something?" She hadn't taken in what he said.

"Tell them?" he scoffed. "Do you think they'd believe? When I was sixteen, love, Space People landed and took me on board *one of those*."

23

"What . . .? You're saying you went on board a *flying saucer?*" She brought the phrase out repugnantly. "You're saying that's what that was? You're . . . you're crazy."

"They blocked my memory. But they told me they could always find me again."

"You're kidding."

"Do you realize what we've seen, the two of us? A starship from the Pleiades! Look up there, love." He pointed at the Seven Sisters twinkling milkily. "That's where. They even took me for a flight in it."

"To the stars?"

"Of course not. Look, let's both phone Deacon. You saw it too. His hypnosis brought it out. There's a lot more that he didn't hear." Michael laughed harshly. "He must have thought it was a fantasy. He'll believe it now all right. When you tell him what we both saw! "

Suzie was a lapsed Methodist; and it was a pragmatic, trimmed religion, without hysteria, almost without miracles. All things bright and beautiful, in a plain brick building. The prodigy of the loaves and fishes translated into a Sunday School tea party. No breath of Hell, no Devil, hardly even a Deity. Heaven was a rather large meadow strolled by a white-robed, bearded figure wearing slightly dusty sandals.

Two firemen were walking up the grass from the road, casting about as they went.

"You're just making up a nonsense explanation. Why should this happen on the same day as your trance?"

"Maybe . . . maybe somehow I drew them to me."

"That's preposterous." Suddenly she made a retching noise. "I think I'm going to be sick—"

One of the firemen waved to them and shouted.

"They'd just think we were drunk," said Michael. "Let's go."

"Maybe you *are* drunk," she panted. Somehow she managed to avoid vomiting.

They hurried off, as the fireman headed towards the lake, switching on a torch.

Suzie woke from a dreamless sleep, squeezed into her single

24

bed alongside Michael. Traffic noises proclaimed it to be a new day. A painful rosy light suffused her eyelids. She tried to open them. She couldn't. Sitting up, she fumbled at her face. Her eyelids felt huge, filled with hot water. They were glued together. Blindly, she shook Michael.

The night before they had neither phoned Deacon nor made love. By the time they had reached her room, they had both felt too limp and drained to do anything more than shed their clothes by moonlight and fall into bed, and sleep.

Michael woke. His eyes also ached. But at least he could open them.

"I can't see, Mike! My face hurts."

"You're . . . sunburnt. Just like I was, after . . ."

"Damn it, what's wrong with my eyes?"

"They're puffed and swollen. Can you make out any daylight?"

"Yes."

"It's just the lids, then. Good job we both shut our eyes last night. I'll soak a handkerchief in milk for a cold compress. That should help." His eyes took in the rest of her body. It was pink all over. Sliding sorely from the sheets, he saw in the mirror over the washbasin how sunburnt he was too.

A half-full milk carton stood on her desk. As he picked it up, he glanced out across the Common. People were wandering about in a purposeful yet random way as though searching for lost property. Several appeared to be carrying field glasses and cameras; bird watchers, but the birds had flown . . .

'Throw a pin to find a pin,' he thought. It was a maxim of John Deacon's.

Deacon had spoken a good deal in Psychology seminars about 'state-specific logics' and the need to develop 'state-specific sciences' to pin these logics down. Each altered state of consciousness possessed its own internal logic, different to a greater or lesser extent from the logic of ordinary baseline consciousness. Each altered state had a rationality that was perfectly coherent, yet could be wholly alien to everyday reason. This was why it was so difficult for the traditionally 'objective' scientist to study these states. Here was a fundamental barrier to communication: an

25

unreportability. Even the subject who experienced the altered state couldn't necessarily explain it, even to himself, afterwards. That was because separate memory systems seemed to exist for each altered state. Whenever you entered that state of mind again, they clicked into place with a shock of familiarity, the sense of being *there* again in a familiar landscape lost till that moment. Thus new psychological sciences were needed that would be specific to each altered state: sciences that would devise their laws within these states, exploiting the logics specific to them—with the ultimate aim of reporting back to states nearer ordinary consciousness; for some states could apparently overlap other states, while these in turn shared features in common with more workaday mentality. Figuratively, then, you had to throw a pin away to get into the frame of mind where you threw—and lost—a pin before. You had to get drunk, to discover what you had (so logically) misplaced when you were drunk. And in order to meet a flying saucer . . .

Deacon. He had to see him. He had news.

Michael poured milk on to a folded handkerchief.

FOUR

TWO FLOORS DOWN, the London traffic rumbled. In his small office Barry Shriver sat opening the morning post, which came from France, Sweden, America, Australia, Brazil, Britain. Soon news cuttings and typed reports littered his desk, to be eyed with a sarcasm which might have surprised his faithful, even fervent correspondents.

The Alabama *Huntsville News* told of 'a spinning disk, like an upturned jelly mould' seen by truck drivers not far from Marshall Space Flight Center. The jelly mould had fled up into the sky, receding at huge velocity . . .

The Hereford *Evening News* reported a 'mystery flying

object' hovering over an R.A.F. camp at Credenhill, seen by airmen on guard duty and a passing farmer.

So it went. Fresh sightings every day, buried in local newspapers world wide. Many hundreds every year. Encounters of the First Kind, mostly—things seen in the sky. A fair number of the Second Kind, where some sort of physical evidence was left, some visible trace. A few of the Third Kind too—glimpses of the 'operators' of these mystery objects and even actual contact with them . . . The third category seemed to be on the increase lately.

Shriver—turned fifty—sported a trim black goatee beard and a rigorous greying crewcut: a mix of colonel (to which rank he had never actually risen) and natty archaeologist or explorer. Fireproof cabinets lined the office walls. An IBM Selectric sat on his desk alongside a pile of *Apa Newsletters,* monthly journal of the Aerial Phenomena Association—to him, by now, so ineptly named.

In the earlier nineteen fifties, fresh from college into the U.S. Air Force, Barry Shriver piloted an F-86 interceptor in the Korean War. In June 1952, flying wing in a squadron out of Inchon, they were paced through the sky by a glowing cylinder as large as a B-26, shorn of wings. When the squadron climbed towards it, it split up like an amoeba into two pulsing disks dotted with portholes. Arcing around the squadron at high speed, these bracketed the American jets. Shriver's radio went dead, his compass spun, his engine cut out. He dived. He saw the two disks closing in around the F-86 on his right as though herding it; then they fused around it, and—as one single fat cigar again—shot skywards, receding to a point of light, and vanishing. (Except that he wasn't positive the cigar had actually shot away into the distance, so much as *shrunk to nothing* right where it was . . .)

He and the others pulled clear. Controls and engines functioned again. Returning to Inchon, they logged the loss of an interceptor in collision with a moving ball of light . . .

Some effort was made to find wreckage, as the ground below was in United Nations hands; none was found. War was pressing. The loss was blamed on massive ball lightning.

Barry Shriver knew this for a lie, a miserable cover-up. Though—of what?

27

After the war he was posted to Edwards Air Force Base at Muroc, three hundred thousand acres of dry lake and scrubland in the Mojave Desert's Antelope Valley where, in 1954, the world's longest runway was being completed.

At the end of the second week in April 1954, in a restricted area of Edwards Base, he'd seen five flying saucers land. And remain on the ground for two whole days, during which scientists, military experts and even churchmen were invited over them by their humanoid operators—the humans bewildered and overwhelmed by craft that could change shape and size at will, become transparent, invisible, even insubstantial so that people could walk through their walls.

He'd seen all this from a little way off. Yet he'd recognized, unmistakably, Dwight D. Eisenhower, spirited in from a supposed golfing holiday at Palm Springs. He saw the President himself, meeting the Space People. He'd spotted Bishop McIntyre of Los Angeles. Many other faces too. Right there.

And he'd known that President Eisenhower would address the nation within a matter of weeks. Then Barry would know where his buddy of the Korean War had gone to, and why.

But nothing happened.

Nothing at all.

People wouldn't speak about those two days at Muroc, subsequently. It was more than a blanket of silence; it seemed an actual subtraction of what had happened from actuality—a deletion of it *ever having happened* . . .

Cold War, then. Red Alerts. He was posted to Germany. Under a pen-name he published a booklet, *48 Hours at Muroc*. Seeing his own account in print, he too had begun to wonder: had it ever really happened? He knew perfectly well that it had, yet as the years went by, each with its own crop of contradictory, paradoxical sightings and close encounters, nothing was ever learnt, and the more he knew, the less he knew.

He married a German woman, later she divorced him. The subtraction of Gisela from his life didn't deny that she had ever been there, though—in the way that Muroc implacably denied itself. He grew angry; then patient and defiant. He left the Air Force and helped found the Aerial Phenomena Association

28

in London, a city he had taken a liking to during leaves.

The phone rang; he lifted the receiver.

"It's Norman Tate here. I've got a really super CE-2 report for you. Local paper—*Granton Herald*. This one could be worth chasing up at source. Alas, I'm off to Scotland on business. A saucer buzzed and burnt some students —"

Enthusiastic Norman—yet the man was a meticulous, fussy investigator. As Shriver listened, he watched a jumbo jet straining heavily through the clouds on its flight path in to Heathrow, and imagined an absurd blob of light engulfing it, and deleting it from the natural world.

What *had* he experienced at Muroc? A hallucination? Or something more sinister: a breach in reality itself? A collapse of consensus causal law, which had sucked into itself temporarily some hundreds of air force officers, scientists and politicians? Including the President of the land himself who, God bless his golf clubs, recognized the anomaly for the treacherous thing it was: a hole, of warped reality, in the midst of Edwards Air Force Base—something which released its captives after a while as normality reasserted itself. Released them so that perhaps even they *no longer knew!* Quite clearly this was different from an ordinary . . .

"Hallucination," he whispered into the phone.

"What's that? Listen, man, *actual burns*. The makings of a classic case!"

"I'm sorry Norman, I was thinking about my book. Do you like *UFO: Buyers Beware!* for a title? *Caveat emptor,* you know!"

"No-o-o." It was a long drawn-out reproof. "Frankly I don't like it. The reading public might take you at your word and never buy the damn thing."

"Well, my idea is that there might be hallucinations of a very special sort, which affect non-psychotics, and which can be shared among witnesses miles apart—"

"That's hardly tenable, Barry. How can strangers possibly share the same hallucination? Everybody has a different breaking point. We all snap in different, unique ways."

"Isn't the Indian rope trick a collective hallucination? This would be a sort of rope trick, without a fakir. The people trick themselves."

"Oh, I've seen the rope trick. That was in Bangalore. I saw it, but did my camera see it? Not likely. The rope trick is some kind of powerful hypno-telepathy. But cameras *don't* see anything because they haven't got any minds, and nothing actually happens. UFOs, my boy, make real holes in the ground, as we all know. They burn people and knock planes out of the sky. Smack. Solid events."

"Mightn't there be hallucinations that are also at the same time, in a sense, real? Hallucinations that have a temporary, conditional reality?"

"Either something is real, or it isn't real."

"But need it be? UFOs seem to act as though they both *are,* and *aren't* at one and the same time. As though they occupy some middle ground." Just as the Muroc episode both was, and was-not . . .

"There *is* such a thing as a law of the excluded middle, Barry. That's basic to all logic. A thing can only be, or not be."

"That isn't true of subatomic particles."

"Of course I mean in the world at large—which is where UFOs operate."

Shriver sighed. "Are UFOs logical?"

He heard Norman laugh, assuming that his remark was a joke. "The public won't buy the book, boy. *Caveat* yourself!"

"Okay, can you give me the phone number of that hospital?"

FIVE

ON THIS MORNING of their discharge, with two days' spare supply of corticosteroid tablets in their pockets, they found the American waiting to meet them. Introducing himself, he offered drinks and lunch. So now they sat sunburnt in a dark lounge bar, Suzie the more disfigured of the two. Her eyes smarted behind fat sunglasses; her skin was peeling into white dead leaves. She looked, she thought, like a parboiled beetroot wrapped in torn clingfilm. Her body stung pinkly. She felt restless, humiliated and angry, and mildly resented the American, laughing at the loud, near-tartan sports jacket he wore under a thin black raincoat; though Michael, pink and peeling too, had taken to him quickly as an honourable confidant, who obviously knew far more than Deacon about what he referred to as 'The Phenomenon'.

"There's a pattern to these phenomena, Mike. Though what that pattern is God only knows." Shriver sounded wistful. "You can't just blithely assume that UFOs are alien spacecraft working on some different principle from any we know. Even if their operators tell you that's what they are! You have to see the phenomenon whole. A large part of it is sheer *misinformation* on the part of the supposed ufonauts. All that nonsense about galactic confederations and hundreds of planets with funny names! It's only paralleled for sheer idiocy by the way these marvellous scoutships seem to be constantly blowing up or having bits fall off them. Not to mention seeming to be navigated by half-witted butterflies—or the nasty tricks they play: kidnapping, scaring, chasing cars, and, oh yes, sunburning people."

"I feel *diseased* by it," frowned Suzie.

"Maybe the sunburn is to prove to us that it's real, not imaginary?"

"Ha. What does it prove, Mike? Like that doctor said, you could have done it with a sunlamp. There's never any proof. Actually this whole thing has been going on for thousands of years in one form or another, and we're still no nearer knowing what it is. You think that's an overstatement, Suzie? I can show you full documentation."

"This lager tastes like piss," she said.

"Suzie!" hissed Michael.

Shriver seemed unperturbed. "I quite agree. Most lager does, to me. Try something stronger."

"Brandy, please."

After soothing Suzie's eyes the other morning, till she could open them a crack, Michael and Suzie had visited a doctor who diagnosed Klieg conjunctivitis. The probable cause was over-exposure to ultraviolet rays. The morning news on the local radio station mentioned strange lights seen over the Common the night before . . . The doctor had shrugged, non-committally; however, Suzie's attack of nausea and the exhaustion they both reported bothered him sufficiently for him to phone the hospital. There they had spent the past forty-eight hours in separate wards, faces smeared with corticosteroid cream, having their blood count monitored and enduring jokes about moonbathing. A local reporter had visited them on the first day, as word leaked out. Later, an interviewer came from the local radio. When Michael finally got round to phoning John Deacon, Deacon had already seen the story in print in the *Granton Herald* and intended to visit them that evening. Michael put Deacon off. He had remembered the trance and what he now had to say couldn't be said in a public ward. So far, Michael had kept quiet about his earlier 'encounter', except to Suzie—and now, to her annoyance, the American . . .

Shriver reseated himself, with a glass of brandy for Suzie.

"The trouble," he went on, "is that the phenomenon constantly suits itself to the frame of reference of *the moment.* Once, that framework was religious. So you got battles of angels in the sky, God walking the Earth, Burning Bushes, Ezekiel's Chariot and whatnot—in Israel, China, Ancient Mexico, wherever."

Suzie coughed on the brandy. "Ezekiel and Moses saw flying saucers, did they?"

"No! They encountered exactly what they *saw*—which is to say a conditioning and manipulating phenomenon. It's no use picturing Ezekiel's chariot as some spaceship and trying to work out what sort of propulsion it used. That isn't the point. Ezekiel didn't meet an alien spacecraft. He met something *of this Earth.* Aliens? No way! This has been here all along. How else can we explain the huge volume of inexplicable sightings of one sort and another down the ages?"

"How about downright ignorance and superstition?" she suggested.

"Take those woodcuts of spinning fiery wheels seen over Nuremburg in the Middle Ages—"

"Cohn's book on cults of the millennium," she began.

" That isn't the answer, Suzie. Our forebears weren't quite so dumb or deluded as we like to think. Life would be a lot simpler if these things were 'just' alien spaceships! How can we explain the huge amount of things of one sort or another dumped out of the sky—ranging from neatly sorted snails all of one species, through blocks of ice and piles of clinker, to gallons of blood—all poltergeisted down on to this world? Orthodox science ignores these events, of course. They don't fit into the scheme anywhere, so they can't have happened. Except that they did."

"That's just, what's his name . . . Charles Fort?" Suzie emptied her glass and sat playing with it, trying to make the rim ring like a bell by dragging a moistened fingertip around it.

"All that Charles Fort did to earn your scorn, my dear, was simply collect reports from perfectly respectable sources—annual registers, weather reviews, meteorological reports. He never invented a damn thing. Now, I just said 'poltergeisted', didn't I? The fact is that UFOs and their kin have a lot in common with poltergeists and ghosts—and with fairies and leprechauns too, and with the angels and demons of the occultists. There's a remarkable similarity of structure between pacts with fairies and summonings of spirits and modern contact stories about the different types of so-called aliens, and what happens to the people who meet them. You get offered fabulous revelations and crocks of gold, then you're systematically hoodwinked, cheated and discredited.

"Did you know that giant dirigibles were flying around the Mid West of America in the eighteen nineties—*before* any such dirigibles existed? Whole towns spotted them. Local papers are full of them. There are stacks of notarised reports by solid citizens. The crews of these dirigibles used to drop in from time to time for cups of water, or to borrow a screwdriver. The damned dirigibles were breaking down all the time, of course! These fliers promised great revelations, real soon—which never matured. They dumped cryptic messages overboard. They

33

winched up cattle—which were found surgically dissected later on. They even hoisted one guy up by the seat of his pants on their trailing anchor! Which is a rather interesting echo, incidentally, of other aerial ships' anchors that got snared in church steeples in the Middle Ages. Bristol, circa A.D. 1200, to name but one—it's in the chronicler Gervase of Tilbury. So what were those dirigibles in the eighteen nineties?"

"Obviously some kind of practical joke."

"Just so! A practical joke. But not one that was quite within the technology of the day, even though it fitted the frame of reference of the time. There's a hoax all right, but the hoax is *by* the UFOs! They're leading Humanity by the nose, now as ever. Busily making themselves seem bizarre and inexplicable in the process!"

Her glass harmonica gave tongue at last, in a cool silver hooting.

"Will you have another brandy?" he offered.

"Perhaps you could try to explain all the hundreds of silent, unmarked airplanes seen over Scandinavia in the nineteeen thirties? Or the rain of phantom rockets there, just when the Cold War was starting up? They generally vanished into lakes, after sending out 'alien' broadcasts in broken Swedish."

"How about the Russians?" she giggled. "A spot of psychological warfare? They captured enough rocket experts at Peenemunde."

"No way, Suzie. No more than the 'foo fighters' of the Second World War were Axis *or* Allied —"

" 'Foo fighters'? What are they? They sound like people who can't stand tapioca. Or is it Fu Manchu's air force?"

Shriver sighed. "It was a piece of pilots' slang in the Second World War. I guess the word was a mispronunciation of *feu*— fire. These UFOs looked like globes of fire. Though the word could have come from a line in the Smokey Stover comic strip: 'Where's there's foo, there's fire.' "

"I've never heard of it."

"I guess you're too young. Anyway, the alien spaceship—the Adamski model—is the same old beast in a new guise. It fits

34

our current frame of reference—of Moon flights, radio telescopes, and the hunt for life in the Universe. Do you realize, the
very same messages, *verbatim*, have been picked up by ham
radio buffs, by Ufo contactees *and* by psychics in trances who
thought they were in touch with the dead?"

"The same structures of hysteria," frowned Suzie.

"Structures I'll buy. But the very same *words?* The very same
sentences? I tell you, something is broadcasting—on the wave-
band of the human mind, and on radios and telephones and any
electrical gear, and right across the visible spectrum too. It even
produces materializations—up to and including a whole
menagerie of apparently living entities. And the whole phenomenon, with this Cheshire cat grin on its face, is constantly
mixing authentic bits of information and true prophecies in with
a whole farrago of nonsense. It plays childish, and pretty com-
plicated, games that quite often turn out nasty—apparently with
the main aim of discrediting itself!"

"Paranoia," she said. "That's all this is. It's the biggest
bloody example of persecution mania I've ever heard of —"

"*Induced* delusions do enter into it. Adamski and the others
aren't all lying. A lot of contactees genuinely believe what
they've been shown, even if believing it wrecks their lives!"

"Everything tied together, from Ezekiel to leprechauns to . . .
to . . ."

Shriver smiled wanly. "How about: Uri Geller? He's another
contactee, did you know? Serving a cosmic metaconsciousness.
According to him there's some sort of super computer in the sky
a million years ahead that helps him do his tricks."

"It's paranoid, don't you realize?"

"It's *happening*."

"I'm not getting drawn into this sort of nuttiness, no thank
you! A sweet, sane life for me!"

Michael sat unhappily. His encounter with Loova no longer
seemed so clear. It had certainly happened. He had no doubts
on that score. The fact that it had happened mattered intensely.
But what was it that had happened?

Shriver read his expression; he knew it well enough. "She's
right in a way," he conceded. "People do get sucked into all

35

kinds of obsessive beliefs and make fools of themselves. That's one way the phenomenon protects itself. Anyway, I promised to buy you both a meal." Appraising Suzie's tattered, blotched face, he added, "In some suitably dark and dingy restaurant . . . Do you figure I could sit in when Dr Deacon next hypnotises you?"

"Heavens, I ought to call him. I . . . we've a lot to tell him."

"I haven't," said Suzie. "Get out of this, Mike, it's madness."

"We promised, love."

"*You* did."

"Just tell Deacon what we both saw—please. We do owe it to him. We wouldn't have seen anything if it hadn't been for the trance, and me telling him—"

"About your space seductress?"

"Christ, don't sound jealous. I don't even know what she was now."

"That's the spirit," nodded Shriver. "Keep your neutrality— but don't let 'em get away with it."

Suzie looked furious, but kept quiet.

S I X

SUZIE STARED OUT of Deacon's window at the jumble of felled, diseased elms. The buzz of the chain-saw slicing them into manageable sections reminded her naggingly of something unpleasant long ago, perhaps a dentist's drill . . .

The intrusive noise reminded Deacon of something else. He searched for associations. This same room, yes. The topic of UFOs . . . There it was—his telephone had rung while the tape was rewinding. He'd heard a screeching sound in the receiver. Then the tape had nothing on it, almost as if the noise had wiped it clean. Surely there was no connexion.

"Mr Shriver, if you were hoping to hear the tape of Michael's trance, I'm afraid you're in for a disappointment."

Shriver leaned forward. "The tape turned out blank? Am I right?" He chuckled. "I can see I am."

Michael rounded on Deacon. "Surely you didn't erase it? You said—"

Shriver laid a restraining hand on the boy's arm. "Of course he didn't. What exactly happened, Sir?"

Deacon explained the circumstances, including the freak phone call which he'd dismissed as trivial previously.

Shriver smiled wryly. "None of that was coincidence, John." Deacon noted the switch to familiarity, as though the American considered that Deacon was now quite firmly enmeshed in his world. "Equipment has a long history of gremlins so far as UFOs are concerned. Films turn out blank. Tapes mysteriously erase themselves. It's as if there's a necessary plus and minus. You find out about Mike, the primed contactee—and God knows how many other thousands of people are primed like him! Mike transmits his information; it comes to light. Immediately you lose the hard evidence. A bit of electronic darkness descends."

Deacon scratched his head. "What you gain on the swings, you lose on the roundabouts?"

"That's it in a nutshell," nodded Shriver.

Michael hesitated, regretting his outburst and wanting to make up for it. "Maybe this is a bit like the 'unreportability' between normal and abnormal consciousness you were talking about?" he suggested. "The communication barrier?"

"Hmm. There's something else that worries me rather more. Michael, do you like Blake's poetry?"

"Not much," frowned Michael, "I couldn't stand poetry at school."

"How about Blake's Prophetic Books? You know, those long free-verse tirades about the Elemental Gods? You might have glanced through them some time?"

"I doubt it. I usually remember what I've read. They don't ring a bell. Why?"

"The reason I ask is simply that your Space People and their

37

blessed planet have names straight out of those poems. That's where you'll find Luvah, and Tharmon. Actually it's Enitharmon, which seems like a nice unconscious joke to me: 'Is there *any* Tharmon?' Ulro too, their world. I'd be most surprised if you find that anywhere in the Pleiades."

"It isn't a very likely locale," commented Shriver. "The Pleiades is a comparatively new star cluster, full of young suns. It's unlikely to have evolved any life yet."

"Ulro is a kind of Hell invented by Blake. A 'Seat of Satan'. Blake also calls it a 'False Tongue', by which I take it he means a Home of Lies. False Witness."

"But those are the names they told me! A person doesn't lie under hypnosis. You said that a hypnotised subject is pedantically truthful. In every detail."

"Ah, of the truth he believes," said Deacon. "Whatever you two saw the other night, I fear that the earlier episode—"

"Quite," said Suzie.

Shriver rubbed his hands. "Whereas for me this makes the whole episode Mike describes *more* authentic, not less. The love episode on board a flying saucer—or a medical examination or whatever—is a pretty standard contact experience. There must be several dozen such accounts—and that's leaving out all the succubus and incubus matings of the Middle Ages! It's a sort of rite of passage. Michael is fed some information that pushes him through a psychological puberty. He's transformed, even if he doesn't remember it consciously. The event presents itself in sexual terms: plausible enough, in a growing lad! But the old UFO hoodwink factor is still at work. The planet Ulro is a hoax. His Space Lady is a hoax. Why's that? Can our dear Phenomenon only do something constructive, if it presents it as a phoney? Friends from outer space, indeed! I'm glad you ran those names to earth, John. Likewise, your tape got erased."

"Oh, come now." Deacon shook his head. "Whatever Michael and Suzie saw in the evening that brought his memory back happened hours after the taping."

"The taping happened before the visible event," agreed Shriver. "Yet the event was already being triggered, through Mike—because of the trance. Obviously it's all linked: the previous 'seduction' incident, the trance and the loss of the tape, then the subsequent 'remembering' event."

"Everything's linked—for you," scoffed Suzie.

"Can you really imagine it's a coincidence, John, that the trance and the UFO event—involving *two* people, not to mention plenty of witnesses—both happened on the same day?"

"If there's a strong enough source of psychological disturbance," ventured Deacon, "one that affects both people involved . . ."

"Plus the Fire Brigade?"

"I ought to tell you something," Michael blurted. "Because it's got to do with Luvah, and there *is* a psychological disturbance affecting us both. You don't mind too much, love?" He took Suzie's silence, unfairly, for assent. "I saw the doctor about six months ago, when Suzie and I first started to, well, go together."

"Christ, Mike," she squirmed.

"I'm afraid I seem cursed with a case of premature ejaculation."

"Uncool! That's really *gauche*."

"Well, I've said it now. It's just a nuisance to us, really. We rest a bit, then it's okay." He grinned sloppily. "It's as if my first one's for the fairies . . . But I know why, now. That first experience, right? The shock of it. Then the way they suppressed it."

"If—it—happened, Michael!"

"But I know that something did happen."

"Encounters do have a lot of physical side effects," offered Shriver diplomatically. "Frequently long-lasting."

"I'm positive it'll be all right now I've remembered."

"Maybe we ought to find out!" flared Suzie. "Maybe we could use this settee? Get out the stop watch. I'm sure we need a couple of impartial observers! I've had enough of this. Are you coming, Mike?"

"I can't, love. I need to know."

The door slammed, hard enough to jar the windows.

"That's a pity," sympathized Shriver. Gisela had quit his own life for much the same reason.

39

"She'll get over it," consoled Deacon, wondering what it felt like to have someone close storm out on you; Mary was too much the good shepherd of her flock. Would it have happened if there'd only been himself present, and not the American as well? Momentarily he felt angry at the intrusion, which he'd permitted at Michael's special request—but also, he knew, because sheer curiosity about a 'UFO-watcher' outweighed his suspicions; curiosity and the hint of a possible new page for the anthology of altered states of mind . . .

First, a shot of sodium amytal in Michael's arm, to give a tighter grip on the trance. (Deacon knew that it was wrong to feel this way—to invest prestige in a hypnotic session. But he felt trapped. Challenged, Tantalised. Over and beyond the fascination of the possible new ASC was the fact that he'd lost control last time, that it was impossible he could have lost control.)

"State?" he demanded . . .

". . . And Tharmon asks me to sit in this padded seat next to one of the portholes. Both men sit at the controls. Luvah isn't here. She went down to the 'Drive Chamber' under the control room . . ."

Id-power, thrust beneath the 'surface' by the Superego twins . . .

"Outside, there's a bright red fog. When it clears we're already in the air. I don't hear any noise or feel any thrust, but the moors are really flying by, down below—"

"Why didn't you describe this part last time?"

"It wasn't there."

"You mean that it didn't happen originally? It only popped into your mind as a fresh ingredient the other night?"

"No! They made me forget it! Even more than I had to forget the rest." The recording needle quivered into the red as Michael's voice rose.

Shriver tapped a finger to his forehead, signalling for a pause, and Deacon tapped Michael on the side of the head.

"You'll sit there quietly. You'll hear nothing till you feel my finger on your head again—"

"Ask him if he can see any writing or any symbols or graphic

40

shapes or anything like that in the control room," whispered Shriver.

"There isn't likely to be a printed label on the repressed material! You have to work out its symbolism in its own terms —like the name 'Enitharmon'."

"Please."

Shrugging, Deacon put the question.

And Michael reported:

"There's a kind of diagram, a circuit diagram on Tharmon's control board. Little lights are bobbing about on it. Either Tharmon controls them by twisting the knobs, or else they tell him when to twist them—"

Shriver held out a notepad. "Can you draw it?"

Michael ignored the question, since Deacon hadn't asked it; but as soon as it was repeated he took the offered pad. Neatly, he sketched:

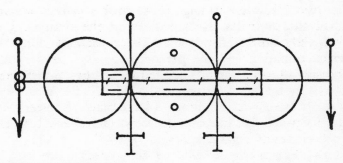

"Ah!" breathed Shriver.

The saucer flew south at high speed, over largely unlit countryside, till it reached the outskirts of London. Slowing then, it dipped, edge on, towards the city centre. The world hung on its side, yet 'down' was still faithfully underneath his seat. The tall cylinder of the Post Office Tower stuck out from the other sideways office blocks and buildings like a long boss from a shield—and interfered with them. Rays from it were disagreeing with their craft. Away spun the saucer, speeding north again, back to the Yorkshire moors.

"Rather a pointless journey," remarked Deacon.

"Not necessarily, John. They travel from one microwave tower to another. They're following a communication network, a sort of main nerve of our technology, don't you see?"

"Hmm. The mentally disturbed sometimes get scared of invisible 'rays'. Not that Michael is . . ."

"Right. He isn't."

"I suppose this 'bouncing back' from London is another built-in denial signal. His fantasy's circular, just as 'Ulro' only means 'Earth'."

Shriver shook his head. "Speaking as an ex-pilot, missions don't always turn out the way you've been briefed . . . But that isn't the real point of the flight, John. It's primarily to persuade Mike. To condition him. *He's* the target, not London. The rest just fits in like so much stage scenery. Tharmon and Company chase the microwaves—well, hell, they talked of the threat of nuclear war, and all your early warning radar data in England *does* go by microwaves through those towers—so, fair enough. And they spun him this tale about saving some human genetic stock. Again plausible flapdoodle. The *important* things here are sexual initiation and the paranormal flight, as they affect *him*. Like I say, it's a rite of passage for the boy—to prime him. It was exactly the same for witches in the Middle Ages: sexual antics and a broomstick flight off to some place of power. Magic and devilry were the frame of reference then—and the effect was: psychic transformations, of a kind. With your poor witches, like as not, ending up hoodwinked and on a bonfire. But they didn't imagine their experiences hysterically. Those *really happened*. The Phenomenon induced them. Today the frame of reference has altered." Shriver grinned down at the notepad, almost gleefully.

When Michael woke from the trance, he remembered everything; and the tape recorder remembered, too.

"Will you just look at this 'circuit diagram'?" urged Shriver. "Do you still think Mike imagined the whole thing? Do you know what this is? This just happens to be an excellent schematic for the field-energies of a spacecraft powered by a bipolar gravity field."

42

"A *what?* What are you talking about?"

"Oh I agree, John, there's *no such thing.* But if there was, what Mike drew just now would be it! Look, the top dot in the middle circle is a gravity point source projected ahead of the craft—into which it's constantly pulled. The lower dot is the same thing in reverse: a repulsion point source trailing the craft, shoving it away. It's this that digs those funny forked holes in the soil at spots where UFOs have supposedly landed. Farmers fall into them now and then. So they call the Army in, and it all gets passed off as mining subsidence or an unexploded bomb that somehow rusted away to nothing . . . This is the UFO's main propulsion system—always assuming that you *can* generate point sources of gravity and antigravity!

"The other dots and bars are secondary field inducers and stabiliser inducers, to trim the craft and give the crew a constant, reasonably level one-G inside. They need that, or they'd be alternately flattened and torn to shreds. Remember how Mike mentioned 'down' as staying constantly below, even when the craft tilted? They didn't even need seat belts, eh? I guess the craft was swinging to the right when Mike drew this, so the gravity field isn't symmetrical, and the little bars along the main axis are all canted to compensate.

"Now, that red fog he mentioned around the craft, and the visual blurring, are both by-products of these fields. You get local condensation—the air dropping below the dew point; and visible light gets red-shifted by the intensity of the G-field. Sunburn, by the way, is caused by the associated electromagnetic radiation; that's induction heating . . ."

The American chuckled bitterly. "So there's your theory of the gravity-powered spacecraft, for what it's worth—the uniquely logical way to fly. Now here we have a classic gravity field diagram! Perfect match.

"It's still baloney, John. We're dealing with an illusion of a 'spacecraft' generated by the UFO entity or entities. It's all manufactured by some idiot-savant 'UFO programme' scripted God knows when, why or how, but still ticking over merrily, still being triggered. Do you know what Tharmon and Luvah and company may be? *Tulpas.* Have you ever heard of *tulpas?*"

"Tibetan . . . somethings," nodded Deacon. Yes, he'd heard of them. Tulpas belonged on another page of the Aquarian anthology. "Part of the old Lamaist mind-science, right? Living creatures created by a prolonged act of thought."

"That's it. Materializations."

"And they're supposed to be actual tangible things, not like children's imaginary playmates—which is all eidetic imagery—or hypnagogic hallucinations. Other people can see them and touch them. They're supposed to be able to function independently in the real world."

"Right. They're independent, importunate sly bastards. Tenacious of the false life they've been given. Conceivably the ufonauts, and even *the UFOs themselves,* are really *tulpas.* It isn't such a mad idea. Translate it out of the jargon of mysticism into scientific terms, and you get something like remote-control holograms. *Solidograms*—that draw their raw material from the air and the sea, from kidnapped humans, from stolen cattle. But what projects them? And from where are they projected?"

Billows of cumulus were drifting eastward, aerial mountains of ice cream. To the west, dirtier sky was advancing along an oblique, sharp divide as a warm front moved in, bringing sheet clouds, rain streaks, thick nimbus. Deacon tried to imagine a hologram projected into the heart of one of the mighty cumuli, condensing and compacting it till it became a tiny flying saucer with a living crew, newly born, programmed with ghost identities: Tharmons and Luvahs bent on a genetic crusade on behalf of their non-existent world of Ulro. Succubi from space. Sent, in reality, for what purpose? Simply to spread confusion? A confusion as great as their own?

Briefly he pitied these putative ufonauts—transients plucked from chaos only to be dissolved back into it again. Then the effort of imagination failed. He only saw a trio of serene cauliflower heads sailing away eastwards before the storm . . .

Yet this image made more sense to him, in a curious sort of way, than an actual gleaming starship whirling down out of the sky.

The simplest explanation of Michael's experience belonged to a pretty threadbare psychological paradigm—the psychosexual. If, however, the Phenomenon could be seen as a new ASC—of a new order which somehow extended out beyond the mind into the real world, as *tulpas* were supposed to . . .?

"What do you really think they are, Barry?" he asked the American.

"Oh, I don't. As I told Mike and his young lady, neutrality's my strong suit. But one thing I'll say is, they're like subatomic particles. As soon as you think you've pinned 'em down, they split up and something new and paradoxical emerges! I don't expect a final theory of UFOs. Frankly, I'd distrust one. I'd consider it planted by the Phenomenon to sow confusion—"

"I hardly see how!"

"That's my personal feeling. As to what other people believe they are . . . Well, primo," Shriver ticked off on his fingers, "genuine alien spaceships, gravity-propelled, investigating us, invading us or just plain visiting us for fun. Two, Earth-based spacecraft from some non-homo sap civilization that predates us by millions of years and arose in the depths of our own seas. That isn't *so* ridiculous! We know damn all about the ocean depths. Three, how about energy lifeforms inhabiting space that wander into our ecosphere now and then? Or four, ancient alien mindforms that got marooned here? Maybe several different races of them all at war, under the banners of God and Satan. This brings in Theosophy and Atlantis: higher vibrational levels, higher 'octaves' of matter, co-existing dimensions. We have to suppose our own world is interpenetrated by a different, and inhabited 'vibrational' space. Which, needless to say, fails to explain the apparent stupidity of those inhabitants! Unless their logic is entirely foreign and ethereal, or unless they've actually *devolved* from a once-high peak into imbeciles, who retain all their former technical toys!

"How about time-hopping intelligences harking back from our own far future . . .? Shall I go on? I seem to be running out of fingers."

The sky had grown dark. Abruptly scudding rain washed the window, imposing a rippling, bobbling second sheet between themselves and the now murky fields.

"How did you get into all this?" Deacon asked.

45

"I was a Captain in the Air Force. My Dad was a successful realtor—real estate. He invested wisely. Then both my parents and my kid brother got killed in an automobile smash, and I left the Air Force. Hell, I was just helping kill people. So it seemed. I set off to chase this pest instead. I tell you John, it offends me deep down. I'm going to catalogue these damned tar babies, because they're a Ministry of Misinformation all around us. But I won't get tangled up in them, like some other Brer Rabbits of the Flying Saucer brigade!"

It was a typical conversion pattern, then. The shock of losing all his family. The search for another family, whose bonding was along other than military lines. A yearning for salvation from some kind of God-force in space; a lurking fear that the order of things was somehow inimical and menacing . . . Despite the American's pretence of detachment, he was stuck in his own personal tar baby without even realizing it, thought Deacon.

"Suppose Michael did draw a gravity field diagram just now, as you say . . ."

"You'd better believe it," chuckled Shriver.

"Only, as you also say, such a thing doesn't exist. So where did he get it from, for *you* to recognize it?"

"Oh, do you think he read my mind just now? No way. That's what Mike actually saw, back then. It's the real McCoy. Mike got it from the same place as he got those Blake names—courtesy of the Phenomenon. Our 'aliens' may claim it's against their ethics to reveal themselves, or similar crap to excuse them vanishing into the wide blue yonder whenever us poor guys seem to be getting close, but oh boy, this Phenomenon sure doesn't mind fishing in all our heads. Quite a few people around the world are heavily into thinking about UFOs using gravity fields. I could list a string of books and articles—and how many people do you reckon have read these and been influenced, eh? I guess William Blake casts an ever wider net. He saw real visions, didn't he? He met angels and demons walking around: obviously the dear old Phenomenon at work. Then he made a poetic mythology out of it. It's all—shall we say?—in the public domain, psychically available for plagiarising by the UFO force."

46

"Supposing that UFOs really are these *tulpa* things," spoke up Michael, "and supposing that an act of thought produces them . . . Well, the trance recreated exactly the frame of mind I was in the first time, when Luvah's saucer landed—and history repeated itself that very evening." He stared at Deacon. *"Why not again?* If you hypnotise me? If you order me to make an event happen?"

"Throw a pin to find a pin?" Deacon smiled appreciatively. "What an intriguing idea."

Rain lashed down. It was a wet Autumn. Rivers, and drains, would soon be overflowing.

SEVEN

THREE WEEKS PASSED before the attempt could be made; two sessions were called off when Michael developed raging headaches. And Deacon had devoured a small library of material about the Phenomenon by now, recommended and partly loaned by Shriver. It had him by the nose—and his nose said that there was an authentic ASC, an Altered State of Consciousness, as genuine and alien to ordinary consciousness as the hypnotic state, the meditation state or the LSD 'trip' state; one which could be labelled for convenience 'UFO-Consciousness': the altered state of mind in which it became possible to encounter, and even to generate, UFO phenomena. If Air Forces spent tens of thousands of dollars on trying to chase these things, and if he could come up with a practical hypothesis . . .

It was sunny enough when they began, but very soon clouds rolled in again, bringing another wet afternoon. Rapidly the weather worsened, and the sky grew obscure.

"Four, three, two, one. Wake up!"

Michael blinked. "Nothing happened? I *am* remembering everything?"

"The lot." Deacon switched off the recorder.

"I'm afraid I've got another headache." Michael smiled faintly. "Just a mild one, this time. I'll go and fetch the coffee!"

Nothing.

Nor had anything happened with Suzie. She was his friend again, but not his lover. She made it plain that she wasn't going to allow her sex life to be a reportable experiment. So he still did not know, about that aspect. For her, the project with John Deacon was taboo; any mention of it made her coldly angry. It was a sort of infidelity which Michael perversely refused to quit . . .

Deacon, left alone, wandered to the window and stared out into the rain. A sense of nervous regeneration, some boost of energy that the rain front had swept before it, was thoroughly dampened now. What had he been expecting anyway? What kind of folly was this? Bottled up with this . . . this choirboy with a sex problem, fondling his head, trying to invoke—*what?* He was still staring out as Michael backed in through the door, a steaming paper cup in each hand.

Through the rain outside glided a huge bird. It was not exactly gliding, though; it was simply floating, ever so slowly. Far too slowly. Not even flapping its wings.

Deacon wiped the window furiously, though the skin of rain was on the outside. The view blurred and wavered like an unfocused TV set.

"Christ, what's *that*—an albatross?"

Michael hurried to his side.

"It looks more like a pterodactyl," Michael whispered. "Something extinct."

The crested, beaked head. The squat body, slung beneath leathery bat-like wings which it held outspread on taloned fingers . . . Thirty yards away, it seemed almost the size of a man. Deacon wanted to smash the glass out with his fist. Except . . . that he wouldn't care to risk letting it hear.

"It must be a kite," said Michael anxiously. "Someone's flying a kite."

"In this weather? Talk sense!"

48

Then the flying thing swung its head in their direction, and they saw its eyes. They were glowing, garish red eyes, not much smaller than a car's brake lights and quite as bright . . .

Abruptly the flying thing banked up and away, dissolving into murk.

"A harpy," mumbled Michael. "Something mythological. From long long ago . . ."

"Damn it, we couldn't see properly! It was . . . It was—"

"It just *was*, and we'd better believe it." There was hysteria in Michael's voice. "It was an object. It flew. We can't identify it. What more do you want? I'm scared, John. Was that a UFO? A vicious harpy with no arms and a tiny little brain —!"

Suzie was lying on top of her bed listening to a Bruckner symphony; the peristaltic waves of the Romantic sublime rolled on and on. The sky and her room were dark, yet she made no move to switch a light on. Rain whipped her window. The stylus tracked across the final groove, the arm lifted off, returned; the longest theme in music began all over again.

Someone knocked on her door.

"Is that you, Mike?"

The handle rattled. The knocking resumed. Slipping off her bed, she turned the latch.

Two men wearing dark blue uniforms with air force wings stood in the corridor. One of them carried a black briefcase with bright metal catches. Their faces seemed stained with liquid suntan; they were long tapering faces. A pair of life-size Action Men dolls, she thought. Foreign-looking: Italian, or even Persian.

"We're sorry to bother you, Miss," said the man with the briefcase in a cheery voice with a note of homely Cockney in it. "We're British Air Ministry investigators. I'm Flight Lieutenant Baker. This is Warrant Officer Jones. We'd like to ask a few questions about your flying saucer sighting a few weeks ago."

" According to what your boyfriend told the papers—" the man called Jones butted in, in an excessively loud voice, so loud that it seemed to embarrass him; he didn't complete the sentence but stood shuffling from side to side. She stared at them in the weak light spilling from the corridor. As Baker slid a foot forward she noticed how clean and dry their shoes were.

Baker held up his briefcase and fiddled with the catches, as though he wasn't sure how to open them. Finally he succeeded, drew out a long printed form and rested it on the side of the briefcase in mid-air. More fumbling, then, to get a ballpoint pen to work; he scribbled jaggedly to and fro, messing the top of the form, all the time edging into the doorway till he was practically thrusting her back with the extended briefcase.

"He's interested in these things, right? He likes to poke his nose into them?"

"I didn't ask you in!" she protested.

"Oh—" Baker looked nonplussed, and leaned against the doorjamb. "Never mind, Miss. Let's see, when were you born?"

"What's that got to do with it?"

"I'd say you're about twenty." He scribbled. "Did you have any major childhood illnesses? Diphtheria, smallpox, TB—?"

"That's ridiculous—those have all been wiped out years ago! You might as well ask if I've had the Black Death. What on earth—?"

"Wiped out, eh?" boomed Warrant Officer Jones. He leered at her. "Do you really think so?"

She took a deep breath. "What sort of joke is this?"

"We're British Air Ministry investigators," repeated Baker. "I'm Flight Lieutenant Baker, we'd like to ask you—"

"You'd better cooperate," blared Jones; and shut up just as suddenly.

Baker said slyly, "We know that there was a full moon on the day, but tell me this, Miss: were you also having a period at the time? And does your period coincide with the lunar cycle? You'll pardon the impertinence. If you can just tell us that, we'll buzz off."

"You're filthy! How dare you come asking that sort of thing!"

With a shrug Baker twisted the briefcase round to face her; the little scrawling he had done on the form was huge and childish, illegible. The print itself was too small to read, in his shadow.

"Look here, Miss, we need to file a report to Central, seeing as your boyfriend's interested in these things, right? Tell you what, you just put your moniker here at the bottom then we'll fill the rest in ourselves. Make it up, eh?" He winked.

"Sign a blank form I haven't even read?" She flipped the light on, and Baker smartly pulled the form away.

"You do ask a lot of questions," he snapped in a petulant, threatening tone. "So why shouldn't we? What time is it?"

"It's time you went!" Suzie swung the door, to force them out. The door resisted her for a while, but at last the spring bolt clicked and she thrust the lock catch down.

She wasn't certain when they left; she couldn't hear any footsteps. She was still trembling with rage and fright as the record ended again, and began again.

EIGHT

MARY LED THE two wet students into the lounge, and pulled the curtains. There were brown leather Scandinavian armchairs and sofa; fleshy flowerless geraniums; a glass cabinet containing her collection of Goss Ware—a hundred miniature Victorian beakers, jugs and cruets with town coats of arms on them . . . So this was the Cupid of John's obsession, she thought —the pretty Gaveston to her husband's pathetic Edward. His channel to the infinite. At least his girl was with him!

Suzie stared back in a hostile yet curiously begging way, deeply resenting this house and anyone in it, yet hoping it might hold some kind of cure.

"What's this nonsense about conjuring up a pterodactyl?" Mary demanded.

The boy smiled primly. A coy mincing simper.

"It doesn't matter! I'll fetch John—he's upstairs."

John was not upstairs.

As Mary retraced her steps she heard the back door bang. She found her husband standing in the kitchen in wet slippers; the uppers were dark with damp. His hands were dirty. Turning to the sink, he washed them vigorously.

"Shep was being a nuisance. He wanted to be out." He fumbled with a towel. Only when she told him that his protégé was in the house did he really sharpen up and gain precision.

"Something happened? Ah!"

She followed through into the lounge and watched him closely, as Suzie Meade resentfully told of the visit by the Air Force investigators, their disconnected behaviour, their threatening manner, their idiotic obscene questions.

"I did telephone the Air Ministry," Michael said. "Then the Military Aeronautical Information Service. They put me on to the Ministry of Defence. But of course there weren't any investigators! They flatly denied it."

"Did you phone the Police?" Mary asked. "They sound like a fairly disgusting couple of perverts."

"They were so *wrong*," moaned Suzie. "A brand new briefcase, that they didn't seem to know how to open. And bright clean shoes." She glanced at Deacon's feet. "It was pouring outside, but their shoes weren't even wet."

"A hoax," soothed Mary. She offered Suzie a drink, and poured gin, ignoring the men.

"It couldn't be a hoax!" shuddered Suzie. "Why should anybody *bother*?"

Deacon shook his head firmly. "Men in Black. That's what they were—MIBs."

Michael nodded. "I knew they had to be. As soon as I heard. I wanted you to explain it to her, John. Though I had the devil of a job persuading her!"

"What on earth are Men in Black supposed to be?" asked Mary.

"I've been finding out a lot about them lately. They're definitely a part of the Phenomenon. They look a bit oriental—typically they're short people with sallow skins. Clothes and

52

equipment are all perfectly new, though often they don't seem remotely at home with it. They turn up, usually in pairs, in the wake of UFO sightings when there's been some publicity. Sometimes they pose as Air Force officers. They ask the damnedest questions. They scare people. They tell them to keep their mouths shut. I'd give you any odds those two characters were MIBs. Did we," he whispered across to Michael, "trigger them too?"

"They weren't dressed in black," protested Suzie.

Deacon nodded. "They're just called that because they often drive around in black cars and wear black suits—though obviously not when they're impersonating officers in uniform. The American Air Force apparently got quite worried about these impersonations! Nobody ever pins them down. They just drive off and vanish. It can be pretty scarey."

"I suppose they're really the Venusians in our midst?" asked Mary acidly.

"Venus is five hundred degrees Centigrade, dear, and the pressure would crush you flat. You'd be boiled, squashed, corroded and poisoned in ten seconds. They certainly don't come from anywhere 'out there'. They belong in the same constellation as ghosts and poltergeists, angels and demons and fairies. Why, that creature we called up in the rain—"

"Called up? You seriously believe that you two saw anything other than a perfectly ordinary bird?"

The egg had hatched: a fabulous monster, a roc, a pterodactyl . . . Deep down, she had known all along that John was only a *tourist* of altered states of consciousness, of the tropics of the soul, snapping away at the various prodigies and marvels of Yoga, Tantra, Hypnosis, and ESP with a camera. He was the Bouvard and Pécuchet of the mental Beyond, and now he was making errors as grotesque as ever Flaubert's two bourgeois clerks did when they got free rein . . . It wasn't so much that he was erecting a pseudoscience as cosmetic for a wretched, squirming affair with this pretty boy; yet he *was* in a doting relationship with the boy now—feeding on his immaturity, and in the process warping both himself and the boy, whom his attention naturally excited. The spectacle sickened her.

53

"What if MIBs are *tulpas*, John?" (The boy called him John.) "That's why their clothes look so brand new, why they talk nonsense, why they can't open a briefcase properly. Because they're imperfectly programmed. Their reality has mothholes in it—"

"What are *tulpas*?" She poured the girl another gin. Michael did his best to answer the question; she only listened for a while, before interrupting.

"Obviously two not-so-funny jokers live somewhere in this town."

"That's a point," nodded Deacon—more in Michael's direction than in hers. "It would be more economical to suppose that MIBs are actually human beings who get used. Without their even knowing it! People who've been . . . infiltrated, preprogrammed. People who can be activated—"

"By somebody else in a UFO-conscious state, you mean? Did we do that to Suzie?"

"Who can be made to hire costumes, rent cars, buy briefcases, make phone calls—without even knowing it! I wonder if a lot of human beings have got such programmes planted in them—buried deep down? How many 'mad' assassins—Sirhan Sirhans or Jack Rubys or that South American who tried to knife the Pope—say a voice ordered them to do it? They couldn't disobey it. They had no idea what was going on, no memory of the episode afterwards. They were in a trance, robotised. Why dismiss what they say out of hand? What if we're all just really some sort of advanced thinking robot, or being *used* as such! Seemingly free to do what we want most of the time, yet liable to be switched on to some other purpose entirely? What if we're all just cells in something larger, a collective with a purpose and ethics of its own? Do we feel qualms about trimming our fingernails or our hair?"

Mary listened, appalled. Suzie darted her a look, briefly, of angry sympathy.

"We need to dig deeper," Deacon said to Michael. "We need to find out if you have any prior 'programmes'—preceding your flight at sixteen!"

"Right!"

"Maybe we're not meant to think about this. I don't mean 'there are things men should not know'. But maybe this over-programme isn't written in such a way that we can appreciate the programming. It's a sort of higher order information. Yet we do catch glimpses—as we see UFOs! Then the MIB aspect, all the negative features, home in automatically, confusing, scaring, destroying, cancelling understanding. So the real nature of the over-programme remains aloof. So it works smoothly—to what end?"

"That's pretty scarey," Michael agreed, infected with excitement—Mary could well see—by the sheer madness of John's improvisations. "Didn't Barry say one of the UFO theories has other dimensions coexisting with our own? What if it's the *mind* that coexists? What if there's another sort of mind coexisting with ours: working through it, inhabiting it, using it? Why, maybe there's the origin of 'The Joke' you've found deep down in hypnosis—the hidden observer apart from the conscious personality!"

The door flew open; Rob stood there, just briefly—"I heard a cry in the garden!"—before he was gone again.

When they reached the kitchen door, Rob, out on the dark wet lawn, was already clutching at a sobbing, whimpering Celia. She broke away from him, stumbling off towards the bottom of the garden. Bursting through rotting chrysanthemums, she sank to her knees in the mud of the border, against the fence. Low, slatted, in indifferent repair, this fence gave on to a boarded-up waste ground of willowherb, saplings and tumbled stones.

"Take a torch, John!" ordered Mary.

A moment later Deacon ran across the lawn, torchbeam wagging. Michael followed him.

Celia, sobbing, struggled with a shapeless mass blocking a gap in the fence. She thrust her brother aside as he ducked and darted helpfully at it, and her.

"It's Shep, Dad," the boy explained lamely. "Shep's dead."

Deacon pulled Celia away, and shone the torch down. He still couldn't tell which way round the dog was lying. He stared, puzzled.

55

"Don't you realize—there's no head!" Celia screamed. "Where's his head?"

This was a dog reduced to a thing, without dignity. Shep was a stuffed giant cushion with four crumpled legs, rear and front ends rendered identical. Parting the long hair, Deacon hunted about vaguely as though he might find the head still somewhere there—intruded, tortoiselike, into the body of the animal. All he found was a pink circular cross section: skin, muscle, bone, windpipe. As neatly cut as a wire cuts butter.

"There—isn't—any—blood!" wailed Celia, a very little girl again. "He's—empty!"

Michael slipped to one side and doused the kitchen light, a conjuror performing sleight of hand, while Suzie was still hugging Celia to her, comforting a fellow victim . . .

"Look—!" he cried.

Above the bottom of the garden bobbed an amorphous ball of green light, bouncing gently along the line of the fence and back again. A blip on an oscilloscope screen, measuring something, a heartbeat maybe, recording . . . their reactions?

"Can you influence it?" whispered Deacon. "Try to make it go to the left. Will it to go!" When Deacon was a boy he had lain in summer fields staring up at a blue sky, to the pock of bat on ball, trying to will the floaters in the vitreous humour of the eyeball to move at his command, trying to influence his own body cells, adrift in that extension of the brain. If there was any truth in psychokinesis . . .

"Left," hissed Michael. "Left. Left." Mary Deacon stared across the darkened kitchen at her husband and the boy with hatred.

The ball of light flicked off perversely to the right. In a wavering zigzag it rose to the topmost branches of the horse chestnut in the nextdoor garden, where it faintly illuminated leafless boughs and twig fingers. As they watched, it vanished quite suddenly from sight.

"If nobody else will, I'll phone the Police," said Mary.

NINE

"It could have been a sword," said the sergeant. "A razor-sharp one. One clean blow." He made a guillotine gesture. "Possibly one of those Jap Samurai jobs. There are some about. It could have been some martial arts nut, with a sick mind."

The Sergeant and Constable had found no trace, in half an hour, of killer or dog's head.

"Kendo," suggested Deacon. "Japanese fencing. There are Kendo clubs, aren't there? Perhaps someone who'd learnt at a Kendo club?"

"You know something about . . . Kendo yourself, Mr. Deacon?"

"Nothing really! Only in connexion with Zen Buddhism. You see, Japanese martial arts are used as Zen disciplines—I'm interested in Zen."

"I see, Sir."

Deacon relaxed. No action of his could have had the effect of a sword stroke. He had indeed wandered a few steps on to the lawn, after letting Shep into the garden. The sky was clearing; he'd simply been skygazing. Seeing if anything was up there. He'd soiled his hands when he shifted a spade, left in the rain, back under shelter. Soil had spattered them. Could it have been the blade of a spade? Quite impossible. The atrocity that overtook Shep came from some outside source . . .

Or—the thought struck him—was this what he was meant to think? That the Phenomenon was wholly external? When, actually, he'd been considering the opposite!

He had nothing to do with the death directly . . . *Except* that he'd been brooding intensively about the Phenomenon. *Except* that Michael, apparently a magnet for it, was by then quite near

57

the house. Except for the events of this afternoon! Could a human being both be responsible and not be responsible at onc and the same time?

Deacon felt as though he was staring down a very deep well, inside himself. At the bottom hung a grinning—or sneering—face, which wasn't his own and never had been. An unhuman face. Simply the sense of a face. Observing. Aware. That it even had human features seemed coincidental—a mere metaphor of the perception filters. If he feared it, it scowled. If he felt it spelled salvation, then it smiled. Suppose that deep down in Michael's mind, and in every other human being's, lurked the same protean creature, somehow existing in its own right, independent of its host? Suppose that the mind-creature was shared equally by all minds!

He was actually, he realized, very tired and already in a hypnagogic state—falling asleep where he stood, on the fringes of exhaustion, with dream imagery welling up while he was still awake, half-dreaming what Michael had said in the lounge an hour ago.

"Are you feeling all right, Sir?"

"It's a terrible shock." Deacon sat at the pine table; he shook his head. "Filthy."

"Yet strangely *clean*, Sir. The lack of blood is very odd."

Vampires . . .? In another age, there was another frame of reference . . . Dogs and cattle certainly disappeared in the wake of UFO visits. There were enough reports of this. But today's frame of reference was one of alien spacecraft, so that vampires were no more; the visitors must be analysing Earth's biology . . . Apparently they needed to steal living matter. Why? To make new *tulpas*?

"Can we keep this from the newspapers?" Mary asked the Sergeant. "I've already heard enough foolishness for a lifetime."

"How do you mean, Madam?"

Reluctantly, she explained why the two students were there that night. The Sergeant looked increasingly nonplussed.

"These two strangers tried to force their way into your room, posing as Air Ministry Investigators—because you saw a flying saucer?" he asked Suzie.

"They didn't exactly force their way, they just scared me—"

He asked Suzie more questions. Suddenly he turned to Deacon.

"So you really think that green light you saw was one of those *things*? And it decapitated your dog?"

Deacon spread his hands on the table. Ten fingers, ten explanations.

"There's nothing that cuts off a pet dog's head and steals it, except some very insane nasty human being!" said Mary.

"A very odd way for visiting spacemen to conduct themselves! If you think that, Sir, why did you mention Kendo?"

"No, *you* mentioned swords first—" The insane swordsman *was* preferable as an explanation, if more immediately frightening.

"Ah. So I did. What do you think that green light really was?"

Mary frowned at her husband.

"A balloon," she prompted. "A luminous one. Whoever did it brought it with them."

"Why should anyone do that?"

"Why do people wreck bus shelters?" Mary asked.

The Sergeant nodded. "I sometimes wonder why people do what they do half the time."

TEN

"WE'LL TRY AND locate any previous contact episode— not necessarily with your space people from Ulro, but any weird, anomalous events which might be a precursor—"

Deacon injected Michael with sodium amytal, and spoke the cue word.

"I want you to fix on any incident in your life, before the

UFO-consciousness event when you were sixteen, that struck you as remarkably out of the ordinary . . ."

The day was crisp and sharp; crows the size of terriers stomped hungrily around the empty fields, wheeling into the air and bouncing down again. After three weeks' tactful delay, the Christmas vacation was due in a week; so Michael sat in the green chair again. Celia had buried Shep's headless body in the garden. The episode, officially, was closed or at least dormant; it was, after all, only a dead dog . . .

In trance, Michael recounted a number of coincidences, which could all be explained as precisely that: coincidences, grassroots acausalities . . .

Yet what had Sheikh Ali Ibrahim Muradi, delivering his lecture on Sufism in the 'Consciousness: Ancient and Modern' series, said about such coincidences? He had said that there are invisible connexions between events. That things happen in succession but sometimes it is a different sort of succession from what most people imagine. Sometimes another dimension impinges upon events, their real cause lying there. Miracles, said the Egyptian (visiting London, en route to America), are really bound up with problems of causality. Cause and effect relationships can be other than generally thought, because of these inner correspondences between things. When true intellect occasionally breaks through, revealing inner causes and linkages, so-called 'occult' phenomena can occur . . . 'Occult', that is, in the eyes of everyday consciousness. But mind could not know itself by force of will alone. You must tap the roots of grace instead. You must seek hidden help. Help would be forthcoming, however unexpectedly, if you entered the right state of mind . . .

Suddenly Muradi seemed very vivid to Deacon. He seemed to hear the Sheikh's own voice—quiet, humorous, incisive—speaking in the room, though in fact it was only Michael's trance voice recounting another trivial happenstance event.

Muradi's voice was talking about miracles. About help beyond comprehension. About help as though from another world. *Karama* was the word for it in Arabic.

"Michael," Deacon cut in, "has a *miracle* ever happened to you? Have you ever been helped—or saved—as though miraculously? If you were told to forget it, you can ignore that instruction now. I say so."

"Yes! Of course! The petrol tanker—it nearly hit me!"

"What age are you?"

"I'm twelve. And five and a bit months. I'm cycling home from school. There's a very long hill with a curve at the bottom. I always freewheel down it very fast. Today there's a big black car parked half-way down with a man standing beside it. He's wearing sunglasses, though the sun isn't shining. It's a misty day."

"What does the man look like?"

"He's short. His skin's sallow. He has black hair, I think—but he's wearing a peaked cap. He's dressed like a chauffeur. He flags me down . . . some trouble with their car, I shouldn't be surprised. It's quite old—a pre-War Bentley, though it's very clean and shiny. Another man's sitting in the driver's seat, wearing the same sort of uniform; sunglasses too. That's odd—two chauffeurs.

"They couldn't have stopped me much further down the hill; I'd have been going too fast. I get off my bike—and the chauffeur grabs me by the elbow. I think it's because something else is coming; but nothing is. I get scared and I try to pull free, but he hauls me round the car.

" 'If you run away, you'll have a terrible accident,' he says to me. 'Get in.' It sounds like a threat, as though they'll harm me if I run away. The man inside pushes the door open, and I'm bundled in with him. The car's incredibly clean. It looks brand new, even though it's such an old model. The dashboard's strange —full of little winking lights of different colours. They fascinate me. I just want to stare at them, even though I'm scared.

"The man in the driver's seat points down the hill. 'Look,' he says. 'You are reaching the bottom just now. Travelling so fast, so very fast—'

"Suddenly a petrol tanker comes round the bend. It's really speeding, and it's right over on the wrong side of the road, against the far verge. Soil is spraying up from the wheels.

" 'That's where you are right now,' the man says. 'You're flying up against it. You're dead. It skids out of control. It turns over. Boom, it explodes. Gasoline everywhere.' That's what he says, but he isn't American. The accent sounds South African, clipped and nasal. 'Flames!' As if he's actually seeing all this! I can believe him too. That's where I'd have been. I couldn't have missed the tanker. But the tanker's coming out of the bend now, and it's heading up the hill towards us. It goes past us with the engine roaring. The driver looks as if he's seen a ghost.

"All those coloured lights on the dashboard start flickering madly. They seem to be flashing morse code. All sorts of different messages. I learnt morse in the Scouts, but I was only in them for a few months . . . Too fast, too many messages at once. They're just . . . very pretty. Pretty patterns.

"The chauffeur man opens the door to pull me out. He stares at me through his shades. The glasses really bend his eyes and magnify them! I ask him, 'Did you just save my life?' He says, 'Forget it.' And I do. That's the strange part. I can't remember them—afterwards. But I always ride down that hill a lot slower. Even if I have to walk all the way up the other side."

Karama . . . Help beyond comprehension.

Michael had received it from two Men in Black parked in an antiquated yet brand new car. (As though, to get their timing right in one respect, to anticipate the very moment when a petrol tanker would have hit his bicycle, they had by some principle of compensation to get it wildly wrong in another . . .)

In Sufist lore, said Sheikh Muradi, a mysterious saint called Khidr often brought help beyond comprehension: a secret guide, whose nickname was The Green One. Dressed in luminous, shimmering green—as though he wore green fire—he appeared at moments of insight and breakthrough. After delivering his message, he would vanish into thin air, disappear from normal cognition.

Was he one of the UFO personae too—elder brother to the Little Green Men, the UFO gremlins? Muradi's lecture! It was even in the book *Consciousness: Ancient and Modern*! Why hadn't he made the connexion till now? The two areas had seemed too far apart to register . . . when in reality they lay side by side, as close as the inside and outside of the same bottle. Had Sufi adepts conceivably achieved a state of mind that tamed and mastered this phenomenon, which he had christened UFO-Consciousness?

If only Muradi were still in the country. The ripples from his unpretentious lecture—which Deacon had thought one of the least in the series at the time—were actually still spreading out, still resonating. Deacon wanted so much to be beside him, asking for a hint of how to proceed . . .

He woke Michael. As he did so, the single word 'ego' popped into his mind.

Michael remembered the 'miracle'. He felt no headache after this trance—all the weight had lifted. However, Deacon felt excited for another reason.

"I have an idea, Michael. A great idea. When you get down to a certain level in a trance, it doesn't feel as though your everyday ego is present any more, right? Your awareness of a personal 'self' vanishes. You feel as if you can be anybody or anything. And deeper still, when you enter the void of the mystics, there isn't even anybody or anything to be."

"I . . . we haven't really explored as far as that."

"We will. I've seen how to. Your ego *is* absent from those deep states—because ego is really only a tag or flavour that gets applied to some mental structures, but not to others. This 'ego-tag' just doesn't attach itself to the deep experiences, so you don't have any sense of volition or control. I suggest this is the case with UFO-Consciousness. You feel yourself manipulated by other agencies, don't you?"

Michael shivered. "Are you saying that the self is just an illusion? That there isn't really any 'I' at all?"

"Oh, it's real enough. Obviously this idea of self is a powerful survival mechanism. It's bloody necessary. *And* it maintains the tone of our being—it keeps our waking consciousness in tune. Yet it only applies to certain mental states—on and around the workaday baseline—while our whole mind is really a bundle of different, coexisting structures. This coexistence comes apart deep in hypnosis, I'd say. The ego gets left behind. Different mental subprogrammes become independent 'minds' in their own

63

right. If only we could graft the 'ego-tag'—this flavour of personal self—on to some of these deep 'non-ego' structures we'd be able to control them consciously."

"But is that possible? I mean, to graft the 'ego-tag'?"

"I think so—using hypnotic commands. There's actually an analogy with our sense of time. All our memories are 'tagged' in our minds with the label 'past events'—or we wouldn't be able to distinguish memory from present experience. Yet we know that this time-tag *can* get displaced. That's where you get the sense of *déja vu*—the belief that you've already experienced something which is actually happening right now for the very first time. If the time-tag can get displaced, why not the ego-tag too? It's just a question of isolating the neural flavour of the ego-tag by a process of subtraction as you go deeper into trance —holding it in brackets, as it were—then ordering it back into the game. If we can graft this 'tag' on to the UFO-Consciousness state, we'll be able to tap directly into this area. That's what was missing last time, with the pterodactyl—conscious control."

And safety. Sufis seemed to know how to tap this area, without being possessed by its devilries, by the jinn locked in the bottle of the soul.

"You want to try this . . . grafting process with me?"

"I don't exactly know how to do it—not yet. It might still be the wrong model, you understand?"

"But you feel it's right."

"Along the right lines, yes."

The telephone rang.

"I thought nobody could interrupt us while we were—?"

"They can't," frowned Deacon. "I switched off. I know I did."

"It isn't switched off now."

"No."

He lifted the receiver and listened.

"Cosmos and Humankind are one," said a voice. The voice reminded him of Suzie Meade's, though the words were nothing she would be likely to say. "All mind and matter form a unity—"

"Who's that? Is it you, Suzie?" ("What?" from Michael. "Ssh!")

"Mind flourishes when the Moon pulls strongest. Why else should a woman void her womb every thirty days, by the Moon? All is synchronised: *mind and matter*! Humans can untune Creation by their actions—"

If it was her voice—and he began to doubt it—she sounded drugged. Or hypnotised. As he listened, he wondered whether this queer, archaically phrased mélange of Tharmon's warnings and the MIB's obscene questions had any essential meaning? Had someone—or something—been trying to convey a genuine message to Suzie three weeks earlier, with utter inefficiency? With much noise in the signal that it turned it into an obscene insulting threat?

"Do you *know* who you are?" he interrupted. "Have you got a real identity?" Michael moved close, straining to hear. He shook his head; it wasn't Suzie, to him.

"A terrible time is upon us. The world might abort itself of embryo, man. For you poison the womb. Then others will come in your place. But there is still time. You can be guided. Only, you must do what you're told exactly. You mustn't question. Mustn't—"

"What terrible time? What others?"

"—mustn't—ask—questions—about—flying—saucer—beings. Must—accept—"

Far away, the words grew more disconnected; as though someone was reading aloud in a foreign language which they only knew how to pronounce, not understand.

Shaking his head to empty his ears, like a swimmer emerging from a pool, Deacon cradled the receiver.

"So they can tap into telephone lines," he murmured, shaken. "They can materialise plasma clouds in the sky, and produce malprogrammed *tulpas*—as well as perfect copies of cars. They can tap into the human brain, deep down. Or are they there— is *it* there—already? And I'm supposed to quit, and not ask questions!" They had destroyed his dog, as an object lesson: an act of vicious, petty intimidation. How did that sort with the purity, transcendence, wise interventions of the Sufi Green Man?

In no way.

Yet it had to. Somehow it must. How?

"We'll try in the new year," he promised Michael "Till then, take care."

PART TWO

ELEVEN

THAT EVENING, NAGUIB Fouad quarrelled with his son again, about the Sheikh and his circle.

At the age of fifty, Naguib had risen as high up the hierarchy of the Ministry of Finance as he was likely to; high enough, though. The family flat, on the eastern, less luxurious side of Roda Island, was proud achievement for one whose father herded buffalo all his life in Upper Egypt. Reproduction Louis Quinze provincial *fauteuils* with cabriole legs, carpentered locally, clustered round the dining table. A pallid oil painting of bathing cabins on some French beach hung over the elephantine sofa, where Mrs Fouad sat whispering interminably into the telephone to her sister about her current stomach disorder. Naguib relaxed in pyjamas in his favourite armchair, frowning at cartoons in the *Rosa al-Youssef*. Ridiculously skinny men in *galabiya* robes were prancing up and down, spinning round and falling over each other while sweat poured from their faces and sinews stood out in their necks.

As soon as Salim came in from the University, Naguib pushed the *Rosa* at his son.

"Are you going out again tonight? Going *there*?"

"It isn't really much like that, Father."

Naguib jumped up and minced round the room, clapping his hands faster and faster. "Hayy! Hayy! Hayy!" he chanted. Despairingly, he sank back into the vastness of the armchair.

"Religion's all very well," he lectured acidly. "Ours is a religious country, God be praised. Of course I'm religious! Not a Communist like some of you students, though sometimes frankly I wish you were a Communist instead. Our country might need miracles—but not that sort! I suppose yours is an

69

attack of adolescent piety; it still grieves me. Mockery is all it brings. Can't you fall in love instead?"

His son shifted from one foot to the other: a tolerably handsome, rather skinny boy, with slightly protruding ears. He wore a freshly-ironed white shirt (which he must have collected from the laundryman on his way home, *for tonight*), loose trousers, plimsolls and a leather jacket. The boy smiled apologetically.

"I should fall in love? With whom? Ibn el-Arabi once said that the lover loves a secondary phenomenon—'whereas I love the Real, the Essential'. It's much the same with miracles, Father. They're a secondary phenomenon too. If all a person hunts for along the Sufi way is miracles, he'll never find the Real that underlies them. They'll always go on seeming merely like miracles."

"How you can attend engineering lectures, and spout this kind of mysticism defeats me!"

"The answer's quite simple. Unlike the yogi on his bed of nails, we work *in* the world. We do our jobs as well as we can, in society; meanwhile, we're part of another current helping to guide the world."

"You're a prig, boy."

Salim tapped the cartoon page. "This sort of self-intoxication is as bad as drink. I know that some Orders indulge in it. But we mustn't try to quit the world. We must behave as though this world is real, even while there's a deeper reality. God wants us to be here. But of course this produces a certain heedlessness of God—"

"I'm not heedless, boy! Don't they tell you to respect a father?" (Could this son, Naguib wondered askance, be *holy*? He rejected the idea.)

"Heedlessness, I mean, because if there wasn't that, and if everyone perceived, the world would be sure to vanish."

"Oh would it indeed? Pray God that sort of foolishness isn't in your head when you're designing a bridge, may God let me see that day!"

"I promise it will be the best bridge I can make."

"God forbid," murmured Mrs Fouad into the receiver. It was her turn, now, to hear her sister's ailments. Kidneys, liver, urinary tract, wherever. Sickness migrated round the body like a band of nomads, pitching its tent in this organ then in that, sustaining a huge industry of laxatives, pills and tonics. Cupping her hand over the mouthpiece, she asked Salim, "Fetch me a glass of water?" and sank deeper in the sofa, clucking sympathy.

In the kitchen, the Nubian houseboy was sorting a heap of giblets on an iron-top table. Salim found a bottle of mineral water, returned and poured it. By now Mrs Fouad was clutching a little yellow pill.

"Isn't it true that you seize your Sheikh's hem to capture *magic*? Don't you all wash your hands and faces in the carpet, for *baraka*?" Naguib flapped his hands in parody.

"For the blessing? Our more countrified cousins sometimes do. It's frowned on. Generally there's just the hand kiss. Come along and see, Father."

"Go there? God forbid. I have a position in life."

"Sheikh Muradi has taught overseas, you know. He's much respected. He has been to Europe and America."

"Pah! America can afford mysticism. It has enough money. What did he lecture about?"

"The hidden currents—"

"Indeed! Well, you can't deny that your people do boast about his *karamat*, his little miracles. I certainly heard you boasting in this very room about that chap who fell off Tahrir Bridge into the Nile—God knows how anyone can be so stupid, is that a hidden current, eh, the Nile? He was worrying how to find the cash for his rent, right? So, while he's flailing about in the water, his hand closes on this soggy banknote that must have blown out of somebody else's hand into the river upstream. He surfaces with this banknote in his hand and hears your Sheikh's voice telling him to be more careful next time. After all that drenching I'm not surprised he hears voices in his ears."

"People get overenthusiastic. I've made that same mistake, Father. In this room, as you say. People get carried away."

"Off bridges, ha! You don't really believe in these hidden currents, do you? Some kind of invisible community governing the universe—headed by some mysterious Axis of the Age, isn't that it?"

"Maybe there *are* events beyond comprehension by reason—*fuq al'aql*, above the intelligence. If there are, then we can't speak of them without producing a nonsense. But they can still be experienced."

"It strikes me as thoroughly blasphemous that God should bother himself with a banknote."

"That's the whole point of that story, Dad! We don't properly see the connexions that produce such an event. Yet events do impinge on our lives from another level. I'm sure of it. Truth is constantly trying to show itself to Men. In the shape of a banknote floating in the Nile—as much as in the Burning Bush. Or it takes upon itself a human form. Remember how Moses had a guide whose actions seemed absurd? They all had a reason, but even Moses got impatient—"

"Thank you for your comparison, but I'm not Moses!"

" 'How can you tolerate that which is beyond your knowledge?' the guide said to him. One day, when we see the connexions—"

"The World will fall apart?"

A smell of grilling hearts, tails and livers drifted in from the kitchen; Mrs Fouad cradled the phone at last.

"That boy says he had to queue two and a half hours at the Co-op to get those . . . entrails. Should we believe him? Do you think he was really at the cinema?"

Naguib shrugged. "Let's assume he was queueing. We don't want to lose him, do we?" He glared at his son. "You might as well go to some *zaf* in a brothel—some séance, as though you were a kitchen maid!"

"Are you two arguing about that again?" Mrs Fouad asked. "God forbid, it makes me ill."

The Nubian youth carried in a bowl of boiled potatoes and tomatoes and a tiny beef salad to go with the giblets. He smiled vaguely at the TV set that he hoped to be watching later on in company with the Fouads. For a new song was promised, from Wafaa—'fidelity'—Wahbi, rising successor to the vasty voice of Um Kalthum.

After dinner Salim caught a number eight bus from near

72

University Hospital along Kasr-al-Aini Street to Liberation Square; here he boarded a second bus bound along al-Bustan Street for al-Azhar.

Gamaliya, ancient crowded bustling quarter of the *galabiya* robe, increasingly was becoming Salim's own personal Cairo, his Cairo of the mind. Every visit to the headquarters of the Order was a voyage on two planes: the spiritual, of course, but on the way there was the discovery, too, of hidden social sources which his father preferred to forget—the *baladi* landscape, village Egypt in the midst of the city.

Narrow streets crazed the quarter like deep cracks in long-dried mud, illuminated by strings of naked light bulbs strung from shopfront to shopfront, by livid neon calligraphies, intermittent lamp-posts like giant matchsticks with glass-blob heads, with in-between zones of hissing paraffin light. Streets and alleys were flickering subterranean canals. Pots, pans, second-hand ball bearings, old clothes, beads, incense, charms, bathplugs cut from spent lorry tyres were up for bargain. Male concièrges squatted on doorsteps of balconied tenements. Men in the cafés played backgammon and chattered, full of protestations. Somewhere overhead ranged the tin shacks of a second, even poorer world which had colonised the sky—farmyards on top of the city, where lambs bleated plaintively in the dark.

He crossed a small plaza fronting a bathhouse of Ottoman design: intricately wrought iron grilles. A crowd was gazing at the large public TV upon a tripod there. An improving romance of young love at the Aswan High Dam was on the screen. A sherbet seller meandered about, clacking his metal saucers. A religious orator was attracting an audience of much the same size as he belaboured superstitions and decried the magic charms on sale nearby.

Salim caught some of the diatribe as he walked past.

"Have you ever bought a blue bead for your daughter to save her from the evil eye? Have you ever begged permission of the Jinn before you used the toilet? Didn't the Prophet—the blessings of God be upon him and his family!—say in the *Sura* called *al-Jinn*, 'Some men sought the help of Jinns, yet they misled them into further error'? The meaning of this is perfectly

73

plain! Even though the majority of Jinns were converted—"

The words faded as Salim walked on, his thoughts not on Jinns that supposedly haunted rivers and streams and even toilet bowls nowadays, but on the mysterious supranormal Guide —the emanation and representation of the unseen linkages in the universe—he who was called Khidr, Green Man, Master of the Saints, Patron of the Orders, and who merely seemed to be outside the world of TV screens and hydroelectric schemes . . . How, Salim wondered, did Sheikh Muradi himself conceive of Khidr? Already he realized that this was a meaningless question. If Salim knew the answer, he would be as the Sheikh was, not as himself who asked the question! The realization brought a note of joy.

He came to an old stone building hemmed by pale cement shops. Hunks of purple buffalo carcass hung outside one shop, bright carpets outside another.

The windows of this building were blocked by thick metal grilles; however, iron-studded doors stood wide open. Beyond a vestibule, naked bulbs lit a courtyard containing a small, railed pool. Water bubbled from the knob of a fountain, sending ripples crossing and recrossing. Ancient blighted stones led to a modern hall with sliding lattice doors. About fifty men were already gathered there. Some wore light suits, others simply a shirt and trousers. There were kaftans, too, and long white *galabiyas* topped by cotton skullcap turbans.

Salim stepped inside, nodding to his friends and brothers. When first he came to the Circle he thought of them, effusively, as the friends of his true life. No longer, though. The world of the engineering student must remain every bit as real as this, or else this was not real at all—then the Work wouldn't be done properly.

The men formed ranks when the Sheikh came in from a side room, interlacing their fingers. And Salim gazed at the Sheikh.

He was a short, black-bearded man with thin eagle nose and hooded eyelids exaggerated by hornrimmed glasses. His eyes weren't lugubrious or fatigued, though. The dark eyes shone. They discerned. They asked a host of questions wherever he looked. Muradi wore the long, full-sleeved gown and long kaftan; his tight turban was wound with the green band of the Order. Yet he wore these robes only for ritual events. At home— a very modern one, so it was said, in the medieval city not too far from the great mosque of Ibn Talun—he dressed western style; likewise in his secular role as Professor of Arabic and Persian Languages at al-Azhar—thus gently emphasizing the truth that there was nothing feudal, reactionary or retreatist about the Order.

How misplaced were his Father's jokes! Even if they did apply to some of the popular Orders! Even as he thought this, Salim realized that the Sheikh's eyes were upon him, reproaching him, so it seemed, for remembering anything other than God at this moment. He composed himself.

Dhikr commenced—the Remembrance of God.

The profession of the Faith. The recitation of the Name. The cycle of the Odes . . .

TWELVE

THE CONSCIOUSNESS RESEARCH Group was in session: the forty-first meeting of the staff seminar. Deacon had invited Michael to sit in, on this dark February afternoon, when he would broach a tentative theory and method for the state of UFO-consciousness . . .

"—How can one 'ego-tag' that mental island-state, so that the UFO-conscious person is consciously aware of his or her role in it? How does one stamp a visa on the psyche, how does one issue a state-specific entry permit to that very powerful and enigmatic island?" Deacon sat back, pleased with the rhetorical flourish.

"One moment," said Martin Bull, a stocky, ginger-headed, rugby-playing man; a neural cybernetics modeller. "I thought flying saucers were supposed to exist in the real world? They appear on radar screens. They get their photos taken. How could you take a photo of something that's purely in the mind?"

"They aren't 'purely' in the mind, Martin! I'm sure their roots are there—but they affect external reality *as well*. Anyway, since you mention photos, there is such a thing as psycho-photography."

"The Amazing Ted Serios?"

"Why not? Ted Serios seemed by all accounts to be authentic. He was well investigated. He could produce photos of distant buildings—ones he'd never even visited—simply by staring into the camera. He had to work himself into a drunken fury to do it. That's to say, he forced himself into an ASC which actually influenced photographic emulsion in the external world."

"But could he knock planes out of the sky and burn holes in the ground? Your flying saucers are supposed to do that, aren't they?"

"This might be a far more powerful form of the same thing. Ted Serios induced an ASC in himself. He didn't know *what* it was—heavens, he was only a semi-educated hotel porter in Chicago—but he knew what it *felt* like. There's one key: the sensations accompanying the ASC. Start by inducing those—suggest them hypnotically, once we know exactly what they are. Naturally this will involve a whole lot of interdisciplinary work: ASC research, kinesics, muscle memory, discrete states of posture . . . not forgetting parapsychology and sensitivity to the 'supernatural'. It's important not to proceed by negative, 'downer' methods. We mustn't make the mistake of all those boring statistical card guessing games that have queered ESP research. Positive reinforcement is the secret. We must make every experiment a learning game with rewards—"

"The supernatural?" queried Tom Havelock of Ethics, a frayed, angular figure with a pinched chin and a caved-in, pink vinyl cheek from plastic surgery; he always tried to walk, and talk, with the false cheek presented the other way. "How?"

"Ghosts could be a sort of UFO, Tom. A kind of projective psychic photography à la Ted Serios, only *sans* camera. We're talking about actual things—maybe just temporary things, but things none the less—getting projected into physical reality by an ASC. In Tibet, before the Chinese took over—and I suppose it was just as well for the majority of ordinary Tibetans that they did!—"

"Hear hear," nodded Andrew Rossiter, who liaised with Granton Psychiatric Hospital; Deacon knew that he tended to bridle at any praise, however indirect, of élitist psychologies.

"—there was a fascinating secret lamaist tradition for the production of just this sort of thing, which I know a little about. *Tulpas*, they were called—"

Deacon shivered, gleefully. Titles of working papers ran through his mind. *Induction and deinduction procedures for traversing into and out of a state of 'UFO-Consciousness'; Limits of stability of UFO-awareness*; *Depth measurement of the UFO experience: a tentative scale and empirical map*; leading ultimately to *The Triggering of UFO-experience: techniques for initiating an Altered State of Consciousness*. This would be only a start. How many million dollars had the US Air Force alone spent chasing reports of lights in the sky? This project would surely deserve one-tenth of those funds, once the first research papers began to appear. Of course, the discovery itself was far more important than the funding or the rather horrifying fame that must attend it. Human *growth* was the main criterion. Unfortunately, little further actual progress had been made with Michael since the events of December. The boy seemed to be holding back—if only subconsciously, out of a false guilt about Suzie. If only he could be freed from it! Deacon had invited him to the seminar to inject more motivation. A breakthrough with him, and he could cast his net wider for other subjects. Though he needed that breakthrough first. It had to be Michael: projector of the pterodactyl, vector of so many alarming events.

Aware that he was on exhibition, Michael somewhat primped and preened.

"Multiple dimensions are just mathematical terms for describing particle behaviour in the space-time which we're already part of," said Sandra Neilstrom of Physics, harking back to an analogy Deacon had made. It was the Neilstrom woman—smart tweed-suited brunette in her early forties—of whom Deacon felt most wary (more so than Andrew Rossiter for his political objections!) yet whose knowledge he most needed to tap.

"I don't dispute there may be 'wormholes' through super-space—through the underfabric of space-time," she went on, "but multiple occupancy of our own coordinates by independent entities which can pop in and out from 'somewhere else' strikes me as unlikely, to put it mildly. No, I don't see squatters in our own subatomic space!"

"Didn't Charles Tart suggest, though," interrupted Tom Havelock, "that *symbols* might actually have an objective reality? They might be manifestations of some spiritual reality outside the mind. Isn't that what John's really driving at?"

"Squatters in psychological space?" She laughed. "I don't feel as though I'm being squatted in. Do you, John?"

"I'm not sure," muttered Deacon, reviewing the events of December. "Maybe I do. What *is* mind, after all? Do we generate it in our brains—or do we simply *transmit it*? William James posed that puzzle decades ago, and there's still no answer. If the latter's the case, and we simply transmit, then we're all like receivers, or modulators, embedded in some sea of consciousness. The same sea."

"I'll offer you an analogy, if you must insist that we aren't what we think we are!" Sandra Neilstrom patted her tight bun of brown hair; she was enjoying herself. "The electron. At its core there's a negative charge—we call it the 'bare charge'—of huge, possibly infinite magnitude. This charge induces a halo of positive charge in the vacuum surrounding it, which almost, but not quite, cancels out the bare charge. The difference between these two huge charges accounts for the small *actual* negative charge we're able to measure. So you might have something present that's far larger than what you actually ever measure or observe. Could you have a similar situation in psychological space?" She sat back smiling, fisherwoman dangling a bright fly.

Martin Bull took the fly, though, and a different species of fish was hauled out.

"I'm always puzzled that people visualize thought as a continuous flowing wavefront, when it's really the product of—

78

pardon me, John, when it's transmitted *through*—an electro-chemical biocomputer. Why don't we think in terms of quanta of thought, Sandra? Of thought-energy existing in discrete units, even though it shows up statistically as a continuous process?"

"There are certainly discrete states of mind," said Deacon. "That's what state-specific psychology is all about. That's why it's so damn difficult to pin down the moment of transit into an ASC. Our body shows definite 'quanta' of movement, too—discrete states of posture. That's why I mentioned kinesics earlier. A person 'jerks' from one preferred state to the next, and he gets damned uncomfortable if he's halted in between! We have a body vocabulary of several hundred of these states. Naturally body posture reflects and influences the different discrete states of consciousness . . . There's a lot of work to be done."

Nothing daunted, Sandra Neilstrom cast her fly again.

"Call this quantum of thought a *gnoon*. Say that it induces a halo of 'positive charge' in matter, in the form of mind. It possesses an enormous bare charge. But all that we can know of its power and magnitude is the tiny little charge left over—the little bit that doesn't cancel out in the equation. And that's us: our individual consciousness."

"Below which is the whole field of mind!" Yes, thought Deacon; this might be why one could never really *know* the entirety of consciousness.

"That's just a wild analogy, John. Let's hope you don't start taking UFOs for these 'bare charges'—somehow rendered visible to us!"

Yet if they *were* that, in a sense? Deacon fretted at the idea, as Martin Bull grumbled:

"The trouble about this whole Phenomenon of yours is that *if* it's aiming any sort of information at us, the signal-to-noise ratio is strongly in favour of sheer noise. Or put it another way. The signal just says, 'I am a signal,' but it doesn't carry any other specific content. How do we distinguish it from noise?"

"Why should it be aiming a message at us," retorted Deacon, "if it's a *state*? What 'message' do hypnosis or an LSD trip convey in themselves? UFOs may seem to present themselves as this

79

thing, or that thing, but that isn't *what* they are. What they actually are," he grasped, "may indeed be akin to these bare charges of Sandra's—enormous forces seen nakedly, telling us something, if we can examine the UFO-conscious state, about what on earth mind itself is! Likewise these unmeasurable 'bare charges' hint at what the root of matter might be. I'm sure the key's in the mind. There's a bridge too, between mind and material reality—or we wouldn't get holes dug in the soil by them, or radar images, or fairy rings where the things land."

"Fairy rings?" Sandra Neilstrom had caught the right fish now. But it proved inedible—distasteful and grotesque. The subject had become too ridiculous. And yet . . . consciousness and physics must come together. This was why she had been moved to join the group in the first place. Any final theory of a self-consistent universe must contain a theory of consciousness too . . .

"Fairies?" she sneered, leaning forward intently.

"Oh, they're part of the same constellation of UFO events!" Deacon assured her. "What do fairies typically do? They kidnap people. They carry them off to fairyland. UFOs likewise! Do you know what percentage of missing person cases are never explained? Do you realize that in the fifteen nineties a Spanish soldier vanished from the Philippines and turned up twenty-four hours later in Mexico?"

"Oh I'd trust sixteenth century colonial rumours—like the plague!"

"Well then, an Argentine doctor called Vidal and his wife, out for a drive in '68—"

"That's 1568?" She licked her upper lip.

"No, of course not! 1968. They were 'removed' from Argentina along with their Peugeot car. They found themselves in Mexico forty-eight hours later—"

"It seems like a popular destination."

"—with no idea how they got there."

"Maybe they drove quickly?"

"During the First World War a whole regiment disappeared in Turkey. The One-Fourth Norfolk Regiment. They were seen marching into a brown cloud down at ground level. They never came out. No bodies were ever recovered! The cloud just moved off up into the sky."

"Quite right of it! That's where clouds belong."

"These events are all on record. They happened. They're not fantasies. They're UFO-events."

She hummed a snatch of tune.

" '*Oh fairyland my fairyland*—' On record with whom, I'd like to ask? With which particular glossy journalist? Do beware the slippery slope of parascience, John! Fringe science perches on a brink. There seems to be some law that always sends it tumbling over before long, into pseudoscience. *Facilis descensus Averno*—it's easy to get into Hell. Getting out again's the difficulty! Now I do think it's time we had some tea and biscuits." She directed a meaningful glance at one of the research students present, who nodded and ducked out. "After we've refreshed ourselves, maybe you could demonstrate some of your induction methods?"

Deacon saw Michael blush. Perhaps inviting him hadn't been such a good idea.

The yellow light from the committee room flooded into the black mid-air, five floors above the paved quadrangle—and Deacon thought of himself as a puny yellow light glowing in a huge dark sea, of infinite negative charge, yet somehow drawing all his power, unbeknownst, out of this sea . . . A halo of thought. Other lighted windows across the quadrangle were other, supposedly private transmitters.

If only he could floodlight the whole! What would be seen then? Or . . . would it blind him?

Michael excused himself after the meeting; he seemed embarrassed by the proceedings.

Sandra Neilstrom attached herself to Deacon on the way out.

"You're working in a vacuum," she smiled, laying a consoling hand on his arm. "Perhaps literally! Did you know that it's respectably theorised that the whole universe is only what one might call a vacuum fluctuation? If you balance the positive mass energy of the whole cosmos against the negative gravitational energy, the net energy of everything that exists may in

81

fact be precisely zero. There's a deep void for you! Particles emerge out of vacuum easily enough on the quantum level. Why not a whole universe? No reason at all why not!"

"But . . . a whole universe? All the stars and galaxies?"

"So long as the net energy is zero—in the mass versus gravity equation. Naturally the universe has to be the huge size that it is, or nobody would be around to observe it, would they? It has to be the sort of universe where life, and mind, evolve. But maybe the whole universe as such just happens—in the vacuum. Maybe your UFOs are other spontaneous emergences inside it?" she teased. "Reflections of this situation?"

"Why didn't you say so before?"

"Ah—" She walked off into the night, mischievously.

Blackness all around; in windows here and there, tiny charges of illumination.

THIRTEEN

IT HADN'T YET struck five, but the Common was dark and deserted. Suzie hesitated, then began walking along the perimeter road instead, brightly lit by high sodium vapour lamps.

Rush hour traffic blocked the road. The air began to stink as drivers revved their cold cars forward a few inches at a time. Poison gas drifted up around her. She felt she was suffocating, her lungs corroding.

Impulsively she turned aside and headed over the dark grass instead. It was still tolerably light, once she'd escaped from the roadside.

The first school she ever went to was at the end of a long high-walled lane, overhung by elm trees; in high winds the boughs fell, littering the lane, and council workmen came to lop and trim. Drone of buzzsaws, plimsolls making sawdust foot-prints . . . Older girls joked that there were rats in the outdoor stone toilets—running out into the playground screaming and giggling, terrifying her . . . She dreamt nightly of a Giant who lurked among the elms, with great grasping hands and a buzzing voice. The sawdust was of ground-up bones . . .

She stalked, lost in that dream, towards the lake and clump of elms, a very small girl chased away from the traffic by its broad saucer eyes, foul urinal breath, throaty buzz. These elms too might have to come down soon, by the saw, diseased.

The buzz wouldn't die away. She started to run, imagining huge hands gripping her, imagining being consumed alive.

A green moon was reflected in the lake, as two swans clapped and battered their way across the water, flailing to take off—then swung skywards on swishing wings . . .

. . . as the original of the green reflection drifted down amongst the trees: a bright ball of green light.

She ran away past the edge of the lake. A glaucous furry fog boiled off the water—and the same fog suppurated out from the mildewed bark of the trees, capturing her, warping the space around the lake and those trees to a malicious involuted curve. She waded through glue; her legs were jelly. Sinking to her knees, lapsed and atheist though she was, she began to pray: "Jesus Christ, dear God, save me."

A devil floated through this fog out of the elms. A goblin that bobbed and bounced as though the low fog was all that glued it to the ground, by a sort of misty adhesive. The creature was green, and as tall as a large child. Its head was huge with stiff piglike ears rising to points, tiny nostrils without a nose, an expressionless downward-sloping slash of a mouth—and two red globes of eyes, set in bulging orbits right round the corners of its head. The eyes were plastic models of fried eggs stuck to its head—in the wrong colours.

Its ears twitched. It turned its head from side to side, as if searching. It couldn't see her except sideways, and would only use one of those eyes when the huge ears had located her. She held her breath, but couldn't hold her heart.

Its shoulders were broad, but slewed askew. One arm hung

down as far as its knees, from an up-tilting shoulder; long fingers tapered to sharp talons. The other arm was as fat and stumpy as a fiddler crab's claw, and dragged the lower shoulder down by its weight. It hadn't spun out to its proper length, but stayed part-formed and inchoate, yet massively crushing. The chest was large, the waist tiny. Its thin legs buckled, and its feet splayed ducklike into a kind of 'fog shoe' foot—a foot, or shoe, for walking over fog. Was the goblin dressed in green fabric, or was this fabric its own skin?

It hovered nearer, ears atwitch, long arm reaching, passing to and fro, swimmerlike parting air that had condensed.

Suzie's crotch felt wet. She was all liquid, slush and jelly, half dissolved herself into the fog.

"Sweet Jesus, I do believe in you—" All things bright and beautiful; deliver us from evil . . . She pulled off her shoes, heavy shoes with thick ribbed soles.

And threw one shoe at it.

The missile hit it in the chest. It rocked backwards, like a wobbly toy. It didn't cease approaching; simply leaned over backwards, slowly righting itself again, all the while drifting forward.

"Away in the name of God and Christ!" she cried. Its glossy, chitinous head turned at her cry, and one red egg-yolk eye regarded her. It stretched out its long green arm further, three tapering clawed fingers and a long thin thumb widespread, to touch her hair. Gently; but the beast stank of rotten eggs.

Flabbily she beat at the thin sharp hand with her other shoe, knocking the arm away. The goblin swung round, brought its other eye to bear. The massive, half-formed crab claw rose. Foreshortened fingers were fused together, opposing a thumb which was almost all thick nail. Flesh had melted and flowed, hardening into stiff gristly ridges.

The crab claw caught the toe of the shoe and held it. She let go of the shoe, pulling her hand back with an effort as though a magnet held her flesh.

Her shoe fell in slow motion from the claw towards the vaguely luminous fog—which now she saw, not as fog at all, but as all the separate blades of grass growing from the soil blown

84

up hugely, fused and interpenetrating one another, all faintly illuminated from within.

When the shoe touched the fog—or the grass—she felt her whole body repelled from the creature, tossed away, rejected. She spun away from it, falling slowly into that inflated, foggy and translucent grass. Away she scrambled then, at last.

She fled. Incoherent. Barefoot. Not knowing where she fled to. Behind, trees creaked and shone as the green fog rolled back among them . . .

On she fled.

FOURTEEN

A CHANTING COUNTERPOINT of rhythms. At first slow and soft, then becoming staccato and percussive as they quickened, binding the brothers into one complex breath . . .

"*Hu! Hu!*" the brothers called out.

He. He. No music, but the Word.

"Eternal!" they shouted. "Assistance!" Fingers interlaced no longer, brothers spun on the spot, clockwise, anti-clockwise, arms aswirl like dancers' skirts. Sweating, straining, but without strain or exhaustion, only accumulation. In what seemed a din they found their peace. Even those who veered out of line, faces twisted, ricocheting off the wall, were only sweating poisons from their blood, which the whole group soaked up as energy and food, while their Sheikh clapped his hands ever faster, conducting.

"*Hu! Hu! Hayy! Hayy!*"

So they whirled and sweated, flicked their fingers, swung about, submitting to the Will.

After half-an-hour Muradi recited the opening of the Koran, to bring the *dhikr* to an end.

As he walked back through their ranks to the anteroom, hands rose to foreheads, brothers called out, *"Madad! Madad!"* Assistance! He exchanged hand kisses with some. Salim stood wishing, hoping. However, Muradi did not look at him; the Sheikh went away through the private door with a few senior brothers. The meeting broke up.

As Salim was stepping out into the courtyard one of these elders overtook him and touched him on the sleeve.

"He wishes to speak to you—will you come?"

Sheikh Muradi sat with his inner council in a crescent of plain cane chairs. (Murmured courtesies: *"Allah yakrimak!"* *"Allah yakhallik!"* May God be generous to you—! May God preserve you—!)

He offered Salim his hand; flushing, the youth pressed kisses. Muradi announced, "Please smoke if you wish to." No one cared to, least of all Salim; it was a token, not a licence. They refused, and refused again. "Praise God," smiled the Sheikh.

"You looked troubled tonight," Muradi said to Salim.

"It's nothing, *Sidi*. Not now. An argument at home—my Father . . ."

"Ah—"

They spoke about Salim's difficulties. Finally Muradi nodded to one of the elders. "I believe Hagg Ahmad knows someone in your Father's office—"

So there was help. Not help beyond ordinary knowledge—though there was certainly perspicacity in noticing that Salim needed it! Simply help that was perfectly adequate to the situation. One didn't take a hammer to crack a nut . . . Salim's thoughts still dwelled on hidden currents and authentic miracles, though.

"I believe there's something else?" said Muradi.

Salim blushed.

"Yes, *Sidi*, Lord. Khidr—how can he be? Where does he come from? Where does he go to? Can a man actually meet him in our century?"

86

Sheikh Muradi rubbed his beard, then smiled. He steepled his palms.

"If a man needs to. If his necessity is great enough. If *the event* needs to occur. Our way, you see, seeks to evolve Man. It establishes communications with an ultimate source of knowledge. But this source can't be known directly. The Whole is beyond knowledge. 'Can you imagine a mind observing *all of itself?* If it were all busy observing, what would it be observing?' Paradox! Is that correct, O beloveds?"

("Praise God!" agreed the elders.)

"Actually there have to be unknowables, or there'd not be any human knowledge. Khidr is this unknowable—who may nevertheless *be experienced.*"

"*Sidi*, have you yourself—?"

"Ah, I'm sure that you know the traps—for yourself—in that question! It's perfectly true that the Masters have learnt to modify their own faculty of knowing so that they can experience space and time, or cause and effect, in another way. Then they can pass from the possible to the impossible, and back again. A true miracle! Yet some onlooker will still see it as deception. Necessarily. The miracle isn't meant to be explained, however hard men struggle to explain it. It's a metaphor, an illustration of what is always—by our very nature and by the nature of the world itself—*beyond*. 'Allah coins metaphors for men. *He* has knowledge of all things,' as it says in the *Sura* called *al-Nur*."

"*Ya, Sidi!*" exclaimed someone, prompting a chorus of quiet acclamation.

"I believe you're studying engineering, Salim?"

Salim nodded.

"A practical art. You can't build a bridge with insufficient supports, any more than you can ride a camel with only three legs—it needs four. Well, the bridge of science is supported by ninety-nine legs, which is enough for almost perfect stability—for practical purposes. There should still be another leg. Or perhaps there are already nine hundred and ninety-nine legs. There should still be another. Khidr is this other leg: the miracle leg, which is outside explanation. He is the leg that actually balances all the others!"

87

"God be praised!"

"Scientists of the very large must leave out the very tiny. Scientists of the very tiny must leave out the force that holds the stars together, isn't that so? This is necessary to reality. It isn't a mere temporary shortcoming. If the whole world was known, it would cease to be.

"Come, you're full of doubts. But not-to-know is a part of knowing. You have to master not-knowing, for not-knowing is part of reality itself. The master of not-knowing will know who Khidr is. Do you recall the story of how Khidr saved a man from drowning?"

Salim recalled it, but waited to be told again, since the telling of this story at this particular moment was quite different from simply remembering it.

"A man once fell into the river Oxus," Muradi recounted briskly. "An onlooker saw a dervish rush into the water to help. The dervish was soon in difficulty with the current too. Suddenly a third man, dressed in radiant shining green, leapt in. Once in the water, he seemed to be merely a log of wood. Our two unfortunates clung to this log till it bore them safely to shore. The log drifted on downstream. Our onlooker chased it down the river, keeping well hidden. He watched it touch the bank—and saw the Man in Green pull himself ashore, soaking wet. Our onlooker raced up to him to beg his blessing. He knew this must really be Khidr, the Master of the Saints. He noticed that his clothes were already mysteriously bone dry.

"The Green Man told him, 'I come from another world. It's my job to protect people who have a service to perform—without their knowing anything about it. And you've seen too much!' The Green Man was gone—whoosh. There was only a rushing noise in the air.

"Later, our same onlooker met the rescuer again. The rescuer no longer looked luminous. Perfectly ordinary, in fact. But there was something about him; our friend still recognized him. Again he begged him to bless him and explain. How could he be a log —and a man? How could he vanish—to reappear in another part of the world?

"The rescuer simply laughed. 'Go ahead and tell the whole

world you've met Khidr! It won't do any good. They'll lock you up as a lunatic.' He picked up a perfectly ordinary pebble and held it out. As soon as our bold onlooker looked at it, why, he couldn't move a single muscle. He turned to stone—while the rescuer walked off. Only when he'd gone, could our friend move once more!'"

The elders, who all knew the story, exclaimed in wonder as if this was the first time they had heard it.

"Well now, Salim, our beloved Master Rumi—who understood the evolution of Mankind long before the Darwins of Western science—once said that 'God most high is not contained within this world of ideas. For if he were contained within the world of ideas, it would follow that the man who formed ideas could comprehend God: who could not then be the creator of ideas.' So: beyond all worlds is God—"

"Praise Him!"

"That is how reality is made, and how it is held in being from moment to moment. Khidr—Guide and Intercessor—must be able to enter and exit again from our faculty of knowing, or the world wouldn't be what it is. In fact, there'd be no reality whatever. Can he be met with in our century? Ah Salim, in what way is it *our* century? Do we own time? Do we generate time?"

"God's century it is," agreed an elder.

"He recreates the world every moment," another nodded.

"Is time 'real'? Then hand me some! Is the world-within-time real? No, reality is elsewhere. It is where Khidr moves. God sustains the illusion of the world for us. Where is your consciousness, Salim? Can you show me some of it?"

Salim scratched his head.

Muradi leaned over and hit him sharply on the knee: Salim jerked reflexively.

"It is not only in your head. But there too—in your knee! And up there!" Muradi pointed at the naked light bulb. Salim glanced up and was momentarily blinded.

"It is whatever you sense. Thus thought is elsewhere. It has no specific place among all the objects which it imagines, because it is itself the imaginer of them. Which is why mind cannot possibly inspect the whole of itself: it is not an 'object'. So Khidr comes and goes—with a whoosh in the air. By disappearing, he proves the texture of reality. Real knowledge protects itself in the same way, Salim—and at the same time forces people to develop new organs of perception; from which in turn it hides itself away. Thus evolution is made possible. However, it's to be experienced—not spoken about! Words aren't the metaphors that God coined for men. Our own lives are that! The world is that!"

"Do you mean that the knowledge is mine already—because I'm alive? Because I have a mind?"

The Sheikh laughed boisterously.

"How could it be yours if you weren't alive, or didn't have a mind?"

He rose, taking Salim by the arm and leading him out alone while the others stayed to discuss the coming festival. The hall was deserted, lit only by a light bulb near the door. They walked out into the courtyard, also in darkness save for starlight and some illumination coming from the street. Salim shivered, as the sweat which had earlier soaked his shirt chilled in the night air.

A schoolgirl passed by outside, still wearing her neat blue pinafore, followed by a fat woman draped in a shapeless black *meliya* out to peddle a few spoonfuls of hot rice. Loud film music poured suddenly from a nearby rooftop. Distracted, Salim stared at the roofs. Only for a moment.

A man was already standing beside the pool, when his eyes returned to it. The water glowed and sparkled as though chemicals had been scattered; it cast a sheen of green light upon the stranger's costume—a cloak with voluminous sleeves, a zouave jacket, floating pleated skirt and tall felt hat. The stranger was wearing the clothes of a whirling dervish from old Turkey, as if in fancy dress for tourists to film . . . except that he was in the wrong city, the wrong country. Salim saw a tight-bearded, ironic face, not unlike Muradi's own; though this stranger was taller than Muradi, and his eyes sharper.

The Sheikh was staring at the stranger, transfixed.

If only the radio hadn't blared out so suddenly, Salim would have *seen* where he came from.

Muradi knelt and touched the stranger's cloak.

"Master," he murmured.

The stranger laughed. "Listen to this reed forlorn," he sang softly.

I'm witnessing a miracle, thought Salim, frozen. Yet what am I actually seeing? If I didn't see how it began . . .

The stranger glanced at Salim. *"Fihi ma fihi!"* he said sharply. "There is in this, what you put into it, child! A demonstration to one man is a bewilderment to another."

Producing a small old book in a worn leather binding from under his cloak, he pressed it into Muradi's hand.

"This isn't for you, but for another more retarded seeker—who doesn't even know yet that he *is* seeking."

Muradi turned the book over.

"A book of magic? Written in French . . . Am I to help a *magician?*"

"Isn't it said, 'Once you've mastered one superstition, you're unlikely to take up another'? But there's no magician in this instance. Don't worry. *Trust.* Do I not come from another world, where more is seen?"

The stranger echoed Muradi's own words. The Sheikh touched his hand to his heart.

"He will come with the first breath of spring, not knowing how he comes, nor why—like Humanity itself. Give this to him, Sheikh. He will find in it what—for him—is in it. It will have a different meaning for him. You see, one moment can serve many purposes. For you the meaning is already here, right now. In this instant. 'Cause is singular, chains of effect are many'."

At last Salim found his tongue and dared to speak.

"Who are you . . . Master?"

The stranger looked amused. "You already answered yourself, child, by giving me a title and a name. What does the name mean to you? *Fihi ma fihi!* A toy is your best answer just now. A toy in words—some poetry!" And he recited:

> "Ever-knowing, as we hide we seek.
> To normal men, we seem other than we are.
> In inward light we roam: making miracles appear.
> —Yet none knows who we are.

"That is me. That is us."

The stranger extended his arms, right palm turned upwards, left palm down; wearing the cloak though he was, whirled.

Overtaken with dizziness, Salim momentarily closed his eyes.

When he opened them only seconds later, he was alone with the Sheikh in the darkness. The pool was only faintly illuminated as before by the meeting hall light, the street, the stars above. The same fat woman in the baggy robe passed by the gate, going the other way without glancing in. She'd sold her rice.

PART THREE

FIFTEEN

ON EASTER MONDAY Michael woke early. He'd been dreaming of cycling uphill, standing up on the pedals while Suzie perched behind, clinging to his waist. She slipped backwards off the seat and rolled down the hill, bouncing like a rubber ball. Immediately the bicycle bounded up and over a crest . . . He was riding on a battlefield now, bearing despatches. Acid gas rolled up, dissolving the rubber of his tyres. Lying in a trench, in stale water, he saw Suzie again—her hair bleached white. She smiled feyly at him.

"Ride to me—to the moor. *Now*."

He had only a vague memory of the dream, yet he saw what a fine morning it was. Birdsong; green gold world. Dressing, he went downstairs, pocketing a couple of apples from the kitchen as he passed.

After Suzie's breakdown, when she was found wandering shoeless through Granton, she went for a while to stay in the Psychiatric Hospital. Michael she had refused to see. Transferred home for a few months' rest, she ignored his letters. Her parents put the phone down on him. And the work with Deacon proceeded nowhere very fast . . .

He'd ridden this road several times since his memory was restored. Wild-coated sheep were grazing the wiry grass. Gorse flared yellow: beads of sun. Little piles of rabbit droppings, like aniseed balls, lay scattered.

He breasted the rise—and saw a big red car, an American luxury model, parked near the spot where Luvah's craft had landed (or come into existence).

95

Elephant-tyred, long-bonneted, massively bumpered, with cinemascopic rear lights and dual exhausts—a beast of unctuous steel—it blocked the road. Its colour, lipstick red.

Was it Barry Shriver, come to investigate the landing site? But Shriver drove an old estate car. In any case, he would have needed Michael to guide him to the spot . . .

Michael coasted closer.

Thunderbird. American number plates: the letters *WYO*, no doubt standing for Wyoming; a logo of a cowboy riding a bronco . . .

A great grey parcel blocked the driver's seat. Something very large, wrapped up. Then the parcel shuddered and twisted into a mass of grey rubber tyres piled on one another, and there wasn't actually a driving seat at all, only this great pile next to the passenger seat, taking up the majority of the space between dashboard and rear seat.

The passenger door swung open and a voice (broadcast, transmitted through some speaker) hooted, "It is safe. It is not one of them. It is something else. Please come! It is safe—"

Bright morning, blue sky, faint cirrus streaks. Sheep were still grazing, unperturbed.

"Safe. Safe. Safe. Please believe." Shuddering, the heap of tyres half turned and something peered at him: through the bulging face-plate of a segmented, grotesque diving suit. Whatever was in that suit could hardly move, jammed into such (for it) limited space. The sheer sense of its confinement made him pity it long enough to look twice, not race away.

He saw a head shaped like a tortoise's . . . then revised what he saw. The entire head *was* a tortoise. The face with its big beady eyes, drilled nostrils and horny beak protruded right out elastically from the plated cranium, like a tortoise's whole head from its shell. The corded 'neck' he saw at first wasn't a neck at all, but muscle and sheathing joining the extruded eyes, lips and nose to the rest of the head, where the brain must be. The eyes seemed quite distant from the brain.

It must react rather slowly, he thought . . . How vulnerable, despite its armour. Back home on the mantelpiece, brought from India by a neighbour, rested an empty tortoise shell with a tiny hole drilled in it so that ants could scavenge the quick from the poor creature and clean it out . . .

"Peace," it honked. "Love."

"All right," said Michael. "Peace." Ponderous and absurd, the thing seemed too confined, too ridiculous almost, to pose a threat. Humanoids, dwarfs, silvery giants, winged 'mothmen' had all turned up in UFO reports, but the phenomenon had never manifested itself remotely like this! This was too far from the phenomenon. Too *alien* to it.

What was it doing at this spot? Squeezed into a Ford Thunderbird! It must be a UFO-thing, after all . . . The UFO programme had gone wildly askew—generating a great plated tortoise-elephant in a pressure suit with only an ordinary 'Man-in-Black'-style car for it to ride in. It must be bewildered and in misery. Again he pitied it. It radiated the pathetic.

"I am not what you think I am," it said. The voice came from a silver grille below the face-plate. The being groaned and heaved; the suit was a boa constrictor. Michael felt excited, as though some resolution was in sight: a loose hem of the Phenomenon, which could be caught hold of and unravelled.

"How do you know what I think?" he challenged the trapped tortoise-head.

"We have a device. A biological machine. It reads the pulse of the Unidentified. You are bright as a light to it, for the Unidentified made you come here to experience an event. The potential is building up right now around you; though we are both still safe for a little while."

"You're an abortion, tortoise. A UFO thing yourself! Only, the UFO programme really got screwed up this time, didn't it? Is this your idea of a flying saucer?"

"No!" The being reared in protest. As it stood inside the car, he could see four stout legs. The forelegs were twice as tall as the hindlegs, though set very close to them. The broad back sloped steeply. The being raised a single gloved tentacle from between its front legs, a soft arm ending in a starfish of rubbery fingers, which it waggled at him.

"I am not part of the Unidentified! We are scared of it too. But we will help you—"

"Why are you all squashed up in that car?"

"We stole the car. We apologise for that. We draw less attention this way—it is a thing of this world. But we have redesigned it. Now it is different. It can fly."

"Oh really? As pigs can fly?" (Yet Michael found himself drifting closer all the time, as if magnetised . . .)

"It harnesses gravity now. This car will be the means for you to get about in your own world, unnoticed—and out to us in space. We dare not stay here too long ourselves, but you are native to this planet." The being wagged its single arm. "It is very easy to fly. You will soon learn. We are not bilateral, you see. We only have one arm. We must needs be simple in our designs."

"What, the car's for *me?*" How soon, Michael wondered, would the monster in its Michelin tyre-suit dissolve into thin air, leaving him (perhaps) with a stolen, translocated American car which was quite undrivable since its driving seat had been torn out? The proffered gift began to fall into place as part of the whole absurd pattern of gifts to UFO contactees . . .

"We have five humans helping us already. We gave them all flying cars. We invite you to be number six."

"But *what for?* What am I supposed to do?"

"Help us understand the Unidentified, of course! Help us to take its pulse, and guide your knowledge of it. For you are part of it, but you know nothing of this—and your ignorance is making it a malign and dangerous force. Don't you want to understand it?"

"I suppose I do. Of course I do!"

"We will show you what it is, but we need your help. We fear for our own lives here."

Michael felt baffled. Was this a UFO contact, or wasn't it? Here was a seeming 'alien' who declared that UFOs existed and wanted them analysed and who moreover was *scared* of them.

"We come from a heavy world, of high gravity. Hence our bulky bodies. We had to learn to tame gravity, to leave our world. This car now generates a constant internal one-G field in flight, for your comfort. It is easily steerable by point gravitational and repulsion sources. Quite fast, too! We can reach your Moon in two hours."

Time looped back; Michael sat in Deacon's office again, listening to Barry Shriver outline the wholly imaginary design of a flying saucer propelled by gravity . . . *The material was already in his mind.*

Shriver had said it was the uniquely logical way to fly. So it could be true.

"There's no air in space. Cars are a bit leaky, aren't they?"

"It only looks like a normal car. Thus it will run normally on your roads, using a miniaturised engine powered by reaction mass. The design was highly inefficient before. But the exhaust pipes are really blocked, and the whole body is airtight—for flight. It is even proofed against radiation. The air conditioner stores enough air for four humans for six hours. This replenishes itself whenever the airtight doors are opened —"

Alien elephant-tortoise as used car salesman . . . It radiated such helplessness and trust. Michael found he was standing by the open door now. Abruptly the creature squirmed about in agitation.

"An event is about to happen. It may not be pleasant now that I am here. Leave your riding machine. Get in!"

Michael stayed where he was.

The creature lurched sideways. Its arm snaked out further than he could have expected, knocking the door wide open. Its starfish hand seized him by the wrist, pulling him.

"Sorry, sorry," it bleated. It hauled him inside, sprawling him across the passenger seat. It whisked the door shut behind him. Its fingers played across the dashboard. As Michael snatched at the door handle, and found it locked, the creature jerked the steering wheel back with an audible snap. The wheel tilted freely like a joystick.

"Ground mode to flight mode," it honked informatively.

From the radio-tapeplayer jutted a block of glass filled with something green and soupy, like pond slime. The radio dial pulsed with red light. One of the stereo speakers in the back of the car was emitting a shrill panic whistle which was growing steadily louder . . .

99

A huge foot pressed forward, quite daintily, on to the accelerator pedal. The Thunderbird quivered and hummed; then jumped into the air, tilting at the clear sky. (But with no sense of tilt!) It sped upwards. (With no feeling of acceleration!)

A gleaming disc was slewing towards them out of the south—while the stereo speaker shrieked. The creature spun the wheel, spinning the moors below, and tugged it right back, racking the car up in a tight turn till they were heading straight up, with the Yorkshire landscape standing on end in the rear window. (Yet 'down' was still underneath the chassis of the car.)

The bright disc darted from side to side behind them, then suddenly split into ever smaller blobs of light, a rain shower, dispersing. The whistling noise cut out; the radio dial stopped pulsing with red light.

"We are safe," sighed the alien creature. It caressed the green glass cartridge stuck in the tapeplayer, sacramentally. "Do you know Tunguska? In Siberia? Do you know of the great explosion there? That is where we lost our first expedition. Your Unidentifieds destroyed it."

Michael clung to the passenger seat; though if he shut his eyes for a moment all sense of motion disappeared and they might have been sitting still.

"You're a . . . *real* alien —?" he whispered.

"They caught our friends in space, on the way in—those jealous, violent energies. We picked up a single tight-beam signal from our ship years later, so we knew that your own human technology was far too simple on its own—at that point in time—to have destroyed us. Our human helpers have told us of the Tunguska mystery. The millions of felled trees. The bright skies around the world for three years. That is where we lost our friends—no doubt about it. We could guess how. The Unidentified! What a danger if we were right! Of course I am a real alien!"

"Where . . . where are we going?"

"To your Moon. Round the far side. It is safe there, masked from the senses of the Unidentified of this world. There is its blind spot—except when humans orbit the Moon. Then it can make itself apparent."

Blue darkened to indigo, then to purple, and black. Stars prickled alight. Sunlight scalded the left hand window, but instantly was cooled and diluted by the glass.

Michael twisted round. Flocks of cumulus dotted England and the North Sea, for it wasn't such a clear day from a higher viewpoint. He saw Ireland and its sea too, then the Atlantic beyond. The glowing, violet-on-blue camber of the Earth's horizon swelled up; then the curve was cut, far out across hundreds of miles of ocean, by the foggy darkness of the westering terminator. An anticyclone coiled its woolly spiral, this side of the darkness.

Then they were in space. Michael stared, in wonder. Black void, raw Sun, jewel stars unwinking. Bright Luna hung in its last quarter, a sickle of mercury cupping a dark rock ball. Outside the windows was vacuum, cold and radiation.

"You say that hostile 'energies' attacked your friends—and these energies are what UFOs are?"

"They are friendly energies, if you can harmonise with them! To call the Unidentifieds of your world wholly hostile is too simple. They still bring some insight to you, as well as folly and malice—but it is blended in confusion, and the trend now is hostile."

"But we humans *cause* the UFOs?"

"All living beings and every living cell in a world's ecology sustain the Unidentifieds of that world. An inhabited world, you must realize, is alive as a *whole*. There is a world mind—a vital planetary aura. It is one unified entity, evolving down the aeons. We call it 'Whole Planet Life'. The web of all living relationships sustains this higher collective existence. It is greater than the sum of its parts; yet its parts influence its nature. The aura can grow sick, and insane, if the parts grossly fail in harmony."

"I can appreciate ecology, but . . . to say that the world itself is a living being! Surely ecology is just about how different, separate things relate? Trees and rivers and the atmosphere . . . food stocks . . . The way cities and industry affect these. Pollutants and so on."

"Your mechanical ecology is only that. This is far from true ecology. Trees all seem to be separate things on a mundane time scale, yet the forest is really an evolving entity, in larger time. Cities evolve from villages and towns over centuries, like blobs of protoplasm growing towards something ever more complex. Cities are alive too, for they are the work of life as surely as an anthill or a honeycomb. They put out veins and nerves—roads, canals, telegraph, power lines. If you speed up the picture of a city's growth over a millennium and compress it into minutes—then you will get the right idea!

"Yet individual beings within the system cannot really know this directly. For I speak of higher-order systems of organization: of higher-order patternings. Lower-order systems cannot fully grasp the Whole of which they are the parts. Logic forbids. It is a natural principle. Which is why, when the processes of the Whole do show themselves, it is as unidentified phenomena—as intrusions into your own knowledge that can be witnessed and experienced but not rationally known: neither analysed, nor identified. Such intrusions are inestimably important. They are the goad towards higher organization. They are what urges the amoeba to evolve towards a higher life form. They are what spurs mind to evolve from natural awareness, and higher consciousness from simple mind. They are the very dynamic of the universe."

"Do you mean to say you're plagued by UFOs on your own planet?"

" 'Plagued' is the wrong word entirely!" The alien tapped the green glass cartridge protruding from the stereo. "We have biological instruments to help us read the Unidentified. This is one such. It is in phase—by way of our bio-satellites in orbit—with the parent Biomatrix up in our ship on Far-Side. Perhaps we found this understanding easier since we are herbivores not carnivores. Plant life precedes animal life, do you see? Plant life possesses the undifferentiated information network from which all animal nervous systems finally spring. The vegetable world possesses Primary Perception. Through this can be sensed the Unidentified. By this means we are in harmony. But yes, the Unidentified is certainly with us on our world, so far away."

The alien tilted the Thunderbird over on its side, rotating the starfield. It gestured.

"If you draw a line from the Andromeda galaxy to your own Pole Star, where that line crosses the central plane of our own galaxy—where it cuts across the thick star river—is the constellation you call Cassiopeia. There is Gebraud, our home. *Eta* in Cassiopeia—the alpha star of the pair. Your own sun we see in your Southern Cross. It takes light eighteen years to reach our home from here. We learnt of the Siberia horror in 1926 by your calendar. We waited for knowledge—for an intuition from our own Unidentifieds—for over ten years. Then we slept in cold another forty years to reach here."

"It seems crazy, sending a second expedition here when your first one was wiped out!"

"Our Unidentifieds indicated that we should."

"You speak as if they're Gods! As if a planet is a sort of God!"

"And your God may be going mad . . . Yes, to a lower-order system the higher-order system effectively seems to be a God. Yet this is not really the case. Whole Planet Life is simply a superior hierarchy. Beyond it lie still other hierarchies, still higher levels of programme and form-fulfilment of the cosmos. We must scan and heal your world's God-programme. If we fail, be warned: a higher programme may yet erase you! But perhaps not soon enough! For the lordly programmes of Galaxy-Beings unfold over long millennia. The harm which might happen in the meanwhile—locally for you, for us, for other nearby worlds—could be vast and fatal. You will understand all this better on the Moon."

Michael felt a chill of suspicion. These veiled threats of doom, these half-promises of salvation: didn't they only amount to a new twist in the same old game? Was he really heading towards the Moon at all, or actually lying bemused in a halted moment of time on a Yorkshire moor, his mind undergoing programming with false experiences from somewhere outside human knowledge?

Clouds shrouded Europe; further south, the ochre landmass of North Africa was entirely bare. The Earth was growing imperceptibly smaller every minute, shrinking at the rate of motion, perhaps, of an hour hand on a wristwatch: a process too slow quite to follow, yet at the same time certainly happening.

"You have not told me your name," remarked the alien gently.

"It's Michael."

"Greetings, Michael. I am Gar-boor-oold-ee." The name dragged out, as if on a tape being played too slowly. It sounded a bit like 'Garibaldi'. So Michael settled on the name of the Italian patriot, discarding all the alien cadences. This tactic made it easier for him to take in the name; it fended off the shock of alienness.

"May I call you Garibaldi please? It's easier."

"If you wish. If it helps."

"How fast are we flying, Garibaldi?"

"Two hundred and twenty thousand k.p.h.," honked Garibaldi briskly. "E.t.a. is one hour and thirty minutes." Its single arm rested inertly on the steering wheel.

Surely he was involved in a hallucination—the most massive one yet, outdistancing by far Luvah's simple seduction of him and the subsequent skimpy, jerky flight to London. But this time there were no gaps in the scenario, no betraying lurches.

"Will you tell me about your world?"

"Later—on the Moon. You will see a film from the memory of the Biomatrix. I am only your pilot."

Could these aliens really be just conjured-up puppets of the Phenomenon? Tulpas? Part of the Phenomenon which it had cast out of its own enigmatic being, charged with the task of probing and opposing and examining itself? Fall guys, whose very grotesqueness forced them to seem genuine?

The nearer to the Moon they got, and the further they receded from the shrinking Earth, however, the more genuine it all seemed—as though he really had escaped from a crazed world-mind into one of serenity and clarity . . .

On sped the Thunderbird.

SIXTEEN

THE RIVER SHIMMERED: brown-bronze, with a catarr-
hal patina of green. Eau-de-nil, thought Deacon vacantly as he
sat on a stone bench looking over a low parapet wall. It was a
dusty bench; he felt dusty too, begrimed . . . Was this the
Thames? Was the long bridge the river passed under Vauxhall
Bridge? Or Lambeth Bridge?

A red and white single-decker bus crossing the bridge, with
passengers hanging out of the door, dispelled that possibility.
Those buildings over the water were what—hotels? Obelisks
rose from the far end of the bridge. Beyond, jutted a . . .
minaret. A small wooden boat with a lateen sail drifted from
beneath the bridge, its helmsman hidden by a hooped canvas
awning.

Laughter burst upon him. Looking round, he took in the
knobbly trunk of . . . a palm tree, then a flag pole with a
fluttering tricolour in red, white and black with green stars on
the white band. Which nation's flag was it? He had no idea.

The laughter came from a family party squatting on arid
grass. They were peeling boiled eggs in the shade of a huge
morose banyan tree, practically a grove in its own right, so
many thickening rooted suckers had it let down. He saw a score
of adults, old folk, young children and adolescents . . . curly
black hair, toothbrush moustaches, long-lashed liquid eyes. Teeth
flashed, and freshly laundered shirts.

Atop a building, the squiggle of a roof sign nudged the sky . . .
in Arabic. *Eau-de-nil*—water of the Nile! He sat a few moments
longer watching those picnickers peel their eggs, waiting for
memory to flood back and explain all this to him. But nothing
came, so he emptied out his pockets. He found loose change (all

English money), car keys, his house key. His wallet yielded a driver's licence, cheque card, library tickets and three English pound notes. A passport? None. If he was staying at one of those hotels over the water, they might have kept his passport at the desk, to register it. He squeezed at a hotel memory, but none materialized.

Rising, he walked past the banyan tree, catching a reek of rotting fish, and on towards the bridge; and for the first time noticed soldiers. Two of them lounged on guard outside a wooden sentry box, dressed in coarse grey uniforms and crumpled bonnets, their rifles held loosely by the muzzle, the butts resting on the pavement. The two guards eyed him vacantly, with detached resentment. He hesitated, scared that it was somehow illegal to walk past them. However, the bridge was open to traffic; pedestrians wandered over it. A wailing noise suddenly keened out over the rooftops, from loudspeakers.

Sirens. War . . .

The guards leaned their rifles against the bridge parapet and unrolled threadbare mats across the pavement. They knelt on these; they bowed in prayer.

Feeling guilty, he hurried past them.

The guards might pray, but none of the traffic had paused. He spied a clock: noon. His own watch read ten o'clock. Then a bus came by with a signboard clipped above the radiator grille. It read, in English: *16: Giza Pyramids.*

So it *was* Cairo . . . A bus route to the Pyramids. Was he supposed to visit those?

By whom, supposed?

Another family party trooped past, carrying more rank-smelling fish with them. As they stared, he pretended to be admiring the river. Some houseboats were tethered along the bank, all in desolate condition except for one where a party was in progress on deck. Fireworks started popping. Small boys scampered.

The soldiers finished their prayers. He must look like a saboteur now, reconnoitering the piers; he hurried on.

Interminably long, the bridge. Upstream, a plume of water burst forth from the middle of the river, rising higher than the

106

buildings. Not a bomb or shell, though. The fountain continued spouting, from a low mushroom-shaped disc set in midstream, somehow hinting at missiles which hadn't yet fallen on the city . . .

On October 24th 1593 a Spanish soldier was standing guard in Manila in South-East Asia. Next day, supposedly, he found himself on the other side of the Pacific in Mexico City . . . In May 1968 Dr Vidal and his wife set out in their Peugeot from Chascomús, Argentina, to drive south. They ran into a wall of fog and blacked out. When they woke they were on a strange side road; in Mexico. Two days had passed . . . Remembering Barry Shriver's tales and forgetting Sandra Neilstrom's derision, Deacon shivered in the warm air. How many days were missing from his life? What year was it, even?

Was this what came from wondering about help beyond comprehension? This absurdity? This joke?

Help, and hindrance, beyond comprehension . . .

The puzzle fell into place.

Ali Ibrahim Muradi, contributor to *Consciousness: Ancient and Modern*, lived right here in Cairo. Deacon had even made a wish: in his own room at the University! If only Sheikh Muradi were still in the country! However: Mohammed and the mountain . . . *He had come here to see him.*

Fronting the Corniche, graciously dowageresque, stretched the long balconies of the Semiramis Hotel. Further north, its back turned on the riverside thoroughfare, rose the Nile Hilton. Probably he would do better there. Crossing the Corniche, he made his way round to the main doors of the Hilton. A great portico of florid mosaics jutted out heavily, fronting a large busy square.

The clerk at the information desk was short and musclebound and tightly packed into his black suit; he looked as though he doubled as a security guard or even worked for the Police.

"Yes Sir?"

"I, ah, need to get in touch with a Professor at al-Azhar. Ali Ibrahim Muradi. *Sheikh* Muradi. He's head of a Sufi Order here in Cairo. It's called the *Fihi'iya* . . . I'm afraid I've lost his home address and I don't know how to read the phone book —"

"You cannot telephone al-Azhar today, Sir. Don't you know this is a holiday?"

So it was still Easter. Yesterday had been Easter Sunday . . . But Easter wasn't a Moslem festival . . .

"Because it's Easter Monday?"

"That is a Coptic affair, Sir. Today is *Sham-el-Nessim*—'the smelling of the breeze'. The first day of Spring."

Hence the picnickers.

"If there's nobody at al-Azhar today, can you phone the Fihi'iya Order for me? Please. It's very important."

A notepad whisked on to the counter.

"If you'll say what your business is with them, Sir? I will have to explain it on the telephone. What name and room number?"

"John Deacon. I'm not actually staying here." He placed one of the three pound notes on the counter. "Can I pay for the call with this?"

"Oh I can't change foreign currency. Impossible. You must ask the cashier. Over there, do you see? The sign?"

"Will you at least look the number up?"

"While you are changing your money."

The cashier's eyes were dark with kohl. She wore a mass of black hair bunched in a fat bun. A stout girl, in a blue twin-set.

"Is this all you want to change, Sir?"

"I'm leaving soon. I only need enough for a taxi," he said, wondering how near the airport was.

"We *do* run our own minibus service from outside the door."

"Ah, I mightn't leave from the hotel —"

"As you please. Have you your passport?"

"Not with me . . . no. Why?"

"Because you are changing currency."

"Heavens, hardly any! They're only banknotes, not cheques."

The stout girl sighed. "A rule, Sir. Exchange Control Regulations. I have to put the number of your passport on the form."

"Even for three pounds?"

"Even for three pounds."

"It's a nuisance —"

"I'm *sorry*." She shook her head.

"I'll have to fetch my passport —" Maybe a taxi driver could find the headquarters of the Order. A taxi driver surely wouldn't refuse hard currency! But he mightn't understand, he might just drive round, ending Deacon up at some small district police station unable to pay the fare . . .

A coffee bar led off the vestibule; he walked in there instead —into a huge, high room supported by massive papyrus columns with swollen bell capitals. It was a room heavy with the silence of an MGM gongbeat just before the boom, full of polished brass, stamped with bas reliefs of sun motifs and wings and eyes of Horus. A thick brass footrail ran round the bar. He sat at a table, and ordered black coffee. When the waiter returned, he thrust the three pound notes on to the tray.

"You don't mind changing this, do you? I left all my Egyptian money back at my hotel."

The waiter hesitated, then the banknotes disappeared into his hand. A quarter of an hour later he finally brought back a pile of tiny frayed brown notes. Deacon removed them all and walked out quickly, back to the information desk.

The clerk looked annoyed.

"I did find your number for you. You wanted it in a hurry."

"I had to take a pill—an aspirin for my headache."

The excuse unaccountably mellowed the clerk. He clucked sympathetically and whisked his pad into sight again. Deacon placed two raggy notes on the counter.

"Please say that I need to see the Sheikh urgently. I'm very sorry for the lack of warning, but can I come and visit him right away? And the address—I need that."

The clerk dialled, talked for half a minute in Arabic, then dialled another number; at last he cradled the phone.

"I have spoken to Sheikh Muradi's assistant. The Sheikh expected you. A car will be sent as soon as possible. If you will wait —?"

"Did you say he expected me? Or expects me now?"

The clerk looked angry, as if his knowledge of English was in dispute.

"A car is coming here, Sir. Just wait."

SEVENTEEN

"HOWEVER CAN WE land at this speed?"

Michael panicked as the car flung itself at the rushing Moon horizon.

Garibaldi swung the steering wheel, foot tapping on the brake pedal. "You will learn. In one lesson—with hypno."

"No hypnosis, thank you!"

"Instead of many lessons?" the pilot wheedled. "You will fly back on your own. I will not fly you. It is the only way to return. So! Talk it over with the other humans. Be helpful."

More slowly now—though still seemingly far too fast—the car tilted round the Moon, travelling low over a massive double ring of mountains enclosing a circular pockmarked grey stone sea. Michael stared back towards Earth, too late. The home planet had already slipped behind the horizon of the Moon.

Garibaldi twisted the car upright again. "Our base is in Tsiolkovsky. 20 degrees south, 130 degrees east. It is quite distinctive. It cannot be missed." Two minutes passed, during which a rumpled, cratered desolation flew beneath them. "Ahead —there, now. Do you see?"

Tsiolkovsky Crater printed a deep, spade-shaped splotch of darkness into the brightly lit, smallpox-blemished plains. The crater appeared dark in its own right, rather than dark with shadow. Puckered, cicatriced walls surrounded it. From its heart rose a white pyramid peak. As they swooped in over the crater rim, travelling slowly at last, Michael spotted a tall black fungoid tower rising to the south of the central peak. It was a dark metal mushroom, a tall stem rooted to the crater floor by three great outspread landing jacks, with a swollen dome-like cap. The space between each of the support legs harboured a long oval dome, three in all, stretching out across the crater floor. The starship rose to perhaps ten times the height of these domes, towering above them.

The car grounded gently, amid a surprising flurry of moon-dust. Garibaldi punched at the controls and snapped the steering wheel forward into 'ground mode' once more. Dust fell back quickly, then, upon the car; Garibaldi cleared it from the wind-screen with a sweep of the wipers, then switched the headlamps on.

"The external gravity point-sources are switched off now. We must drive normally into the dome." The car's pseudo-engine whined faintly. The Thunderbird bumped forward towards the nearest of the domes. Pressing his face against the window, Michael stared up the long column of the starship. The under-side of the dome-like cap high overhead was vaned, mushroom-like, with metal gills.

"Do you see those vanes underneath the hood up there?" asked Garibaldi. "Those are to radiate waste heat. The ship has to be cold while we sleep between the stars."

"Oh —"

A triangular mouth opened up at the end of the dome they were approaching. They drove into this dark mouth, illumi-nating a short tubular tunnel with their headlamps, and halted. Behind them, the mouth closed. Garibaldi waited a while then switched off the 'heater'—a heater no longer, in this recon-structed car. The 'door-ajar' warning light blinked green. Im-mediately Michael lost nearly all his weight.

"The internal gravity is off now, and this airlock is pres-surised with Earth atmosphere. So our car doors will open again. But wait."

Ahead, a second triangular mouth opened up, revealing a small car park. Three cars stood by a transparent wall that rose to the upcurving roof of the dome. They were a Pontiac, a Mercedes and a Volvo, bearing American, German and Swedish plates. A second transparent wall divided the entire dome down its long axis, into two separate halls. The left hand hall was nar-rower than the other, subdivided by screens and partitions, and brightly lit in yellow. In the larger, right hand hall, illuminated a sickly green shading into blue, a gutted Peugeot hung on chains among much heavy machinery. The engine of the French car lay discarded beside it. Several aliens, wearing no suits, were working on the Peugeot. For the first time, as Garibaldi pulled up beside the other cars, Michael saw the aliens in the raw.

Their legs were of wrinkled grey hide, their feet stout and stumpy with thickly horned toes. Their plated backs sloped steeply, and umbrellas of bone roofed the brain, from under which the snout-faces poked out. The single, tough, flexible tentacle sprouted from the chest wall as though an elephant's trunk had slipped down into the wrong location . . .

Each alien wore a tool belt around its right leg. Strapped to the other leg was a pouch-like holster holding a glassy green block identical to the one slotted in the car stereo.

Such preposterous creatures to have built a starship! Yet they moved so gently, as they nuzzled in the guts of the Peugeot, deftly remaking the car to fly through space . . . Two of the working aliens glanced up. Their small faces seemed pathetic and tender.

A woman stood at this end of the yellow-lit hall, by an airlock, in conversation with a suited alien.

Garibaldi tapped Michael on the knee. "I have been in this suit too long. Will you go over there, please? Your people and mine will explain."

The pilot flipped Michael's door open and prodded him in the ribs, as if playfully. Michael climbed out. How light he felt upon his feet, how bouncy and elastic!

Seeing him, the woman waved. She left the alien's side and skipped into the translucent, circular air lock. There must be human air on both sides of it, but obviously the larger hall held alien air.

She seemed in her late twenties. She was rather plain, with an odd disproportion about her body: a skinny upper half, then kangaroo hips and big legs. She wore slacks, an old suede jacket. Her hair was brown, and bobbed. Her jaw jutted.

The airlock cycled; she hopped out.

"Hi there, I'm Helen Caprowicz." Her accent was American. She stuck out a hand. "Welcome to the gang. Isn't this really something? It's quite a responsibility."

"Hello, Helen. I'm Michael Peacocke. How many people are there in the, er, gang?"

"Six. You're British, I guess? I'm from upstate New York myself. You're the last in, Mike. That makes six of us, counting you. Think of it! Just us six guys to distribute all those bio-sensors."

"All those what?"

"Oh, they haven't told you yet? Come on through —"

As the airlock cycled, he whispered, "I thought it wasn't real. I thought it was a hallucination."

"Mike, if this isn't real, neither am I! And I feel real enough to me! Do I need to kick you to prove it?"

"Oh now, that wouldn't prove —"

But she did turn and kick him, playfully if sharply, on the shin. Recoiling, he actually left the floor for a moment.

"Or do I get a Gebraudi to kick you in the butt?"

"No . . . You're real!"

She led him to the waiting alien.

"Meet Boon-ap-aat-oo, Mike. I guess that's how you say it! He's our instructor." Garibaldi—and . . . and? . . . and Bonaparte! Its bones were certainly 'apart', so far as its exterior cranium went.

The alien stretched out its arm. It took Michael's fingers in its glove and wagged them limply up and down, as if inspecting for breakages.

"Welcome," it hooted. "We appreciate you. Please follow me."

Bonaparte led them to a temporary room run up from a few free-standing partitions. A milky glass panel, the size of a very large television screen, stood on the floor. Its base was an opaque prism, fitted with a keyboard printed with alien symbols. Helen Caprowicz promptly sat down on the floor, sprawling out her large legs.

"You do the same, Mike. They've got no use for seats." So Michael squatted.

Bonaparte grounded itself in a heap of tyres beside the glass panel. It removed the green cartridge from its leg pouch and slotted this into a gap in the prism base. Then it tapped the keyboard; the panel lit. A picture appeared—an animated cartoon —of two stars revolving round a common centre of gravity, but quite far apart in space. One star was larger than the other.

"First I must explain about our home, and origin," said Bonaparte methodically.

"I just love this film show," whispered Helen. "I've seen it twice already. You spot something new each time."

"Our home sun is part of a binary system. These two stars average six billion kilometers from each other—three times the distance from your own sun to the planet Saturn, which is enough room for both suns to have planets of their own. A great incentive to develop star flight! Imagine if you had another sun with a family of worlds where the planet Pluto is. Consequently our Unidentifieds thrilled with the hope that there might be Whole Planet Life around the other sun, and spurred us into space. In the event, alas, that second sun was barren." The alien paused. "How would you explain the term 'Unidentifieds', Helen?"

She whistled. "I guess they're like symbolic entities. Bits of the symbol language of the cosmic programme being glimpsed by us, the programmed. Though the programme isn't written by some Big Programmer in the sky. It's within the nature of reality. So we can glimpse a bit of it."

"Or you can fail to," grunted Bonaparte. "Which warps it into evil."

The picture zoomed in upon the larger of the two stars. A family of planets orbited this. Here there were three small moonless worlds, a larger planet in fourth position possessing twin moons, a fifth small world, followed by a gas giant with many big moons.

"Gebraud is number four—"

They watched the weather patterns of that fourth world as it turned in space. Thick clouds cycloned and anticycloned, boiling and streaming apart, constantly disappearing around the world's camber in accelerated time.

Abolishing the clouds, now, the picture laid the planet bare; and one world-continent appeared. The seas were all contained by land chains, quite the opposite of Earth. The camera eye drifted down across this world-continent—and the picture switched from cartoon format to actual scenes. Mountains were quite few, quite low. The light was faint and sickly green. The air was adrift with spores and mists and scudding showers.

A swampy plain extended to the horizon, studded by low knolls. Fungus trees sprouted on these outcrops: cups, bells, parasols, twisted turbans, coral branches, puffballs, morels, chanterelles. Great segmented worms hatched in these fungi, munching through them and burrowing into the soil as the fungus trees rotted down to jelly. The worms ate out waterlogged tunnels, spraying dirt and eggs behind them, drowning themselves in their own tunnels, rotting.

Beasts grazed the swamps. They watched a stump-legged, scaly platypus with a shovel-beak scoop up and sieve water monotonously for weed. Fungus sprouted in a rubbery mat upon its back. Worms hatched in the fungus. Dissolving, the vegetable jelly rotted the seams of its scales, and worms dug into its body. The platypus thrashed about; it rotted. More platypuses mated cumbersomely on the edge of a knoll. The male's semen dribbled over the stream of eggs tumbling from the female. These eggs crystallized, glazing as soon as the liquid semen washed them. They rolled into worm holes, to lie there ripening. Hatching, soft-bodied platypus babies waddled underwater quickly (those that got that far) and in the water grew their scales that would ward off spores and worms and other parasites . . .

They watched a four-legged, thick-hided beast with a flat, bone-plated skull. A flexible leathery face thrust in and out beneath the skull. A single arm snaked among puffballs, breaking off chunks of fungus, pushing them into its mouth. In between bites, it tucked its arm back between its legs in safety among the folds of hide, and withdrew its face to chew, presenting only hard leather to the world. Fungus sprouted on its back and fell off and sprouted again. Storms drenched the land. Rain cascaded down the slope of the beast's back, washing it clean. Mud fell from the sky. A giant chanterelle sprang up upon its broad neck. Straining the single arm over its shoulder, it pushed against the fungus till this snapped and fell away. It broke it up and ate it.

When the beast met a female, the pair coiled their single arms

115

together and hooted in each other's faces. Thus, face to face, they mated. The male stroked the female's orifice till it opened and the female squeezed the male's leathery pouch till it spilled its seed. She transferred the seed manually, smearing it into the passage he pressed open. Which then shut fast.

"That's how octopuses do it," whispered Michael to Helen. "I think it is. It's all done by hand." She hushed him.

The two beasts grazed together now, thrusting food at one another. The female began to swell, in calf. Eventually, straddle-legged over water, she gave birth, the male hauling the baby in its thick birth caul clear and tearing up the afterbirth, then pressing it into the female's lips. Wearily she chewed this down, reincorporating her spent self.

"However did they *get* these films?"

"You'll find out. Just watch."

The female sickened and died. Her womb was rotten with worms and fungus. The male reared the baby instead—its sucking lips triggered milk from the male nipples.

The picture reverted, now, to a simulated landscape. As the imaginary viewpoint receded, the binary system of Eta Cassiopeia fused into a single blob of light, swimming through space among other slower and faster stars. One of these other stars suddenly bloomed blindingly. Circles of light radiated from it. They washed out across its neighbours. In their wake, rather more slowly, a halo of ionised gases expanded.

"There was a supernova, very near to us in cosmic terms. We believe that it affected your world too; but more distantly. The stars were in quite different relative positions seventy million years ago."

Once more they watched the swampy plains. But now the dumb predator worms and other soft parasites were withering in the flux of cosmic radiation. The armoured, thick-hided platypus and the proto-Gebraudi sickened. Some died; but many recovered.

Was it possible for less complex life to die off and more complex life to survive? On Earth, it had been the dinosaurs that died out . . .

Michael felt the pair of apples nudging in his pocket and

realized how hungry he was. He took both out and offered one to Helen. She reached for it momentarily then shook her head, frowning at the screen. Famished, he ate one of the apples, getting rid of the core by standing it neatly on edge against the wall. The other he returned to his pocket. His watch, he noted, read 9:15; he had left the house around 6:00 . . .

(Was Helen Caprowicz conceivably lying asleep—sharing the same dream as he was—somewhere in upstate New York?)

The particle flux from the supernova altered the climate drastically. Cyclones tore across the land. Snow fell. Swamps became *taiga*, slushy tundra. The platypus and proto-alien trudged through white wilderness, hunting scant vegetation. Some died of starvation. Nearer the equator, however, was more temperate land, carpeted with rubbery green mushrooms, where the pools and lakes were rich in algae. Patchily, mistily, the sun shone through. The platypus grazed dumbly on, unchanged, however the Gebraudi cranium began to enlarge. The grooves at the tip of its trunk-arm grew suppler; in time they became plucking analytical fingers.

Eventually, culture dawned. Sprawling villages of roofless houses with thick walls and long gentle ramps arose. Vegetation grew everywhere, bred and tended by the elephantine gardeners. By night, towns were softly lit by phosphorescent moss and luminous algae in irrigation streams . . .

Centuries flowed by.

At last, an alien dipped an array of metal plates and wires into trays of chlorophyll and salted water. It recoiled, its starfish fingers stung by an electric shock.

Another alien laid out arrays of green glass cells wired to a mechanism—which began, ponderously, to turn.

"Here we have the first solar batteries," explained Bonaparte proudly. "Chlorophyll yields up electrons to a metallic semiconductor. Next you will see generated the first radionic waves—radiations which plants detect, which influence their growth and health." Broadcasting antennae loomed over thriving alien fields. Inside botanical workshops, wires fixed to alien vegetables recorded the reactions of the plants to stress and noise, to music and vibration . . .

117

"We begin to understand the nature of Primary Perception: the root sensations and energies of all living cells. We learn how energy patterns interact with matter."

On the screen, an alien with a tool kit strapped to its thigh was projecting 'aura films' of the energy fields of different plants upon milky glass plates.

"It is pattern that organises all living matter, and ultraviolet rays that carry the patterning information from one cell to the next. Yet it is not only living matter that transmits. All the vibratory atoms in the whole universe—whether in living cells or in non-living cells—transmit information. So it is hard to say where the boundary is between life and non-life! Or even if there is any true boundary at all. Here our understanding of the living universe—a universe that is itself a living entity—really starts." Bonaparte touched the keyboard, and images came more rapidly. Towns, then cities arose: green cities all of them. New machines and devices were put together: a mélange of the organic and the inorganic. Biological sensors were built—and grown. Biomemory systems came into being: data etched in living cells . . .

"The whole cosmos is vibratory—from galaxies to single atoms. Every molecule of matter broadcasts and receives on its own wavelength. Sensitive beings can perceive these broadcasts—"

"Like dowsers, you mean?" chipped in Helen. "My grandad was a dowser. I guess I might have some dowser genes myself. I've a real knack for finding things that go lost. Is that how you picked on me? My vibrations?"

Bonaparte made a circular gesture: of acceptance and inclusion of her words. "The natural currents of the world flow through the living body. The Unidentifieds follow these world currents. Certain patterns of relationships—certain shapes—can tap the currents too . . ."

Now the screen showed pyramids and stone circles and great vegetation mazes on Gebraud, and canal mazes brimful with green water.

"Don't they say the Great Pyramid in Egypt has a special shape?" squeaked Helen. "A shape of power? On account of its proportions?"

The alien's fingers executed the same approving twist once more. Cosmic Mutt and Jeff, thought Michael—Helen and alien Bonaparte.

"There are indeed patterns of power which draw corresponding cosmic energies towards them. We commune with these."

"There you have our UFOs, Mike!" grinned Helen. "These guys are way ahead of us."

Michael nodded. "So that's what the saucer shapes we see in the sky are. They're cosmic energy patterns—I'll buy that. But I've met alien-seeming *people*, on board a saucer—"

"You've been contacted by a UFO? Gee."

"*And* I saw something else that looked more like a pterodactyl!"

"That's spooky. Still, why not? I've read a bit about magic, Mike. Magicians were forever trying to conjure up powers—under the name of demons. These demons took all sorts of hybrid animal forms. A strong magician could command them to take a human shape that was easier to communicate with. But they'd try to change back and slip away. That's because these powers are really higher-order forces, whereas we—"

"We're lower-order systems. So I was told. Garibaldi—I mean the pilot who picked me up—he was saying that."

"We only learn something from the Unidentified, Mike, if it presents itself in a reasonably identifiable way for the sort of creatures we are. It isn't likely to appear purely human, because it's something more. All the same, they can come spontaneously —because they're necessary to us. *It's* necessary to us. You don't have to be a magician. You've proved that. So they came to you, looking like alien people, and something like a pterodactyl—I guess you couldn't control it. I guess it just scared you. But you've been privileged! That's why the Gebraudi picked *you*."

Bonaparte honked: "The Unidentifieds that work within the life-aura of a world can sometimes be seen as energy patterns in the sky, but when they come closer they will generally take on the shapes of that world. Indeed, the more in harmony you are with them, the more ordinary they may seem—though they still make their entrances and take their exits from your knowledge in extraordinary ways."

"If they look crazy," added Helen, "that's because *we're* crazy —screwed up with fear and hatred and paranoia. It's us who see them out of focus."

Michael took a deep breath. "Do you mean to say that UFO beings can look just like *you*, Boon-ap-aa . . .?" The name came apart in his mouth.

Bonaparte's hand rotated; there was something mesmeric about the gesture. "On Gebraud, they must surely seem like us, if we are in true harmony," agreed the alien. "Though I admit that is a generalisation. Unidentifieds belong to *all* life on a world, not just to the leading species. So they may sometimes appear as hybrids if their message concerns our relationships with other life. They always choose the most appropriate form when you are sensitive to them. Usually it is an ordinary form: our own form."

The admission that UFO beings could well look just like these aliens from Eta Cassiopeia chilled Michael. Could the Phenomenon invent its own perfect alienness—out of all the human brooding upon extraterrestrial beings throughout the twentieth century?

Bonaparte seemed to sense his alarm. "Tell me of your own meeting with the Unidentified, please?" the alien asked gently.

So Michael described Tharmon and Luvah, and his impregnation of her—Helen nodding admiringly, while he talked.

When he had finished, Bonaparte wagged its trunk in acknowledgement.

"So they pretended to be from another world, in the Pleiades —far from Gebraud, many hundreds of light years distant across the sky? A rich alibi! Yet that is the pattern on your world, from what Helen and the others have told us. You humans need such metaphors to cloak the truth of miracles. Of course, these visitors spring from the mind of your own world—for their form is your own, a little out of focus. Even these ones hurt you a little, since you are so resistant to the miracle on your world."

"You mean that they weren't—how shall I put it?—a 'bad' UFO force?" asked Michael, puzzled.

"The aura of your world is sick, but there is still a continuous spectrum between good and bad. Good and bad light are mixed together—even in the same encounter. Your world, alas, is fast

120

moving towards the dark end, yet this particular encounter was still bright, it seems to me—though not unmixedly so, as you discovered."

"But why did I have to mate with Luvah? Was that good— or bad?"

"That was to produce a more perfect man. It is a noble metaphor. Your seed goes into a blank template and makes another, more perfect You. That is the true meaning of this. But the more perfect man should really be *you yourself*. Obviously there is no baby imitation of you, safe elsewhere out among the stars. You yourself must do the work."

"It's like alchemy," said Helen, thrilled. "Alchemists weren't really trying to change lead into gold; they were trying to change themselves. If they did change themselves, power would be theirs —access to a higher order of experience, with magical-seeming powers—but that wasn't the main aim, ever."

"A more perfect You is what the Unidentified aims for," agreed Bonaparte. "A transmutation."

"But we're too confused, Mike, too blind. So you failed and forgot it all, and you got your body burnt like a clumsy apprentice. Still, you wouldn't be here at all if you hadn't started out on the road. The Gebraudi can show us how to carry on. With their help we can transform Earth's aura—and ourselves."

Michael had been feeling increasingly uncomfortable for the past ten minutes. Edgy, awkward, tight.

There was, he realized, a perfectly simple physical explanation.

"Excuse me, Bonaparte—I mean Boon-ap-aat . . . I must go to the toilet right now. I'm sorry if this keeps you locked up in that suit any longer than need be—"

"My suit is self-sufficient. Do not concern yourself. I will show you where to go. Helen, will you please serve food and drink for yourselves?"

Lumbering upright, Bonaparte led Michael through a maze of screens to another temporary room set against the main dividing wall. It was transparent to the blue-green hall. The floor was inlaid with a carpet of green moss. On the other side of the glassy main wall he noticed an identical patch. Beyond, an alien was helping seal one of its comrades into a space suit. Their two trunks co-operated like a man's two arms.

"Do you see how we help each other in our clumsiness? As in our mating, so in our work! We are cripples. We must perform in harmony—in peace and love. Thus our awkwardness becomes our joy."

"What do I—?"

As though on cue, the unsuited alien of the pair made its way to the other green moss patch. It straddled its short hind legs, while its fingers plucked thoughtfully at tools in its leg belt. A steamy cascade poured down on to the moss; to be soaked up.

When Michael also had watered the moss, he smelt the tang of Christmas trees and fallen pine needles . . .

Chimes sounded through the dome.

Bonaparte reached for the glassy cartridge in its leg pouch, as the other aliens were doing on the far side of the wall. The glass block remained in the other room, however, still plugged into the screen. Bonaparte lowered its tentacle, instead, to touch the patch of moss; and stood silent. For a while no alien moved.

The same chimes rang out again. Bonaparte withdrew its arm.

"Communion. Harmony," the alien honked. "Do you see how any living green matter can serve as symbol for the Biomatrix? Now Helen must surely have your food ready. Can you find your way? I will rejoin you soon."

EIGHTEEN

THE SHEIKH'S ASSISTANT proved to be a skinny youth with wire brush hair and ears that protruded rather. His eyes were large, soft like a deer's, the eyelashes luxurious. He was wearing a black leather jacket.

His eyes met Deacon's. Smiling intoxicatedly he walked over and introduced himself, in slightly hesitant English, as Salim

Fouad. To Deacon's astonishment, he kissed his hand. The information clerk glared at them.

"You're part of a miracle, Professor Deacon," the youth murmured, drawing Deacon outside to where a ten-year-old Mercedes stood under the portico. The driver wore a long white robe and skull cap.

"A miracle? That's one way of putting it! I don't even know how I got here."

" 'Not knowing why you came, nor how—like infant humanity.' You're perfect!" The youth blushed. Was it proper to say that someone was 'perfect'? They drove off just as a flower seller was rushing forward flourishing pink roses. The youth almost looked ready to buy some as a bouquet . . .

"This is Republic Square," Salim said conscientiously, assuming the easier role of guide. His initial hesitancy had been less a matter of language than decorum. "Our Revolution is celebrated here every twenty-sixth of July. Thousands gather. Many tents! That's Abdin Palace—it's now the Ministry of Land Reforms. Our Sheikh is highly contemporary, you know!" he added. He made Muradi sound like a piece of furniture. "Other brotherhoods fail to adapt to modern times. This is the time of science—I personally am a civil engineer." Salim flushed again. "That's to say, I'm training to be one."

Turning right, they drove up a broad straight thoroughfare lined by tall ugly lamp-posts. "Port Said Street, this: a canal flowed here a hundred years ago."

When they left Port Said Street, turning left, Deacon saw domes and minarets covering a hilltop in the distance.

"Yet there is another science too! The threefold science—of Man. We say that it consists in a science of ordinary knowledge, then in a science of extraordinary knowledge: of unusual inner states. That's your special work, isn't it, Professor? That's why you're part of the miracle . . . Sidi Muradi explained your work just briefly before he sent me."

Deacon nodded.

"That's right. Normal psychology—then the altered states of consciousness. What's this third science?"

"Ah, that is the science of true reality, that lies beyond the

123

other two. The other two are hollow without it. So the real work lies in seeing how all three sciences need one another. I think you're verging on the third science too? The science beyond ordinary human knowledge?"

Deacon shook his head, as if to dislodge some water from a buzzing ear. The gesture reminded him of some other time, but he couldn't pin it down.

"The Sheikh will see if it's so," Salim promised. "Even if you and I don't. He's been visited—" the youth's voice sank to a whisper—"by Khidr, the Unseen Guide. Do you understand who Khidr is?"

"Yes I do! You mean visited metaphorically?"

"I don't know that word."

"What you're saying is a picture. A symbol. Like a piece of poetry—not an actual event."

"No! I saw it happen. I was there. It's the great event of my whole life. Over that way," Salim waved a hand northward, "is the city gate we call Bab Zuweyla. Where criminals were put to death long ago. It used to be named Bab al-Mutawalli because of a saint who lived there. He could lift himself through the air at the speed of thought. He could be in Mecca or Baghdad instantly with no sense of passing from here to there. Though of course today we have aeroplanes, by which you travel," Salim hinted.

"Yes we have aeroplanes—" And unidentified flying objects that supposedly accelerated to ten thousand miles an hour in a single second, that were said to vanish from sight and reappear out of nothing. Was there really a 'third science' to explain those?

"It was near Bab al-Mutawalli that we met Khidr—"

Through crowded streets the Mercedes crawled up to the open gates of a mosque. Inside Deacon glimpsed a flaxen desert area parched by sunlight, with black-shadowed crenellated arcades around it. Passing by, they entered a jumble of ancient houses and zigzagging alleys. After several minutes of maze-threading the old Mercedes halted outside a whitewashed, shuttered building.

The rooms in Muradi's house were unornamented save for calligraphies printed on cloth and carved in wood, and bright arabesque carpets yielding layer below layer of interlocking pattern, as though the floor led down and down, tier below tier.

A lunch too large to finish was served, of mutton *kufta*, rice, spiced vegetables. Sheikh Muradi ate sparingly, Salim hardly at all.

"I've no idea how I got here," Deacon said again. "No passport, ticket or money. It's as if I was just picked up off the street in England and set down here on that bench by the Nile—"

"Money is no problem, John. As to a hotel, you shall stay in my house. I insist. I agree that the passport is a nuisance. You will have to visit your embassy. Of course I shall vouch for you to our own officials, but you must accept some embarrassment. How can one explain what lies beyond explanation?" Adjusting his glasses, Muradi peered at a text on the wall behind Deacon's head as though it was an optician's chart—which it was for him, perhaps, in a spiritual way, whatever he could read in it representing a quality not of eyesight but of insight.

On the last occasion that Deacon had met him—in London two years earlier, at the time of the lecture series—the Sheikh had struck him as urbanely cosmopolitan, if personally austere. His urbanity was the politeness of soul of some undisclosed, non-political prince. It had seemed like Renaissance *virtù*, belonging not to State but rather to states of mind. Deacon had thought of a sixteenth-century Pope of power and authority, but one whose statecraft operated entirely within the sphere of a relationship with the Infinite—a relationship which wasn't private, but communal, social, shared with all human beings, yet visible to his eyes alone. Muradi had said then that God makes metaphors for men: which are their lives. He seemed to live his own life as though what most people saw as facts and absolutes he saw as metaphors for another sort of event, occurring in another way entirely. Life's events were shadows cast by another species of Being, even though they were perfectly solid shadows. He saw through the trapdoor depths of the carpet at the same time as he stood upon it firmly.

Deacon understood, as the Sheikh sat looking at him, that he was being seen as a meaning behind the metaphor—as the real import of himself, the hidden substance that cast the

125

shadows which Deacon, being the shadow, could not see.

The real question wasn't whether a UFO 'event' had shipped him here, like the real or legendary Spanish soldier from Manila to Mexico; or whether he'd 'actually' stepped on board an aeroplane and flown here in a kind of trance—in some state of mind not accessible to baseline consciousness. As he sat facing the Sheikh, still tasting the charred, fatty savour of the minced grilled lamb, he knew that in a sense *both* had happened so that one explanation cancelled out the other. No wonder he had no ticket, no passport to record his entry point! He simply wasn't located at an event-viewpoint from which ticket or missing passport could be viewed. Which was how all UFO events must relate themselves to the *sensus communis*, the common world! They withdrew their meaning at the moment that they yielded it. Their credibility always vanished on the point of being proven. Yet, while he might be in a state of not-knowing, for Muradi at this moment he represented knowledge—the very knowledge of which he had to be deprived.

Muradi lifted his glass to sip some iced water. "I think you can *see*—how you come to be here."

"I know *you* can see it! I'm just a thought in your mind, aren't I? A thought which you can know in its entirety—objectively—because actually I'm out here in flesh and blood—and very well fed, thank you! I needed that. But did you somehow cause me to come here? Or are you only a sort of target for me, the arrow, to hit?"

"Calm yourself, John. You're losing the moment. Knowledge is a matter of keeping the moment just as it was before you opened your mouth, seeing the world through those eyes, holding that vision."

"Where does it all lead?"

Muradi shook his head. "It doesn't 'lead'—except out of the world, beyond the world. 'Leading' is a matter of the causes and effects within the world. The true answer is the *event* of your being here, not some explanation for that event. The event is already a metaphor. You proceed the wrong way if you make it still more metaphorical, by attaching an 'explanation'. At that point explanations proliferate endlessly, all equally paltry."

"I have to know! Tell me, how much do you know about flying saucers, Sheikh? About unidentified flying objects, as they're called?"

Muradi smiled.

"As much as I know about flying carpets!"

"I thought Salim said that some local saint—what was his name, Salim? The one who was supposed to fly—"

"Al-Mutawalli," said the Sheikh.

"You do know about 'flying carpets' then! Are you saying that you *do* know, or don't know?"

"I answered you, John, in exactly the same style as the 'answer' you seek to this event! Don't you see that the event is the answer?"

"It may be for you. I believe I've been captured by a UFO event. I don't say captured by a UFO—that isn't the same thing." Deacon laughed harshly. "That's how those who undergo this experience often interpret it. It's the story they tell themselves—the metaphor their mind tosses up. It's the tree they make up out of a green blur in the distance. They can even go closer and climb into its branches and pluck apples from it. They go away and tell everyone about this fine tree with luscious apples. So people come and there's nothing there; they seem mad."

"You could become quite a fair Sufi story-teller," nodded Muradi. "Let us drink some coffee to celebrate. Or perhaps you'd prefer mint tea?"

"Mint tea sounds different."

"Therefore it is better! Salim, would you please—?"

As soon as Salim left the room, Muradi took an old leather-bound book from his pocket and placed it face down on the table.

"Let me tell you something, John. He who does away with causal law does away with *mind itself*—with the human mind we know, the mind which knows the world of things and so permits us to live here. Our human mind can't cease to think of the things around it. That's our activity in the world. Only God truly exists—outside causes. The extracausal, the miraculous, is always present, though—within everything, for the world only exists while God keeps it in being from one moment to the next, with its freight of causes and effects that our minds feast on. The . . . disparity between our thoughts and His Thought—the inexplicable vacuum that would suck all causes and effects into it, if we weren't so imperceptive of God—is actually what draws us on, to higher states. So new organs of perception—new states of consciousness in your jargon, John—come into being. Out of necessity! I say therefore increase your necessity! Your own necessity has already been increased wonderfully by all this. But don't impose false causes."

"UFO events are simply meant to breed . . . the need to understand? Not to understand *them as such*? Is that what you mean?"

Muradi slid the book across the table. "A gift for you. From Khidr, the Green Man. Its meaning, likewise, is for you."

"Salim said that you met Khidr! I thought he was just being poetic—"

"Salim saw with his very own eyes, precisely what there was to see."

"How did Khidr appear? Out of the sky? Out of a—" Deacon felt embarrassed: a hobbyist, a stamp collector trying to mail first day covers from Hiroshima on the evening of the Bomb.

"Out of a flying saucer? Why shouldn't he be his own flying saucer? Why should a flying saucer not be he?"

Deacon took the book and opened it.

> *LE LEMEGETON*
> *ou La petite Clef du Roi Solomon*
> *Dictionnaire Infernal des Esprits*
>
> *Paris, 1856*
>
> *Tirade limité à 20 exemplaires*
> *No. 8*

The figure 8 was written in faded red ink. Dried blood? No, blood would surely blacken. A mimicry of blood, perhaps.

He turned the pages, and saw curious diagrams. They reminded him of electrical circuits with looping wires, aerials, resistances, gates and switches. Little symbolic light bulbs sprouted from the circuits. If they were all somehow connected up to each other in the correct way in some three dimensional array, all these shapes that apparently conjured up power . . . Was it possible to put them all together? To write a computer programme to sort all the millions and billions of possible ways of interlinking them . . .?

His heart thumped. On one page was a diagram he knew well.

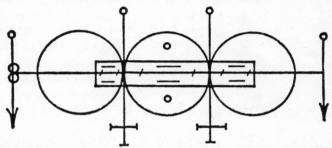

Michael had drawn it under hypnosis! It was the schematic for the gravitationally propelled space vehicle! The circuit diagram for a UFO!

He read:

FORNEUS a l'apparance d'un monstre de mer, bien qu'il devienne humain si l'opérateur le desire. Il peut enseigner à l'opérateur tous les arts et les sciences. De plus, on peut apprendre de lui tous les langages.

So the shape that Michael saw on the control panel of his 'flying saucer' was really an occult sign for conjuring up some devil called Forneus which looked like a sea monster—though it could change its shape to suit whoever saw it. A devil which could teach all arts and sciences and every known language . . .

The Sheikh seemed to recede physically, becoming part of the wall, an abstract text. His reality waned. Meaning leaked out of all he had said. An ethereal edifice which had been building in Deacon's mind dissolved into a mirage in a hostile or, worse still, an indifferent desert. The desert didn't invent the mirage, the desert simply existed—with the mirage a mere byproduct of men's eyes.

A book of black magic.

Of trashy superstitious spells.

Salim came back. "Please smoke if you wish," invited Muradi. "Please do." Salim shook his head firmly, face full of protestations; to win a smile.

A dark wrinkled man of indeterminate age—the servant—followed with a beaten brass tray bearing three cups of aromatic mint tea.

"The answer is that UFOs operate *by magic* . . ." The answer was no answer.

This might just, still, be a joke. A teaching joke staged—in all seriousness—by Muradi who saw life permanently from a different angle. Suppose Deacon discounted Salim's pious avowals that he and Muradi had indeed encountered the Green Man slipping into this reality continuum then out of it again . . . Could he discount them? Hadn't Muradi experienced, in his own way, a UFO encounter? He might have done—and still the gift of *Le Lemegeton* could be a teaching joke, to prove by shock to Deacon that the answer is no answer! Weren't the Sufis notoriously fond of sending pupils away with apparently idiotic advice—which, years later, would suddenly take on an entirely new meaning, once the pupil's inner state had changed? Weren't they notorious for sending fools away with blessings in disguise? Famous for deliberately absurd behaviour? For their shock psychotherapy? The gift of this book could easily be one such absurdity grafted on to whatever had really happened earlier to the Sheikh. Indeed, the Sheikh's message might be that he had no need to know about UFOs, or about ineffable phenomena—and no capacity either. So he was given a child's conjuring set, a book of magic spells.

Except . . .

. . . that the diagram was exactly the same as the one that Michael saw! So it was genuine. Which meant that the truth was: occult nonsense. Forneus can teach . . . all human knowledge. Forneus indeed!

'Why should a flying saucer not be he?' Muradi *knew*; and wouldn't say!

Bitterly, Deacon slipped the book into his pocket.

"I really should telephone my wife. I ought to have thought sooner. I'm afraid it could cost a bit—"

"A few pounds."

"I'll repay it. When I get back to England I shall wire the money."

"You merely say that because now you resent me, John." Muradi sipped his tea equably. "Salim will take you up to my study and put the call through for you."

Deacon followed Salim upstairs. The Sheikh's study was a large shaded room lined with Arabic books, Persian books, French and English books. On a broad mahogany desk sat an IBM typewriter with an Arabic typeface. Salim proudly showed it off—its automatic script processor, its simplified keyboard, its logic circuits—to prove how up-to-date his Sheikh was. A small three-legged rosewood table held a large Arabic volume, its binding densely illuminated with floral forms: a carpet in miniature. The Koran, no doubt. A black and white photograph (the only picture in the house, it seemed) stood on the desk—of a coffin upon a catafalque covered with an embroidered shroud. A large black turban perched on the coffin with an eel of fabric hanging loose.

"What phone number in England, Sir?"

Deacon said. Salim dialled the operator, talked a while.

"It might be half-an-hour. They'll call back. When you speak, Sir, you must only use English, French or Arabic."

"What do they expect I speak—Venusian?"

"That is _the law, Sir. Russians must speak to Moscow in French or English. Japanese to Japan. It's to hinder spies."

"Oh, I suppose I could be seen as a spy! No passport. No logical explanation for how I got here."

"Ah, but we know, Professor Deacon. I know. _Sidi_ Muradi knows."

"What's the photo, Salim?"

"That is the tomb of Shams of Tabriz! The dervish who intoxicated our Master Rumi. It's at Konya in Turkey. Shams seemed like a wild man—yet between his mysterious appearance and his disappearance three years afterwards he inspired sublime poetry and thoughts and transformed our Master's life. It's said," Salim hissed, "that actually Shams was Khidr . . ."

"Khidr certainly gets around! I think I'll stay up here till they phone back. I'd rather."

Mary sounded furious with relief: the tight anger of a mother chastising a child for tumbling downstairs.

"I've no idea how I got here!" he protested sheepishly yet again. "I'll be back with you all as soon as I can book a flight."

Static crackled, relays of clicks. Was this call routed beneath the Mediterranean, or was his voice flying into outer space and bouncing back again? Had he too been transmitted through outer space, and reassembled—by means unknown?

"I don't have my passport or any money, you see. The embassy might have to repatriate me—"

"Like a lost child, with a label round your neck!"

"I can't talk too long. This is someone else's phone . . . Will you give my love to Rob and Celia?"

Click-click-click . . .

After he'd put the phone down, he slipped a sheet of paper into the Arabic typewriter and played at tapping out simplified characters for two or three minutes, watching the IBM processor conflate them into Arabic script; though as he didn't know the language the words must needs be absurd, lacking any true existence.

Then he went downstairs. The Sheikh was putting him up, after all. One must be polite.

NINETEEN

A BLOND MAN with big bones and a long stubbly witch's jaw was sitting on the floor by Helen Caprowicz. He wore a ski sweater, jeans and tan boots. They were eating cold frankfurters, vegetable salad and pickled onions off paper picnic plates, using their fingers. Helen pushed a third plate towards Michael.

"Meet Axel Moller—our food bringer! It's his fifth solo trip to the Moon already. Imagine that! That's his Volvo parked out there."

Moller nodded, still eating. "I'm from Kiruna, up in the north of Sweden," he munched. "A mining engineer." He swallowed and grinned, displaying large loose-looking teeth, noticeably bare of gums. "What do you think of our friends?" he asked Michael.

Michael smiled wryly. "I think it's very . . . harmonious of them, to help us."

The Swede nodded. "Of course, there's the long-term threat to them—and to anyone else in the vicinity—if we get loose outside the solar system in our present state. Just imagine if we sent a starship of our own out to Gebraud—then another and another, I don't doubt. What a fine colony Gebraud would make! Especially as they're non-aggressive. We'd treat them as we treat the whales and dolphins back home. Then we'd leapfrog on to another world, and another, over their bodies—and souls."

"But it's such a long way to their star," protested Michael. "My pilot said it took them forty years to reach us."

"I imagine there's a faster means. Gebraudi technology's fine, but it's always been pretty linear—while ours is exponential. I'm talking about the next few *centuries*, boy. The next millenium. Our aura would be growing blacker all the time, expanding like a metastizing cancer as we carved out an empire—till eventually we met something too big and wise to be crushed and poisoned. Or till it eventually registered us. There are lordly beings that pervade whole star clusters, out there! The entire galaxy is an even higher level of being, slow and vast. These are hierarchies of existence we can hardly comprehend! We'd be surgically erased in the end, believe you me, and it would *still* only be a tiny tragedy within our galaxy, but the local cost could be incredible—whole worlds and races lost because of us. And yet actually self-interest hardly enters into it, for the Gebraudi— that's the wonderful thing. They come here as much for our sake, as for themselves. No, even more so." He picked up a frankfurter and bit the end off. "Did they tell you how their own Unidentifieds inspired them to send this second expedition to us? Just as a human being might see a vision and hear a voice telling him to go on a pilgrimage . . . It's in the Gebraudi nature to help and be helped. Altruism's a genetic thing with them."

Helen shook her head. "Not exactly, Axel. It's outside the actual genes. It's an 'idea-gene'. It's a way of thinking that gets handed down. That can be just as formative as any piece of DNA, once a species reaches a certain stage. Given their physical shortcomings, they really need it—so the idea survives too."

"Shortcomings?" echoed Michael. "They don't seem overly functional, do they? To have built machines and cities and starships . . ."

Helen turned to him, pursuing her hobby-horse. "We don't really understand the genetics of ideas properly yet. But they do get passed down like physical characteristics. Thought patterns get inherited. They mutate and evolve—only, in society not in the germ cells. Thank God we've got a bit of an idea-gene for harmony, ourselves—or we wouldn't have survived as long as this! We just don't have enough of it. The Gebraudi can inject a whole lot more into our system if we only let them!"

"I said they don't seem very functional. Or very realistic—"

Moller glared at him.

"I mean evolutionarily," Michael added hastily. "They've got the absolute minimum, haven't they? One arm. It doesn't even seem to have any bones in it."

"Is a giraffe 'realistic'?" demanded Moller. "Was the pterodactyl 'realistic'?—they couldn't even take off from the ground. Nature is prodigal with her shapes."

"Giraffes and pterodactyls don't build starships, though," said Michael.

"You saw the film of how they evolved," insisted Helen. "They belonged perfectly in that environment. Then after the supernova, when all those filthy pests got wiped out, it became a lot more favourable."

"Some might say too favourable. Where was the challenge to evolve?"

"Challenge?" snorted Moller. "Nature isn't an enemy, to be fought and beaten. That way lies planetary suicide—and it's been our way far too long. Oh, once it was different! Primitive Man felt at one with Nature, in all her moods—foul as well as fair. Power flowed through him because of this, and he enjoyed a psychic oneness with his fellows, too, that we precious individualists can hardly credit. But Man became alienated from this power and this oneness. He couldn't come to terms with his awakening intelligence within the bosom of Nature. He rejected the Mother, then repressed the guilt of it. It was a self-alienation —but he turned it outside, don't you see? Man is the ultimate obsessional neurotic—and this split has been widening ever since, so that civilization is one long fight against untold evils 'out there': devils, or other nations, or natural 'disasters', or the plain 'stubbornness' of Nature in making us sweat for her fruits. And all the time the evil is inside—it's the denial of Nature and the rhythms of the world. The Gebraudi never denied Nature, though. They awoke to intelligence within her bosom, and stayed within it, all together. They didn't need two meaty fists to belabour the world; one soft trunk is enough for their needs. So Nature guided them upwards, softly, gently."

At that moment Bonaparte returned. The alien went to the blank screen, unplugged the green glassy block and laid it delicately on the ground before Michael. It was a honeycomb of tiny transparent cells, layer upon layer of them full of green matter, linked by fine, barely visible wires. Copper prongs stuck out from one end. Michael touched it tentatively.

"Yes, it lives," said the alien. "It senses the vibrations of the world around. Molecularly—vibrationally—it is highly sensitive. It is nourished by sympathetic radionic resonances from the parent Biomatrix up in the hood of the starship, with which it is in tune. We can modulate it with our various instruments to tap the memories of the Biomatrix—as on this screen—or make it an extension of the perceptions of the Biomatrix, as perhaps you saw Gar-boor-oold-ee do . . ."

"Those were *live* films of your evolution that I saw?"

"Apart from the star and planet diagrams, yes. They are recalled from the world-memory with which the Biomatrix is primed. We can see into the past history of our world this way. All vibrations are recorded and stored."

"I told you you'd learn," smiled Helen happily. "It's a kind of dowsing—not of where lost things are, but of everything that happened in connexion with them earlier in their history. Stones, places, tools, skeletons, fossils . . . All the vibes they've been imprinted with. My grandad used to pick up a brooch or ring he'd never seen before, and he could tell you all sorts of things that checked out afterwards about who'd owned it. What the person looked like. How she felt—even though she was long dead. These guys have got it down to a fine art. Live archaeology."

Bonaparte retrieved the cartridge and slotted it back into the keyboard. "Now it is time to show you the Biomatrix itself, through this access point. You may not enter our ship yourselves on account of the hostile atmosphere and pressure. We do not have pressure suits for humans, and our own suits are far too large even if we tanked them up with your air—"

Helen giggled.

"Besides having four legs apiece! We'd look like a pantomime horse with only one guy in it, dragging the empty hind legs around!"

Michael chewed his last frankfurter. Such squashy things these Gebraudi must be under their thick rhino hides! Full of guts and giant entrails busily digesting ropes and balls of green fodder, with cud passing to and fro through chains of stomachs. He felt he was seeing right into Bonaparte for a moment, just as he'd once stared at a cow in a field, trying to see right into it and *be* it. He realized that he hadn't yet seen any of the aliens eating. Yet herbivores are hungry all day long, aren't they? Their alien stomachs must really be packed with cud. For a moment he felt that he was living in the alien's guts himself, being pressed back and forth in peristaltic surges. Obscurely he sensed that he and Helen and the Swede had somehow been swallowed by the beasts, taken in by some oozy digestive process . . .

The image of a pantomime alien teased him. He imagined Helen, wagging kangaroo-hipped behind him, with her head burrowing blindly up his backside so that they could actually fill a Gebraudi suit: *blindly,* not seeing her way. There was some principle of compensation at work here. Two humans equalled one 'balanced' alien—yet the alien had only one arm . . . A curious equation of plus and minus seemed to be in operation. Once more he wondered: were they genuine star travellers at all?

The notion of the American girl burrowing into him made him realize that it wasn't she who should entwine with him at all, but an English girl with a ziggurat of crinkly red hair—who had been driven away and separated from him by a goblin that frightened the wits out of her . . . Why had the twisted UFO-being separated the two of them? Was it so that he could be free to be driven here, to learn all this about the true harmony of life? If so, what a seemingly cruel means. Had he first to lose something, in order to gain something else? Had he first to be wounded, to be healed? The principle of compensation again: galaxies race away as we chase them with our telescopes; what we gain on the swings, we lose on the roundabouts . . .

"The Biomatrix constantly reads the whole vibrational status of the ship and every being in it. So we can view the ship by sending a query-impulse through the Matrix—a viewpoint 'Ego' to inquire upon this status. What you will see is not the ship directly, but its primary awareness of the ship: the image of reality, which it dreams."

The image which it dreams. Michael felt dizzy and afloat. Maybe it was the fault of the low Moon gravity. He took another bite, to ballast himself.

"How does it monitor anything between the stars?" he asked hesitantly. "Surely it must sleep in the cold too?"

" 'Awake' and 'asleep' are not correct terms for the Biomatrix. Plant cells do not sleep or wake; they always do both. Their awareness is primary; it precedes the split into conscious and unconscious modes. The Matrix simply waits in chilled dormancy between the stars—matching the dormant ship. That is its wintertime. Then comes the star, your Sun, and Spring."

Something nagged at him. Something Bonaparte had just said. About sending a viewpoint 'Ego' through this strange living matrix of awareness. Wasn't this what John Deacon had been hoping to do? To attach an 'ego-tag'—to UFO-consciousness! Was this, then, Deacon's experiment *succeeding*?

The screen showed a ship's interior, seen by a disembodied eye drifting along a corridor which throbbed and pulsed as though to the dance of atoms in its walls. The eye passed through a solid wall: a grainy, densely-packed kaleidoscope of quivering, intersecting dots—a pointilliste wall. Beyond the wall stood an alien, doing something. The eye passed sheer through its body; and the screen jumbled with throbbing forms of light —fluorescent balloons squeezed into one another—which he took to be internal organs.

"They cure illnesses that way," Helen boasted. "Their Biomatrix reads the vibrations of sick organs and adjusts them. It's beyond our medicine—except for a few psychic healers."

The eye drifted into a lift shaft, a long vibrating tunnel boring up through the stem of the ship.

Bonaparte stroked the cartridge, as the eye drifted upwards. "Basic awareness does not 'think'," the alien said. "Rather, it *knows*. Existence is primary, individual existences are secondary. Our Biomatrix puts each individual being in touch with the Whole."

The eye glanced out through a porthole across Tsiolkovsky crater, then down at the roof of a leathery, paunch-like dome, perhaps the very same dome that they were in. If it dived down through the dome, thought Michael, he would see himself on the screen, watching himself . . . throbbing, shimmering.

"Knowing is everywhere. It is the texture of Whole Planet Life. Conscious thought only need to learn to tap it—"

On the screen, several aliens grazed round tanks packed with fleshy, vibrant plants resembling water hyacinths. They trunked up clumps of greenery, and fed. More tanks repeated, mirrorlike, as well as machinery that hinted more at an engine room. The eye drifted roofwards, and passed through the roof into a hall that glowed with blue-tinted sunlight. Honeycombing the domed roof was a translucent cellular mosaic. It was a fly's many-facetted eye, hugely swollen, seen from within. The viewpoint eye dipped.

"Behold the Biomatrix."

Michael saw row upon row of U-tubes, hundreds of these racked in series and in parallel. Each tube was as large as an upturned pair of human legs. Each one was brimful of green clotted glue. From a spider grid overhead, silver wires dipped down into the stiff green juice. Pipes and cables ran about like roots and branches. Spaced round the perimeter of the Matrix were screens similar to the one he was watching. Aliens sprawled intently before them, observing vibrating lattices and hierarchies of complex patterns unfolding.

"Doesn't it all shut down during the lunar night?" asked Michael weakly. "That's two weeks long."

The Swede bared his pink, withdrawn gums. His mouth looked false, like dentures in plastic on a dentist's tray, as though it was only a model of a mouth, detachable from the rest of his head.

"Time is sensed in a different way by Whole Planet Life," he grinned.

For a moment Michael imagined that Bonaparte was speaking through the Swede's lips, and Moller was merely an extension of the alien, a pseudo-human with a false mouth. Whereas Bonaparte was too solid, too thick-hided, too full of rumbling guts and cud-packed stomachs to be anything less than wholly real! How strange that a human should seem less authentic than an absurd alien from the stars! A moment later, Bonaparte did indeed take over Moller's lead.

"Whole Planet Life is an entity, child of your star as ours is of our own star. You are its cells. So are the fishes and the birds, the trees and grass. Your communities form its organs. As do the forests, and the coral reefs. You, however, are its brain cells, its higher consciousness centres. Yet you remain unconscious of the world-field within which you operate!"

The screen became bobbly green: a jelly aquarium stiff with frogspawn. For the eye had drifted down into the Biomatrix itself, completing its journey of observation by re-entering into its own vision of itself—whereupon everything became amorphous, formless, indecipherable.

Bonaparte blanked the screen.

"Its time sense is radically different from yours. Its memory comprises all the timeline of cellular life from the very beginning! So the world does not ever forget itself. What, then, is the nature of the 'present moment' for it? Very much greater than your own personal present moment, *Mikal*." Bonaparte made his name sound like an Old Testament prophet's. "Time is only a construct of consciousness. How long does the present—the 'now' moment—seem to you to last? How long before an event feels 'past'? Perhaps a single minute by your watch? Not much more."

Michael glanced at his watch. Perversely it had stopped and was recording no passage of time at all. He rewound it.

"Your personal 'now' spans a moment of the past, and an instant of the future. It must—or you could not think continuously."

"We all share this same 'specious present'," said Helen. "That's the best name for it, because it isn't absolute. It isn't written into the universe. Other viewpoints can have a different time sense. Ours last a few minutes at the very most—not long. It's funny: personal time's a kind of Moebius strip. All the information we get comes to us from the past—the sound of my voice, the light of a distant star: they've already happened. So we're always living in the future of everything else, inside ourselves. That's how the knot of time gets tied, that binds us in the here and now. Past and future tie themselves together in our minds to make the specious present. There's only one surface to this Moebius strip, though. So there's only one direction. We can only go forward."

"You express it well, Helen," honked Bonaparte. "We are proud. We enjoy." 'Enjoy' sounded utterly the wrong word: conveying a gloating, almost. Perhaps it was just an unhappy choice. Just then a suited alien poked its head between the partitions and gobbled at Bonaparte, then began hauling the screens away. As the walls vanished from around them, Michael could see into the parking lot again. Another alien was fitting an entire new petrol tank into the boot of the Thunderbird which he had thought so seamlessly welded.

"Whole Planet Life binds time far more vastly," went on Bonaparte. "Its present moment extends much further than yours or mine. For this reason the Unidentifieds—which are the go-betweens of the higher-order system—seem able to tamper with time, appearing and disappearing mysteriously as they cut across our narrow viewpoint. Or they may take time away from creatures they meet; or add it on."

How long was it really since he had left Swale Moor? A minute—or a day? How long could one disappear, into the UFO-state? Forever? He panicked.

"What's happening to my car?"

"They're renewing the reaction mass," Helen said sharply. "I don't know what it is—plain water, maybe. That's for the gravity-field. Of course it runs the normal engine too. From now on, friend, your only filling station's on the Moon."

"The units are sealed," sighed Moller. "We aren't ready for such technology yet. We shan't fly to Jupiter and Pluto in our cars, trailing our unstable UFOs with us. Bearing false witness, half the time, because of our own poisonous blindness!"

It was all a film, a solid three-dimensional film where the events and actors were real, living and tangible—yet somehow projected from elsewhere. Michael felt full of wind. Covering his mouth, he burped, and tasted pickled onions again. By the 'thirty-plus' level in a trance, Deacon had said, you could experience false tastes as perfectly real . . . How deep down was he now? Michael stared at the Thunderbird—*which must still be parked on Swale Moor!* It was his re-entry vehicle to normal sane reality. However could he learn to drive it back?

John, where are you?

TWENTY

THERE WAS NO surcease, no let up.

"The briefest moment of time for the Whole Planet Life of Earth, continued Bonaparte, "must extend at least twenty-four hours, to equal the period of rotation of your world. Otherwise the spin of your world would rule all its other sensations."

"Put its head in a spin," laughed Helen.

"Which means that events which seem to possess sequence for you are blurred and averaged out for it. They do not necessarily have the same strict order. What is more, this is only the *briefest*

141

moment in its experience. Many such moments make up its own 'specious present'—amounting to days or weeks on your time scale." Bonaparte spoke swiftly now, as though time was running out. Beyond the transparent wall, the alien serviceman slammed the boot lid shut and ran a nozzled machine, a hand vacuum cleaner, around the joint, perhaps welding it by acoustics or vibration . . .

"Wait a moment," interrupted Michael. "If we humans are its higher thought centres, and if we only feel that the present moment lasts such a short time, how can it last so much longer for Whole Planet Life?"

"How long does it take one of your brain cells to fire, then inhibit itself and be ready to fire again?" demanded Bonaparte. "Microseconds! A time too short for you to register—compared with the time a thought takes! You are all separate brain cells, but you are not the Mind. You cannot fully grasp the Whole Planet Life system when you are merely the thought cells in it. Yet you can certainly upset its balance, and very sanity, by your collective attitude—just as a poisoned brain makes the mind schizophrenic!" Bonaparte wagged its trunk in distress.

"Take your attitude to death. Life and death are really a dialectic process. Cells must die so that new ones are born. Older species must pass, that higher species may arrive. What does death signify to a Whole Life that stretches back a billion years? Not the constant, nagging. anxiety that it conveys to you. What does death mean to a creature properly in harmony with Whole Planet Life? The hunted prey accepts death with a kind of frozen joy once death becomes inevitable! But your abject fear of death—ignorant as you are of the Whole Life system—imprints a virulent death programme upon the nervous system of Planet Life. This death programme wins over the life programme and becomes its master, not its partner. You are murderers! Killers and poisoners of beasts and forests and seas. Killers of yourselves. No wonder so many Unidentifieds are hostile and hurtful!"

Axel and Helen were bobbing their heads in agreement. The technician had finished fusing the Thunderbird back together; now it waved to Bonaparte.

"I suppose this is the new mystical ecological frame of reference for UFOs!" Michael said acidly.

"What are you saying?" cried Moller. "Do you think *we* aren't real people? Listen to me, boy. Whole Planet Life is ancient and powerful—and it's becoming bloody autistic because of us, its brain cells, and our death and power crazes. That's why it wiped out the first Gebraudi expedition with an energy attack or something. *We* couldn't tolerate it if the aliens came. We're too self-centred. We've infected the world. We've malformed it. It's a mass of festering wounds. Thankfully, Whole Planet Life isn't just *us*. It's all the creatures that dwell on Earth. We aren't even the only higher brains around. Why do you suppose so many UFOs are seen diving into the oceans? That's not because of bloody Atlantis. It's because of the whales and dolphins—they're wiser than us. We just happen to be the dominant race right now, because we're cuter at manipulating things. And it wasn't always this way. Primitive Man was in key —so we still have some credit balance from our own past, too. The life programme's strong. It fights back—"

"With its saviours!" Helen burst in. "With its prophets and saints, with its miracles and signs."

"We can help you," vowed Gomorrah. "First we will examine and diagnose. There are natural pathways in the world, as in a brain: networks that the Unidentified will follow. These are the lines that link life centres, where you once built pyramids and shrines and temples. We have some maps of these 'ley lines' already. Axel and the others have helped with this. Here is where we must take the pulse of your world, on the primary level. We will feed this information to our Biomatrix to make a model of your world. Thousands of biosensors need to be laid out, to read the rhythms along the ley lines that Ancient Man knew—before you unlearnt all this. But we Gebraudi cannot place these sensors along the leys ourselves. The Unidentifieds would soon try to crush us. We must rely on you."

"It's like taking an encephalogram," said Helen helpfully. "Or placing acupuncture needles, to read the body's energy field. Only, using living biological equipment—extensions of the Biomatrix. This isn't hostile to UFOs, you understand?

We're not setting traps. We're just taking the pulse."

"The pulse of a tiger," growled Moller. "But we can do it. We are tigers too."

"When we understand the pattern of your planet, we can begin to think our way into the soul of Earth and heal it. We can pour energy into the world pattern, then, through the bio-sensors you deploy. This will bring you friendly understanding of the Unidentified. You will gain knowledge from it."

"Then there can be proper UFO landings, Mike. Genuine contact. Real visions giving proper guidance. We'll have the chance of tapping UFO power positively. A visible God force. A new dawn."

Michael stared at Helen. "Don't you realize this would mean the end of human science?"

"Of the limited science we know!" snorted the Swede.

"It will be a magical time, Mike," she assured him. "Just as Early Man knew it. It will be what the Aborigines call the Dreamtime, brought back to us again."

"More like a new Stone Age, I'd say!"

"You won't help? You won't believe?" Bonaparte waved to the alien standing by the Thunderbird. It entered the airlock, cycled it and lumbered over to them. Michael felt scared. He feared the squashing power of the two great bulky beasts. He backed off. However, the other alien came not to him, but to Bonaparte.

"You don't believe in our reality? In our truth?"

For a moment Michael said nothing. He stood there; his fingernails dug into his palms.

"No, I don't," he said at last.

Bonaparte burbled at the technician, which reached with its trunk to help Bonaparte unfasten the seals on suit and helmet.

"Bad, thin atmosphere. There is poison in it for us, *Mikal*. It is a slow, painful, messy death. You will see enough pain to believe that we are real. You will smell enough vomit and voiding of the bowels."

The helmet came off. A gluey rheum of turtle tears flowed from Bonaparte's eyes. The alien's throat crowed stridently. As other seals came loose, the bulk of the suit flopped open. The technician nosed it apart till it lay surrounding naked Bonaparte in a flabby heap of tyres. Bonaparte subsided to its knees, hobbled by pain.

"For God's sake don't let him!" begged Helen. "You bastard! How can you do this—when they chose *you*?"

Axel Moller bunched his fists, helplessly. "They're such beautiful beings. A hundred of them died at Tunguska. They'd still give their lives for us—from pure altruism. And—you—kill —him!"

The alien vomited: a thick stinking green pool. It shook and whined.

"If we cannot persuade you," honked the technician, "what use was there in our coming?"

Bonaparte began to grovel pitifully, squeezing its hind legs together. Abruptly its bowels voided, staining its hide and the floor.

"A long time dying, *Mikal*," it wheezed. "This is only the beginning—"

When he was five years old, Michael had seen a ladybird dying slowly in a patch of DDT. Twitching, fumbling, trying to die. He'd tried to put it out of its misery by crushing it under his heel. His heel was only soft crêpe rubber. The squashed broken thing just went on dying—only, more broken and agonising than before. It had been a trivial thing: the agony of a ladybird. Yet it had branded his soul. From then on, he'd had a horror of killing anything. Flies or snails. A rabbit with myxomatosis, wandering blindly around in the corner of a field. The creatures never seemed able to complete the act of dying at his hands. The time of their agony stretched out hugely, and it was he who drew it out: a torturer who loathed such suffering as the worst thing in the world.

Seconds were hours now. He was a little boy again, wanting desperately to help that ladybird, and only hurting it intolerably. He felt completely vulnerable to the other's slow agony.

"We'd never have had Pearl Harbour bombed," hissed Helen, "if we'd only trusted and believed. It was our fault. One Japanese guy cut his bowels out in front of the U.S. embassy in the Thirties to persuade us that we *must believe*, stop treating

Asians like gooks, stop banning them from the U.S.A. Did you know that? He thought we'd understand. That was the strongest argument he could put—his own death by hara-kiri. It's the same with the Gebraudi—because self-sacrifice is so deep down in them. Don't you know what hell there'll be if they don't help us? Oh, the Gebraudi won't *bomb* anywhere! The only violence they can do is wound themselves. They only use force against themselves. It's our own UFO-evil that will bomb our hearts and souls."

Dying ladybird! Dying alien! Michael couldn't match this trump card. Something within him stretched—and snapped.

It was all true. He began to cry. He begged:

"Save him. Help him. Let him live!" The alien was a thing no longer. Bonaparte was a person: real and true and living. "Our friends . . . they're beautiful. I didn't realize!"

Later, the technician returned.

"How . . . how is Boon-ap-aat—?" asked Michael humbly.

"He is very ill, naturally. But he will get better. Now I must show you how to fly your car, *Mikal* from Earth."

The technician led the three of them through the airlock. The white vinyl driver's seat of the Thunderbird had been bolted back in place and the passenger seat removed to make space for an alien driving instructor.

"It is time to be on your way, Helen and Axel. Your bio-sensors are all loaded, on the back seats and floors."

Helen—a small figure, rather drab, rather homely, rather brave—walked to her Pontiac. "Take care!" she called. She backed the car out and turned into the open exit tube. Nodding more curtly to Michael, the Swede got into his Volvo and followed after the Pontiac. No exhaust fumes came from either car. They were sealed; powered by reaction mass—by the total energy conversion of, perhaps, plain water . . .

The triangular door of the exit tube closed. When it reopened a few minutes later, the tube was empty.

"I have to hypnotise you, to make the learning faster and easier. Normal functions remain unimpaired, I promise. Do you agree?"

146

Michael nodded lamely. Since the alien still waited for an answer, not understanding the gesture, he said aloud: "Yes."

The alien slipped the glass block out of his leg holster. He fitted this into what looked like a large, boxlike inspection torch that was resting on the hood of the car.

"Please watch."

A bright green beam of light shone into Michael's face. The light was flickering very rapidly, too rapidly to notice at first. Yet as Michael stared into it, increasingly he became aware of all the individual pulses of light . . . He felt fully alert and brisk, supremely receptive—though in a passive, volitionless way. He noticed, peripherally, how the movements of the aliens in the blue-green chamber over on the far side of the wall had somehow lost the knack of fusing smoothly and were jerking along instead, like frames in an early movie. But this didn't worry him.

Soon enough, he was learning how to fly the Thunderbird.

TWENTY-ONE

THE VC-10 WHICH Deacon boarded in Cairo was crowded with a large party of Kenyan athletes and many tiresomely boisterous expatriate children returning to their English boarding schools. As they flew to Rome, then Paris, Deacon turned the leaves of the *Lemegeton* of Solomon.

The curious diagrams in the book—those shapes supposed to conjure demons—still looked to him like fragments of circuit designs torn asunder from some giant plan . . . *of mind*. Patterns of relationships, bits of a mental map. Each of the 'demons'—AGARES, AINI, ALLOCEN, AMDUSCIAS, seventy-two of them in all, through to ZAGAN and ZEPAR—apparently stood for a particular parapsychological type: bestowal of unusual power in some normal (or quite abnormal) area. Love, warfare, skill in mathematics or poetry, in dowsing for treasure, foretelling the future and understanding the language of birds and beasts, in knowledge of powers in plants and stones, in fireraising, the influencing of people unawares, in invisibility, speed-learning, the raising of mirages.

Here were fragmentary sketchmaps of a more evolved mind that could manipulate reality directly by seizing hold of its underlying forms, precursors of some kind of superconsciousness which men could tap into, for good or ill. He remembered Tom Havelock's comment weeks ago that symbols might have some sort of objective reality . . .

And one of those diagrams had been programmed into Michael's mind as part of a UFO control panel.

At last south-east London spread below, dull under clouds. Rain flicked down the window.

The jet descended, bumped, roared its tail engines, taxied. Grey concrete, grey buildings, even the grass looked grey. He hadn't changed his clothes for the last five days. His most recent shave was twenty-four hours out of date. Sticky stubble grated against his collar, but he couldn't bear to loosen collar or tie and so appear even more seedy and reprobate. He was a tramp in an airliner.

In his wallet was an extraordinary visa from Egypt with fingerprints and photograph on it, an identity card issued by the Consul in Cairo, a special permit to enter the U.K., a letter of authorization to Immigration, and five pounds sterling (to be refunded) . . .

His visit to the Embassy in Garden City had been so embarrassing that after a while he became anaesthetized, a human parcel to be probed and prodded, left standing in corners or resting endlessly on hard seats till eventually relabelled.

He had told the Consul a story about amnesia; overwork. He must have thrown his passport into the Nile, without registering at any hotel. He sincerely hoped the tension had all been released by his absurd flight from England.

Police checked; his passport wasn't lodged with any hotel desk. The Embassy checked. No John Deacon had flown out of Heathrow in the past week; so he must have given the airline a false name. His wife supplied a list of personal questions to identify him. 'How did our dog die?' was one.

He was lectured, like a little boy before a headmaster, by a Consul maybe ten years younger than himself. Deacon, the parcel, submitted to all this tamely, the price of help—within comprehension. Though, when he got back to the Sheikh's house where they let him stay while enquiries were pressed, he had telephoned Reuter's Cairo office.

On board the VC-10 the stewardesses kept a frigid watch on him, as though he might suddenly molest one of the schoolboys, shout racial abuse or fumblingly try to hijack the plane.

"Was there any need," asked Mary tightly as she drove the car northwards, "to have reporters meet you? Did you think I was going to spank you in public?"

"I had to set the record straight with myself! I told a lie in Cairo, at the Embassy. Just so I could get back here with the minimum of fuss. You can't know how humiliating it was."

"Can't I?"

"Only the Sheikh and Salim knew the truth. But as they say, the truth conceals itself! Maybe I ought to have been bolder . . . I was just redressing the balance, a little, at this end."

"The facts are that you went to the Bank, John. I know because I went along and checked our account. You drew out just enough for a one-way ticket. Two hundred pounds that we can ill afford!"

"Oh, I might have got there by plane. That doesn't matter, you see! That wasn't *how* I got there."

"How can you pretend that your flight to Egypt was courtesy of flying saucers, when you didn't even travel in one?"

"I travelled in a UFO-conscious state. It's the same thing, as I told the gentlemen of the Press."

"God, John, you're about to fall off the edge of a cliff. I'm trying to keep a grip on your collar. Yet you tear it out of my hand as though you hate me! Have you any idea how this'll come over in the newspapers?"

"Those reporters struck me as a fairly shy bunch. I always thought all reporters were brazen extroverts."

"Probably they were as embarrassed as I was. Cub reporters set loose on a crackpot tale. That doesn't stop them going to town on it." All the King's horses and all the King's men, she thought bitterly. John's cranium gleamed stickily; but the fairy only gave one wish . . .

Deacon patted his pocket complacently. Wherein reposed the Little Key of Solomon. Muradi, he was now convinced, had been an honest intermediary.

"Sorry, darling. I can't give up. Not now that I'm so close."

"You utter fool."

TWENTY-TWO

MICHAEL BUMPED DOWN on the moor road exactly one day after he'd been taken from the Earth. His bicycle wasn't lying there any more.

He drove to a disused little quarry over the moor in Goosedale and hid the car among a mass of leathery rhododendrons. It was a three-mile walk back.

He stepped out joyfully. He'd lost a kind of virginity up on the Moon, been initiated into a splendid, appalling secret. The world smelt different now. Invisible lines of force were everywhere, binding together the vegetation, the birds in the trees, worms underfoot, all the works of the human race into a plenum, a whole which—alas—was purblind due to men. It threw up miracles and atrocities alike as it struggled towards knowledge, its higher centres crippled and dwarfed by the death programme. Orgasm was once called 'the little death' . . . and he had always died too soon, full of anxiety. Humanity was crippled by anxiety too, full of self-hatreds, out of touch with the rhythms of life. Thus had grown up an epileptic palsy which bred monsters, at the very same time as the life programme projected, inchoately, signs of transcendence in the sky, sometimes even coming down to Earth to try to deliver a message: from life to itself. Men's eyes saw, from time to time, but the hands were forever fashioning more weapons in the service of death.

This elation tided him through other embarrassments, at home. For he had gone off without a word and not come back that day or that night. His father had found his bicycle upon the moor road in the evening, and called the Police. He had actually cycled into Swale, lied Michael, and locked up his bicycle (or so he thought—someone had obviously taken it) then caught the bus to Otway and the train to Sandstairs. He'd been in Otway overnight, at a youth hostel; he missed the last bus home. He'd had to see Suzie. Love. Impulse. He had a day's stubble on his chin . . .

Recriminations followed. Because he hadn't even bothered to phone from Otway.

It was a tight, horrid morning—when a few hours earlier he had been on the far side of the Moon, talking with aliens, learning to fly over Tsiolkovsky . . . No connexion existed between the two segments of experience. Home and mother and father became increasingly unreal as the morning wore on. *They were the dream.*

Ordinary life was a dream. A solid, real dream—a dream none the less. It was so hard to step outside the ordinary, which sucked you back so cloyingly, reasonably and anxiously. What had really happened could simply not be said. He had no alibi save Suzie Meade, adolescent passion, callousness.

His mother stared, red-eyed, into a garden sunbright with daffodil trumpets, mere wax or plastic to her eyes now, drained of joy; while he wolfed toast and coffee that she'd duly made for him. It was so long since he'd last eaten, from Axel's food hoard on the Moon. She sat (black curls overcast by grey) so absorbed in her own unhappiness that it seemed impenetrable. To reach out a hand . . . To comfort . . . To apologize. No use! A lie had come between them; she sat on the far side of it, in the falsehood of the ordinary, the illusion of the normal . . .

If he took her to the Thunderbird or brought the Thunderbird to the house and . . . went off with her into the sky—she would be ruined, devastated. She would scream for help, from the ordinary world.

He spread ginger marmalade thickly. Daffodils wagged in a rising breeze. A thrush trod the lawn, tap dancing to pull out a writhing worm and chop it with stiletto stabs. His father came back from the telephone and hugged his wife in her isolation. "Why? Why?" The question had no answer to it, save for an answer so absurd that it was no answer. When you rode the route back from fairyland, thought Michael, if you as much as touched the ground with your foot everything would turn to dust and you would suddenly be very old . . . If you wed a fairy bride and as much as hinted at her origin she would flee from your arms. Gold would become lead, the magic ring brass, rubies mere coloured glass.

No alibi existed for this world, except Suzie convalescent in Sandstairs by the sea.

'Alibi'—*Elsewhere*. That was where the flying saucer and all its avatars came from: from elsewhere—out of the essential elsewhere implicit in any whole system. So the Gebraudi aliens had shown. A system could never know itself wholly within its own terms. Yet it was driven to do so—its very failure being the force that evolved it. So the Unidentifiable quantity within the system became briefly visible, only to flee constantly away. You could only learn by going elsewhere too, to the blind side of the Moon. In everything there was a zone of elsewhere. In every kettle of boiling water were a few microscopic crystals of ice; in every ice cube in the refrigerator were a few atoms at boiling point. Or else the world simply wouldn't be. It would lock rigidly—and lose its existence. The UFO was the boiling atom in the ice cube, the seed of ice in the kettle. It was the invisibility at the edge of the universe—without which there would be no universe. It was the indeterminacy of the particle—without which there would be no matter. The Gebraudi understood this far better than the Human race did. All those bio-packs loaded in the Thunderbird, in tune with the Biomatrix behind the Moon, were sense organs to perceive the hidden rhythms of the world. While men built missiles to destroy it.

"I'm very sorry," Michael apologized to them, dabbing at his mouth. "I really am."

He went to bed exhausted and slept, wounding his mother

152

even more. Because he could not have spent the night in a youth hostel, to be so tired.

He dreamt of being on the Moon again with Bonaparte. He awoke within the dream, realizing that this was a dream and he was still asleep. He tried to tell the alien that it was actually a dream being in his own mind as he lay abed in Neapstead, Yorkshire. Bonaparte was wearing no pressure suit, yet he wasn't dying! As soon as Michael pointed this out the alien started to bleat and choke and die again. Still aware it was a dream, Michael willed Bonaparte fiercely to stay healthy and coherent so that he could question him; question his own alien knowledge, the alibi zone within the mind which mind must struggle in vain to know. The struggle turned into Bonaparte's death throes. Michael could no longer keep himself awake within sleep, or preserve the alien's health. Ordinary dreaming flooded back.

Helen Caprowicz, wearing a spangly leotard that emphasized curious lumps and bumps in her body and her large pear-shaped bum, mounted the alien and galloped him round what was now Suzie's bedroom—much enlarged—in the Hall of Residence. Outside the window lay no Common. In its place he saw leprous blanched craters, jagged black mountains, blinding stars reflecting the spangles of Helen's acrobat costume. He thought of her as Suzie, though she didn't remotely resemble her.

He noticed the Earth hanging in the black and starry sky. Helen/Suzie cried, "Catch me if you can!" Digging spurs into the hide of her lumbering mount and flicking its rump with a riding crop she galloped it into the window and through in a spray of broken glass. All the air suctioned out of the room, suffocating him, spinning books and records, cups and saucers, and himself through into lunar darkness.

He thought he was dying; in fact he was waking up.

TWENTY-THREE

SINCE HE HAD used Suzie as his alibi, he went to see her in reality. He drove over Otway High Moor, by way of Scawby and Bridleby, the forty odd miles to Sandstairs.

The embarrassments of the Thunderbird! Lipstick red, as wide as many country lanes, rear seat and floor piled with glassy biosensors under a groundsheet: why couldn't they have stolen a less conspicuous car?

Outside Bridleby, a few hundred yards uphill from the road, rose Worm Rigg, a ragged edge of rock with standing stones around it.

He pulled over and unrolled the map given him before he left Tsiolkovsky. The map recorded the ancient ley lines, the lines of power linking sacred and numinous places: holy stones, mounds, dewponds, hilltops where prehistoric man met his 'Gods'—those lines which the ancient Chinese had called *lung mei*, the dragon lines. It marked out the probable nervous system of Whole Planet Life, the pathways of the Earthworld considered as a living system, those loci where Unidentified events would most logically occur.

Worm Rigg was one such node on it: a primitive God-spot, a locus where the Unidentified could be experienced.

The ridge of the worm: of the dragon, of the serpent power —of Quetzalcoatl and the Lambton Worm. For a serpent with its tail in its own mouth formed the UFO disc, the mandala, the circle of being of which man was part—and which man could not stand outside, to see entire. He could only see its shadows in the sky or meet its 'solid' echoes on the ground.

Michael took the first biosensor from under the groundsheet and clicked it into the slot of the modified tape player. Beeping tones sounded from the speakers, fore and aft. He fiddled with the fader and balance controls to synchronise the tones while the tuning bar tracked across the radio dial, which was calibrated with the 360 degrees of the compass. He checked this reading against the dashboard compass.

Yes, Worm Rigg up there was a place to plant a biosensor.

He pushed one of the channel selector buttons, and the beeping faded out. No warning whistle howled. At the moment the potential for a UFO event in this prime location, this prime acupuncture point, was quite low. Currently the area was inhibited, not excited. It was safe. Otherwise, it could be like fixing a lightning conductor to your roof just before a thunderstorm. In the presence of a higher thought centre of Whole Planet Life—himself—the sensor might draw down a discharge of the UFO force that would zero in on him, alerting the planetary consciousness to the 'tap' planted in its nervous system. Remember Tunguska, the Gebraudi had warned; and Michael remembered Garibaldi dodging the gleaming UFO that appeared just as they took off from Swale Moor. Garibaldi had only been able to locate Michael, a sensitive, by exposing himself where an event involving a human contactee was highly probable. Now, though, Michael knew how to steer clear of such a probability. He was cautious. He pushed another button which sent a vibrational signal (so he'd been told) towards the Moon via a biosatellite in space, to say that this particular biosensor was now on line.

He hiked up Worm Rigg through spiky grass and heather towards the unshaped boulders which his map identified as standing stones.

He hid the biosensor beneath a tangle of gorse inside a rabbit hole.

It needed no sunlight, nourished (they'd explained) by primary vibrations from the main Biomatrix on Luna.

He could just make out the blue line of the sea from the top of the Rigg. A fresh breeze brushed his hair. He listened a while, to hear the haunting of this spot, the tune of energy. However, there was only wind. Just as well.

He went back to the car and drove on towards Sandstairs, stopping once more en route to plant another sensor.

He hid the Thunderbird in among hundreds of day-trip cars and holiday coaches, where it looked quite plausible, almost fitting into place.

He found a phone box. The equipment inside seemed creaky and medieval compared with Biomatrix, Thunderbird and sensors that could read unidentified world patterns which had shaped human religions and mythologies.

Rather to his surprise, the telephone worked; and she answered it.

"Suzie? It's Mike, I'm back home." Yet he hadn't said he was in the same town as her; indeed his words implied the opposite. He'd concealed the Thunderbird; wasn't going to show it to her. He couldn't. It would appal her just as it would appal his mother.

They talked inconsequentially.

After a while he asked casually, "There haven't been any more odd events, have there?" He received no reply.

"Are you still there, love?"

He heard an exasperated intake of breath. "Haven't you given that dirty nonsense up yet?"

Yes? No? What could he say?

"You haven't," she accused.

"You did see something, Suzie. It reached out and touched you. I know it did!"

"So does madness. Madness reaches out and touches people. Witchcraft too, if you're fool enough to get involved."

He thought of Bonaparte, on the far side of the Moon; of the Biomatrix, and of Whole Planet Life . . .

She was saying, "I don't even need sleeping pills any more. I'm coming off the Valium too. I've got a job in a café, would you believe? I'm clearing tables for the Summer. The debris of people's holidays—you get to feel quite aesthetic about clearing it up. Reality therapy! I'm ordinary now, Mike, and it's lovely." He heard her fingernails tap the mouthpiece. "So you're still up to your neck in it? That's what you rang to tell me?"

How could he not be up to his neck in it?

"You are. Oh dear." It sounded such a mild reproof; but she

had put the phone down. The receiver buzzed in his ear, white noise.

Bonaparte . . .! Moaning, agonising alien.

He settled into a routine, cycling to the quarry of conceal-ment, driving to the nearer loci on the alien map, hiding bio-sensors. He had to fly the car by night to some points on the map. Those far afield. Glastonbury Tor. Dragon Hill, by Uffington. Stonehenge. Silbury Hill. The Gebraudi had promised that radar couldn't pick him up; somewhere under the welded bonnet was a jamming device. He flew, he landed, he drove, he scaled locked gates and wire fences, hid his sensors. He never saw a single strange light chasing him in the sky; the speakers never whistled out a warning. He led a charmed life, as though he was as invisible to the UFO force as he was to human radar. Nearer home, he succeeded in never being seen by any friends of the family. It was all surprisingly easy. Perhaps, looking up into the sky, late night travellers saw a dark enigmatic flying object, soundless, wingless. To them, of course, the car and human pilot would be a UFO. He lived perfectly though feverishly; he began losing weight. At home, a truce prevailed, while his parents willed his motiveless cruel rebellion and his sudden passion for hiding himself away to burn themselves out. His mother smiled bravely, his father went about the daily business of managing the land.

He got no University reading done; but one day his mother handed him an old newspaper, unread at the first time of grief three weeks before. "Don't you know him?" she asked.

He read about a psychology professor's flight to Cairo in a state of 'UFO-consciousness'; and rejoiced.

It was time in any case to return to Granton for the new term.

TWENTY-FOUR

"CARL JUNG WAS perfectly well aware of the risk to his reputation in speaking out about UFOs," said Deacon. "He didn't do so with a light heart."

"What a pity you didn't share his scruples," sighed Bruce Fraser. "It isn't just your reputation you're putting at risk. It's the Group's—and the University's." Fraser, Dean of Social Sciences, attended this forty-third meeting of the Consciousness Research Group distastefully. For some others present, too, it represented a calling to account of the Group's director.

"Jung only wrote about UFOs as psychic myth," objected Martin Bull. "Yet you claim you were spirited off to Egypt by them—when we all know you flew there by scheduled jet! And as for this notion of your dog's head being taken in some kind of Devil's exchange, so that you can conjure UFOs up by magic now . . . it's sheer sensational crap!" He tossed his head. "It beats me what you think you're doing."

"Jung spoke out because he saw that a major psychic transformation was on the cards. By that, I mean a shift in the whole structure of knowledge—in the episteme. Jung saw the UFO 'sky wheels', quite rightly, as focal patterns for the breeding of, let's say, a new kind of transcendent consciousness—a fusion with some higher order of mental information. And I assure you there's a lot more to UFOs than just sky wheels! Anyway, the papers misinterpreted me."

"What did you expect?" asked Fraser. "If you feed them a sensation story, it'll have precious little to do with the nature of sense perceptions in their eyes."

"You do honestly maintain that you conjured up a 'devil'?" asked Tom Havelock. He covered the vinyl of his cheek with a cupped hand. It seemed to be blushing furiously in the neon light.

" 'The Devil Rides a Flying Saucer'!" snorted Martin Bull. "That's a good one."

"It wasn't a devil, Tom. It was a UFO that looked like a harpy or pterodactyl or something equally devilish. The Phenomenon does adjust itself to our frame of reference, but we're still trailing phantoms from the religious past. We all have our ingrained images of Gods and Devils. I'm certain that the whole phenomenon is connected with the very nature of knowledge: a knowledge that stays hidden."

"Occult, in other words." Havelock rocked his head against his hand, sympathetically but nervously, hiding his stigma.

"Wrong connotation. 'Occult' suggests devils and pentacles and dancing witches and things. No, my view is that the Phenomenon has always been with us in one form or another because it really relates to what you might call, information-wise, the 'knowability' of the cosmos. It's a kind of evolutionary learning programme which exists because of the way the universe is. It teaches by means of what is *unknown*. How else? It uses the medium of what is, at each and every stage, unknowable. Obviously the science for this has to be a very special breed of science."

"Doubtless," said Sandra Neilstrom dryly. Deacon's folly angered her now.

"A science of consciousness."

"How about this *Lemegeton*?" asked Havelock uneasily. All those shattered circuit diagrams . . . As though a machine could be built for tapping God's thoughts. The new hubris. Something very different from true God-centredness.

"Magic is about the unknowable too. It's an attempt to tap it through symbols and geometries which even you, Tom, agree are *objective*. Though if you just stop at that point and imagine you're actually summoning up demigods—Forneus and his crew —from other dimensions, you're lost. Superstition swallows you. The programme eats you up instead of you drawing nourishment from it. After all, the whole point about Alchemy was to transform the mind—not to make gold or a miracle longevity

159

drug! I want to appeal for people like my student Michael Peacocke, people who are sensitive to what I'm calling 'UFO-consciousness effects', to join in a new sort of research programme."

"Using black magic?" winced Sally Pringle. She worked with the Psychiatric Hospital, her métier being the shapes of psychosis. A tall thin brunette, she wore charm bracelets and heavy silver bangles on her wrists as though to ward off and earth any encroachments into her own personal life; although in her own mind she regarded her ornaments merely as bringing a touch of sympathetic elegance into the dim tattered lives of the prisoners of madness.

"That's not what I said. We need to develop a new state-specific *science*—directed at the unknowable. At the Unidentified. 'Surely some revelation is at hand.' That's what Jung believed. I trust I know how to uncover it. The way to do it is to attach the ego-tag, somehow, to those 'non-ego' psychic areas. Those areas, dear Sandra, being ones which bridge both mind-space *and* the material world."

Bruce Fraser cleared his throat.

"This simply isn't *on* at a university. I'll rephrase that: it's not on at this one. Really, John, your razzle-dazzle approach so far!"

"I had to set the record straight in public. I'd be a coward otherwise. Strange and remarkable things have happened to me. What use is this damned Group if we're not bold? We still haven't the foggiest idea what mind and consciousness *are*. We're still no nearer learning."

Fraser stroked his chin, which seemed to wear the permanent blue bruised blush of a fresh shave, as though he ran an electric razor over his face three or four times a day to maintain a perfect fresh polish. A suave, burly figure, with an air of elegant brutality about him—as though quite prepared to strip to the waist and put up bare fists like some gentleman Regency bully—he had supported the Consciousness Research Group strongly in the past.

"If I might introduce a note of business, John? The Group's application for a research fellow?"

"Held over from last year! That's long overdue."

"Ah, you know how priorities compete . . . Normally I'd support this request to the hilt. But we all had the impression you were working on hypnosis. Now this turns up. In one of those newspaper interviews you as much as said that *we'd* be advertising a flying saucer fellowship! That kind of thing really puts people's backs up. Academic Board's collective back, for instance."

"Are you threatening that we don't get a research fellow unless I drop the Phenomenon?"

"Frankly, John, it will have to be a bit more than that. This isn't exactly the place to wash our dirty linen." He glanced at some of the research student members of the group, who contrived to look demure. "You've raised a lot of eyebrows with these wild assertions . . . This isn't Esalen, you know. I always strongly supported the concept of the C.R.G. Consequently you've had your teaching load relaxed to almost nothing. So has Tom for that matter, and Andrew. You have these postgraduates doing dream research and whatnot on your say-so. Not to mention a lot of behind-scenes help: secretarial, library, floor space . . . The C.R.G.'s been your pigeon—and a fine flier it's turned out to be. But it isn't *all you*, John. It isn't your own personal property."

"Right," nodded Sally Pringle. "It would rather queer out present excellent relations with the Hospital if we seemed in need of psychiatric treatment ourselves."

"One of the C.R.G.'s real achievements is its interdisciplinary character. Look round this table: Biochemistry, Physics, Computers —"

"That's not an achievement! That isn't a discovery!"

"When you involve other disciplines you have to consider your working relationships."

"Physics and flying saucers aren't the best bedpartners, Bruce," said Sandra Neilstrom. "It makes it just that much harder for me to propose a meaningful synthesis of Consciousness and Nature."

"Do you *see*, John?" Bruce Fraser patted his bruise-blue chin. "I was even talking to the Vice-Chancellor on the phone —"

161

That evening, after a rather meagre dinner, Deacon bit into a Cox's Pippin. Apple of Knowledge, he thought wryly as he savoured the sweetness. Already that sweetness was biting at the enamel of his teeth, eroding them like old sandstone buildings exposed to car exhausts and acid rain. Ghost toothache haunted him. He cut a wedge of soft Wensleydale, and sucked the cheese around his mouth to clean his teeth again.

How to halt the rot?

He was in the right, God damn it!

So why should knowledge eat a man away, consume him?

There were people in the world who already *knew*. Who had known for a thousand years and more, maybe far longer. Who had anticipated. Who had goaded the knowledge gently on. There was an invisible college of them, fluent in the paradoxes of the unknowable. One of the latest of these being Sheikh Muradi, to whom Khidr had come, out of the collective psyche of Humanity to communicate an ambiguous, teasing truth to Deacon . . .

The phone rang; thankfully he quit the table.

It was Michael Peacocke who spoke.

He talked excitedly of a rendezvous. In his room, the following evening at five.

"I've asked Barry Shriver to be there too. It's the most important thing, John! I'll show you something remarkable —"

PART FOUR

TWENTY-FIVE

"You're expecting an event?" Shriver chuckled. "It won't happen. Not if you expect it to, boy. You've been hooked!"

"There's no point in me telling you beforehand," said Michael, unruffled.

"Spoken like a true believer!"

Deacon turned to the 'G-field diagram' in the grimoire; but Michael had never studied magic nor even heard of the *Little Key* of Solomon. The diagram obviously puzzled him. However, he soon recovered himself.

"Well, it *is* the uniquely logical way to fly, isn't it?" He wouldn't elaborate.

"And this is how the Phenomenon indicates you ought to investigate it?" mused Shriver. " Through magic? Typical! The old trickster! You'll end up diving under tables to hide from etheric fiends who live in the hollow Earth. You'll count the cracks in the sidewalk. And you'd not be the first one!"

Dangling car keys, Michael hurried them downstairs and out of the Hall, after making the curious request that they should all empty their bowels first; they were going a long way. ("I *can* pee by the roadside," Shriver said. "I'm not shy." Michael shook his head. "Not by this roadside you can't.")

As they walked along to the multistorey car park Shriver said, "Look, suppose some UFOs actually landed by prior arrangement at a U.S. Air Force base. It's said they did, only it was all hushed up. Dammit, I even *knew* that they did, myself, once upon a time! Well, if they did and there was still no way of knowing what they were, whatever their operators said —"

"No full proof," Deacon nodded. "There never can be."

"—if they just dipped into what you call normal cognition and out again, then I'd say it would be very wise of any government to clam up about it. It's one thing for us poor guys to go chasing these will o' the wisps and living—or ruining—our lives accordingly. But for a government to succumb, God Almighty, we'd be like a banana republic run by voodoo then! If I was the President's adviser and a whole fleet of UFOs landed at a base I'd say to him: *don't you believe 'em, Sir.* Honest to God. You can't run governments by miracle. This isn't the Middle Ages. If the President suddenly upped and announced that UFOs really have made contact, and come from Star X or Dimension Y, he'd be utterly wrong, and I'd be scared shitless. Goodbye to rationality forever."

"I thought that way," said Michael. "Once."

"Satan and his crew would be loose in the world, monkeying with history. That's why your book of magic's so damn dangerous, John. That's what it hints at!"

The carpark lift, aswirl with aerosol graffiti, smelt of urine.

"Supposing you interpret these shapes as the 'circuit diagram' for a special kind of consciousness, though," Deacon began.

Michael led the way through the concrete gloom to a parked Ford Thunderbird.

"*That's* yours?" exclaimed Shriver. "With Wyoming plates? Where on Earth did you borrow it?"

"Oh, I got it from someone. You'll meet them soon." Michael tipped the driver's seat and Shriver climbed in the rear.

"Someone's been messing about with the instrument board," he said over Deacon's shoulder, as Deacon settled himself in front.

"My window's jammed," complained Deacon; Michael switched the air conditioning on.

"So is the clock, John. It's stuck too. It says nine."

Michael navigated the large car with some difficulty round the tight coils of the down ramp. Once, the bumper hit the wall. Braking, he swung the wheel, overcompensating. At the exit barrier he switched the remarkably quiet engine off and opened his door to push the ticket in the toll machine; apparently his window was stuck too. Then they swung out into a queue of

166

evening commuters, heading out of town. Drizzle began to wet the windows, insulating them.

"We'll suck in all their exhaust fumes, you know," Shriver told Michael.

"Oh no, we won't." The air in the car did smell faintly metallic, but it was clean and refreshing.

"Getting back to the subject of miracles, John. Take the miracle at Fatima. Portugal, 1916 to 1917. A luminous lady appears to some kids inside a hovering globe of light. She says she comes from Heaven. That's a religious context, right? She promises to return again. That's the initial contact—the pre-conditioning phase. A small crowd gathers at the appointed time. They see these kids go into a trance. Our Lady promises them subsequent light-shows in the sky, and passes on some secret prophecy that never gets revealed—though leaks out of the Vatican suggest it really horrified the Cardinals. End of the world stuff! She says the First World War will soon end—that's true enough—and goes on accurately enough about the coming 'conversion' of Russia. *That* has already begun, though these peasant kids aren't aware of it—and it surely isn't a religious conversion. No Sir, it's the Bolshevik Revolution that's busy 'converting' Holy Russia! She uses all sorts of technical theological jargon which these kids couldn't possibly have known. The crowd don't see her, they just hear a curious buzzing noise. But she promises the kids a real miracle for everybody —"

A motorway patrol car blocked the road, its red lights flashing. A policeman was setting out warning cones, while another waved cars through the bus lane. A motorbike lay tangled with the fender of an estate car. Crystals littered the tarmac. Death and wreckage. The traffic speeded up and spaced out after this.

"And so, on October 13th 1917, about seventy thousand people turn out. *The miracle damn well does happen.* A great whirling disc bobs up and down over their heads. It puts the fear of death into them. Mass hallucination? Not likely! The thing could be seen over twenty kilometers away. The disc becomes like the Sun itself, a great blood-red Sun falling down from the sky upon their heads! Its heat even dries their wet clothes bone dry.

"Plenty of photos of that crowd survive—with people in it pointing cameras at the sky. And not one single picture of the disc itself! Did all those cameras jam? It isn't unknown, with UFOs around. Maybe photographic emulsion and shutter speeds weren't up to it back then . . . Or did the Vatican grab all the exposed film—just as they watered the event down by making a fuss of the kids' saintliness, keeping the whole thing a holy mystery and suppressing the major prophecies? Very wise of the Vatican, say I! Not just because it wouldn't do to have our religions seen as engineered and manipulated by the Phenomenon, with God in the back seat—if in any seat at all! But to keep miracles where they belong, in the pages of piety—not loose in the real world. I bet the Vatican could see the danger. They've a lot more experience than any other government!"

At the roundabout marking the city limits Michael swung eastwards along the ringroad between fields and farms. As dusk thickened, he flicked the headlights on. A mile later he turned off down a deserted country lane. Brambles reached, scratching, from the hedgerows. No other car followed. He pulled up.

"Here?" whispered Shriver, mockingly.

"Not here."

Michael jerked the steering wheel back roughly and dabbed at the dashboard. Tilting the wheel a few degrees, he touched his foot to the accelerator.

The car jumped forward, and upwards—without motion, acceleration or tilt. It rose above the hedgerows.

Squeezing the accelerator and pulling the wheel sharp back, he flew the Thunderbird upwards.

"Oh Christ." Shriver clung to his seat, slowly relaxing as he realized where the locus of gravity still was, then tensing again as he fought the knowledge of how this could be so. Deacon stared blankly ahead as they cut into the clouds, sweat like teardrops on his cheeks.

Michael smiled shyly. "You see, we're going to the Moon."

The swelling Moon ahead was crescent.
Black space.
The milky spatter of stars.

The Void.

"Why didn't you hand it over to somebody in authority?" protested Shriver. "Any air force, British, American, whoever you please? Somebody who could have copied it and built new ones. Gravity control . . . anti-gravity! My God, we could reach Mars in a few days in one of these. We could fly down the gravity well of Jupiter and out again!"

"I just told you. I had to do things for them. For us all! Because our Whole Planet Life —"

"The metaconsciousness," shivered Deacon. "That's what it is."

"It's becoming deathly. More beasts and fish and forests are wiped out every year, and there are always just more people, more cities, more machines. Our . . . yes, our *metaconsciousness* is becoming a deathly mechanical thing, a kind of plastic devil because of us. That's why I spent the last few weeks laying out the biosensors where they told me instead of having the car sawn open. Who'd have done it if I hadn't?"

"So these aliens, these Gebraudi, left their own metaconsciousness, their own Gods, behind them when they left their star system? That's like leaving your soul behind. What strange pilgrims . . ."

"No, they're safe. The 'moment' of the metaconsciousness is much longer. Its present is much vaster than for its individual components. It's spread out through time. The Gebraudi are still part of that same moment. They still belong."

"Even though, at the same time, they don't?" Deacon stared out.

The appalling vacuum, beyond the windows. Even this vacuum was crowded with atoms, compared with the emptiness further from the Sun.

"I could write volumes," said Shriver, "on the implausibility of your aliens. Plant eaters have to spend almost all their time grazing."

"I know. I saw them eat."

"No arms, just one elephant's trunk? Even if it has got a whole starfish of fingers! They can pull, but never really push hard. That makes technology pretty unlikely for simple

169

mechanical reasons. And yet they're not like any UFO operators I've heard of."

"They look outrageous—because they're genuine. I thought the same as you at first."

"Why do they look outrageous?" worried Deacon. "If the timespan of this metaconsciousness is so great—well, just suppose there are ultra-intelligent machines up ahead of us in our own future, conscious computers that we'll build to design other superconscious ones . . . and they become part of this metaconsciousness. They would have to, wouldn't they? They'd be part of it *already* then! They'd be thought-centres more complex than ourselves! I wonder, could your Gebraudi possibly be how these superconscious machines of the future would view the biological life that originally designed them? As pitifully hamstrung, clumsy, and limited?"

"No! They're from Eta Cassiopeia. They want to help us. Their 'Gods' would befriend our 'Gods'."

"They may just as well be all the lost souls of whales and dolphins, and elephant and chimpanzee, and the souls of the forests and prairies, and even of humans too—which have all been superseded. They could still be UFO beings, representing the dying flesh in the only way the programming allows!"

"They can't be," explained Michael, exasperated. "Because this isn't a UFO we're in now. This is no *tulpa*—no materialization. This is a car built in Detroit and rebuilt by alien science so that human beings can fly, line of sight, to the Moon base."

"One of the darling features of the Phenomenon," said Shriver, "is its way of using human equipment. What else could it use?"

"It's for camouflage, so that their agents—*us*—can move about easily."

"Dowsing, and hiding boxes of telepathic algae? Sure. I recall that a couple of Men in Black driving a *car* saved you."

"Has any human being ever been given a UFO to pilot, Barry? Or do you suppose I'm some *tulpa* masquerading as myself?"

"Don't you see, you've been programmed by them in the past? Now your own personal Fatima miracle has happened!"

"Your miracle too!"

The emptiness, outside. Deacon's head ached with it. The tiny, vastly distant beacons of light . . .

"You've been given the good news, Mike. By messengers from the backside of the Moon. *Angeloi*, angels. You ought to have handed the car over. Were you scared it wouldn't really work? Aren't we mainly here to prove to you that this isn't only a dream? What would you have thought if we hadn't taken off from that lane?"

"We did take off."

"You ought to have handed this car over! Damn it, with this baby we could get right down into Jupiter!"

"It doesn't carry enough reaction mass to get that far."

"Mars, then! We could colonise Mars with just one of these."

"Not even Mars."

Shriver laughed brusquely. "Somewhere, somewhere!" One belief was oscillating wildly with another—scepticism with utter conviction—as he gazed at the huge Moon crescent and the smooth dark circle of the Sea of Crises pocked by craters· Pierce and Picard, so close now, less than a singe Earth diameter away. Michael swung the steering wheel to the right. Great Luna moved gently over.

The sheer static precision of every rumple and bend of airless ground, the clarity of the brown horizon . . .

The inky floor of Tsiolkovsky loomed ahead, with its bright peak casting a jet shadow. As they flew in over the crater wall Michael hunted for the tall mushroom of the alien starship.

In its place, he saw flattened wreckage.

TWENTY-SIX

DESTRUCTION.

Of starship; of domes.

Not by explosion, but somehow by compression, by a squashing flat—as though a giant hand had squeezed the Gebraudi expedition into shapelessness. The ship was a small splayed hill of metal less than a tenth of its original height; the volcanic basalt underneath was cracked and riven by the pressure.

They landed in a brief flurry of dust; Michael switched over quickly from flight mode to ground mode. Not far away, at the end of tyre tracks, the wreckage of Helen Caprowicz's Pontiac lay squashed into a car-size crater.

"But," said Michael. He drove to the crater. A bare human arm poked stiffly out of sandwiched metal; it must be Helen's.

Michael swallowed. "But we need more reaction mass. The clock doesn't measure time, you know, it measures the fuel level. We left at nine by the clock and now it's ten . . ."

"That's okay." Shriver was flying over Korea again, one eye on the fuel gauge, calculating the reserves, the other hunting for MIGs—or for a cigar of glowing light . . . "We took two hours real time to get here. That's equivalent to sixty minutes of fuel. We've still got plenty left. Let's look around—I've never been to the Moon. I want to see if there are any alien bodies."

"God, they got Helen. Maybe they got everyone."

"They?" sneered Shriver. "Who's 'they'? Let's find something out, boy. One thing I'll tell you for starters: someone forgot to get the gravity right. It's the same as back home."

"Oh, I left the internal field on. Here—" Michael switched

off the 'heater'; then they were only an eighth of their proper Earth weight.

"Wup." Shriver pressed himself off the seat on the palms of his hands. Michael switched the internal gravity back on.

"Okay, okay, realistic. My body is convinced."

"Is your head?"

"If only you'd handed this damned car in, Mike! Then we'd *know*."

Michael steered the Thunderbird away from the crater where Helen had died, towards the flattened things that once were domes and the putty mound of metal which had flown from the stars.

Jammed into a pocket crater no bigger than its pressure suit lay a solitary alien, faceplate missing, trunk-tentacle squashed across the rim as if vainly fending something off. Its dead face was plain to see.

Shriver gripped the door handle impulsively, then jerked his hand away; from his lips came a popping, nervous noise. "Christ, I nearly did it there."

"No, all the doors are power-locked while any G-field's on. That's why I switched it on again. Poor aliens," mourned Michael. "Poor clumsy brave things—"

"Dammit, if only we could grapple the body! Confront NASA with an actual body and tell them where."

"Ah, you do believe in them!"

"Seductive, isn't it? I stand corrected: if only we could show NASA *this* . . . There looks no way into the ship or those things you say were domes. Pulverized . . . but how?"

"What the hammer, what dread grasp?" murmured Deacon.

"Yes, it does kind of become mythological! Out of the window with reason, that's the risk. Except, luckily, the windows won't open or we'd all be dead . . . This surely wasn't any shock wave from a nuke at altitude. No air. No medium to propagate in . . ."

"Maybe we're looking at all this upside down," said Michael. "Everything looks squeezed flat. Couldn't it have been sucked flat instead? They do have gravity control. Did have. Suppose it went wrong? Suppose they accidentally generated a point source

173

of a hundred or two hundred gravities—or a plane source, if that's possible—and all this happened before the generator destroyed itself! It could be a terrible accident."

They drove right up to the starship. A pressure-welded hill, now, driven a little way into the solid rock. A snapped landing jack splayed flatly from the mass along the surface, indented into the basalt . . . Michael pressed his cheek to the side window, staring up at where the vaned mushroom cap had been: the Biomatrix, too . . . All the biosensors back on Earth must now be lifeless, rotting.

He stared up . . .

At the bright veil of the Milky Way, the white shroud of stars above . . .

There was a hole in the shroud.

A hole that swallowed one star then another was swelling darkly upon the field of light. The silhouette of a great wingspread bat was free-falling down towards the Moon . . .

"Look up there! What's *that*?"

They squirmed against the glass.

Or the outline of a pterodactyl . . . Something ancient, extinct. Hooked black wings, spread wide, were falling, falling down upon them. There were no features apart from the outline. Dozens more stars disappeared. The shadow of this thing which seemed like shadow itself brushed the white peak in Tsiolkovsky. Eclipse began, winging over the crater floor, casting the alien base and the car into the darkness of burial underground. The darkness was only relieved by their headlights.

"Focus the external G-point above us fast, Mike! Can you do that without driving us into the ground? Use it to shove against *that thing*?"

Their headlight beams crept closer, lighting far less space. A bubble of vacuum shrank about them.

The car hummed. It sang. Michael pressed the accelerator pedal and the car lifted vertically from the ground for a moment, then was pushed back again. The suspension creaked. He shoved the pedal right to the floor. The creaking stopped, but the car failed to rise. Their headlamps played now upon a formless solid ink a few feet from the bumpers; though the darkness came no closer.

"For Christ's sake don't let your foot move—hold on," Shriver hissed, as though the blackness was swallowing the sound of their voices too. Michael thrust his foot against the floor. His ankle and calf were already trembling, dissolving. Bones be rigid, he willed, flesh be firm. He held on.

"You're doing fine, Mike. You're keeping it off us. The crater floor ought to be clear ahead. I don't remember any wreckage. We can't fly out because it's holding us down. But it can't overcome the G-point either—and we can *drive* out."

"No we can't! We're in flight mode."

"We damn well can. We can let the gravity point draw us out. Tilt the point forward a fraction. Not too much or the Dark will crush our tail. Tilt the wheel . . . Hold it there. We're moving, Mike. We are moving. Stones are creeping past. I can see 'em. We'll get out—"

A shock ran through the car; the hood dipped to the left.

"We've burst a tyre. No sweat. We don't need tyres. Let the point source pull us."

Shock; the hood dipped to the right.

"Don't panic, you can drag us out. Slowly, slowly."

Michael wanted to say, but I feel like a jellyfish; only his jaws wouldn't unbind. He heard a gargling noise in his throat.

"All right—keep on," urged Shriver.

Shock. Shock. The rear tyres burst.

Stones and the pockmarks of microcraters still crept past, though.

"Don't slacken off that pedal! Not for a fraction of a second, you hear me? Fine, you're doing real fine."

Deacon licked his lips; he thought he tasted blood on them.

Slowly, interminably, the car crept forward. The chassis had begun to croak faintly like a pond of distant frogs.

Deacon saw the minute hand moving slowly round the clock. Quarter past, sixteen minutes past.

"We're losing fuel!" he cried.

"Using it, you mean. The stronger the G-field, the faster the reaction mass goes!" Complete conviction sounded in Shriver's voice now that they faced this blackness, this negativity; absolute certainty that the gravity drive was authentic—and alien. Their

175

death would be the same death that the aliens had died.

"We're hardly moving," mumbled Deacon.

Seventeen minutes, eighteen minutes past.

"You fool, we're under full power. There's just *nowhere to go*. Not yet! Except just a little—way—ahead. A little—at—a—time. I can see the damned clock as well as you!"

Nineteen minutes.

"When we do reach the edge, Mike, be ready for us flying up *fast*. And how."

At last a seam of light was prised loose from the Dark. Sunlight existed again, a rising sword thrusting the black weight aside. Their hood nosed forward into it.

Abruptly the car tore free. It was fleeing from the crater. Already high above it. Pitching, rocking, as Michael clutched flabbily the steering wheel. The face of the Moon was a mile behind, five miles behind . . . At last he let his foot off the accelerator, moaning as muscles knotted in cramp. He kneaded and massaged his leg. In free fall they flew on, faster than escape velocity. Away from the Moon, but away from Earth too. The Earth now rose, white on blue, around the bumpy bend of lunar horizon.

Far behind them the dark floor of Tsiolkovsky stirred; and rose. A shadow of bat wings flew westward across craters in the direction of Gagarin, Cyrano, Paracelsus. The source of the shadow rushed up after them . . .

"Shit, it's following us."

"It'll cut us off," squeaked Michael. "It'll get between us and the Earth."

"Bring us round gently, under full power. I'll watch it."

Deacon dabbed his mouth, and tried to think clearly about the nature of *tulpas*. Tibetan adepts were supposedly able to sit in their cells and create autonomous thought creatures with independent—and often malign—lives; creatures which could travel about the real world. It was also said that adepts could create thought landscapes. In his cell the Tibetan monk could think an entire forest into being, which he could then journey through, thus proving the superficiality of our perceptions. Yet the mind creation was regarded as none the less real, for all that! Even Westerners had vouched for the reality of these creations. If the forest in the room was real (as real, the Tibetan lama insisted, as any other illusory reality!) why not a phantom journey to the far side of the Moon, occurring within a parked car—or even, for all Deacon knew, in a car racing at this very moment at speed along a motorway? Why not a phantom journey which had its own equal force of reality, one where driver and passengers could all be crushed to death against lunar lava or burst open in the emptiness of space at the very same time as the car impacted with a juggernaut lorry somewhere in England, upon the surface of the real Earth?

"Have you thought," said Michael, "that we brought it here ourselves? The destroyer! We're its sensors, aren't we? The Gebraudi never considered that. Or else they took the risk. *We* snuffed them out—me and Helen and Axel . . ."

Deacon groped for the entry point to this *tulpa* reality, but couldn't locate it. He could remember every moment of their journey with entire clarity from first stepping out of the smelly lift in the multistorey car park, before they had even set eyes on the Thunderbird. He could discover no seams in cognition, no gaps in the continuum of reality . . .

Who was projecting the *tulpa* reality? Not himself! Michael? Barry? Or was it all of them together, unwittingly, possessed by the deep-down Joke?

If they died here, it was real . . .

He groped fiercely for the exit point, staring out of the window, willing himself to see another reality in which they simply drove along an ordinary road. Where would they re-enter? London, Leicester, Leeds, somewhere on the Yorkshire moors? Meanwhile Michael kept the accelerator flat on the floor, using up their fuel far too fast, and the American stared through the rear window at that tiny pursuing black shape which he only saw as it occluded one star then another, speeding after them across the star field.

TWENTY-SEVEN

EIGHT MINUTES TO midnight. Only eight 'minutes' of reaction mass remaining.

Night was swinging across North America—by now the nearest landmass—as they re-entered the atmosphere. Ionised air shimmered in a ball around the car; sparks and milky streamers of white hair spilled out a meteor trail. Cocooned in their own gravity pocket, the atmosphere scarcely slowed them. The muzzy terminator was nearly at the Rocky Mountains. They headed down upon the mountains and across, bellying out from their panic dive.

"I've lost the black thing . . . The destroyer. I think it's gone back to roost in space . . ."

Barren brown ground swelled up: mountains, canyons, plateau.

"Don't we use reaction mass decelerating?" Shriver asked suddenly.

"Hell, yes." Michael pressed his foot to the brake pedal. As rapidly as their speed slackened, however, so did time on the clock contract. He eased off the brake. They slowed less rapidly, more economically. He squeezed and eased.

There was desert below them. Alluvial wasteland fanned out from high faulted escarpments towards sand hills. A dry lake glinted with baked salts. Buttes poked up. Broad flat basins opened between rubbed-down hills. A railway line and highway stretched thinly ahead; an aqueduct pipe led the way west. Matchstick trucks were crawling along the highway, pitching their desert crossing for sunset.

Two minutes to midnight.

"Listen, Mike, it's the Mojave Desert we're over. We've got a whole lot of military installations up ahead. George Air Force

178

Base off to the south-west about sixty, seventy miles. Edwards A.F.B. is right ahead along this road, about a hundred miles. We're really close to Muroc! If only we can put down there—if we can be seen bringing this crazy flying car right in on the main test runway!"

It would be a disaster, Deacon knew at once, an earthquake in human history. He was about to remind Shriver of his very own words. The irrational and the absurd would well up as they had done already once this century in Hitler's Germany. *Welteislehre.* *Hohlweltlehre.* Frozen heavens and hollow earth . . . Only this time there would be evidence. Or would there be?

Shriver was intoxicated now. The hollow in his own life had been filled up at last—out of the vacuum of space.

Yet how could Deacon himself deny that they'd indeed been to a solid, authentic Moon? Could he still pretend, seeing not some English motorway below them but an interstate highway running over the Californian Desert, that they'd 'only' been outside normal cognition, outside ordinary space-time relationships, ordinary causality?

Yet that's what the Inconceivable is, he realized. It is and yet it isn't; at the same time. It isn't to be thought of in terms of NASA and 'The Eagle has landed' but in Sheikh Muradi's terms —those of *Mu'awanat,* magical annihilation of space on the journey to *Arif,* to knowledge; in terms of *Karamat,* wonders; of the journey to fairyland, which isn't located some*where* in consensus spacetime but rather some*how,* outside ordinary cognition; to be thought of in terms of flying carpet journeys to—

"Bagdad," pointed Shriver excitedly.

"What did you say!"

"That town down there. Back there. It's called Bagdad. They mined gold. What's the matter with you, John? I know exactly where we are. Next on there's Ludlow, then Daggett and Barstow . . . I don't figure we'll make Edwards but we should make George A.F.B. down by Victorville. Stick to the highway then peel off to the left when I say so."

"Can they see us up here? The drivers?"

"Doubt if they're looking up, Mike. People don't look up much. They'd see a lot more if they did."

"Trip up and bruise their noses!" snapped Deacon.

"Cut it out, John. We're nearly home—"

"*You* might be."

"—and we have a gravity-drive spacecraft with us."

"Only if they see us landing. It mightn't work ever after—like the old grandfather clock. That's why you want to get to an air base, isn't it? The ordinary road won't do. They'd say the truck drivers were drunk or dizzy or saw a mirage."

One minute remained. Shriver paid no attention.

"We'll make it, Mike. We'll bring this bird down in style. Peel away to the left now—ten o'clock to the highway."

"But it's a wilderness. Then mountains."

"The Ord Mountains. We'll cross 'em."

"No, we ought to land on the road."

"Do as I tell you, boy! *This matters*."

So Michael swung the wheel away from the highway and they turned towards the Ord Mountains, across the sunset wasteland.

For a moment the car fell forward instead of flying. The hum of the drive picked up again. Michael feathered the brake pedal.

"I'm going to land."

Again the drive cut out. They could all feel their stomachs falling. They flew again, but down.

"Mike, I beg you—!"

"I'm going to."

By now they were eight or nine miles south of the highway; and fifty feet above a scrubby monotony of brownish-green creosote bushes. A few yucca daggers poked up, their black shadows pointing eastwards. In the west the Sun of warmth and life was setting, something golden, warm and calm. Again the drive cut out, and again they fell, to within a few feet of the ground. The drive picked up for a second or two. Michael stamped the brake. They hung briefly, all forward motion stilled. Then the car fell the last few feet into the creosote scrub, jarring them all. A kangaroo rat jumped from the shade of a bush back to its burrow . . .

Silence, and stillness. A few faint creaks of metal.

"Empty," whispered Michael, as much of himself as of the car. He leant his head on the steering wheel and shivered.

"It'll never go again," said Deacon quietly.

"Nonsense," snorted Shriver. "Shift your butt, John. I want out."

Deacon opened the passenger door and stepped out. He tripped on some burroweed; his feet were uncoordinated. The air felt oven-hot after the cool car. Peeling his jacket off, he hung it over his shoulder. Loosening his tie, he kicked his legs out to stretch them. For a moment he thought he heard the car hum again, but it was only some grasshoppers singing in the bushes.

All four steel-ply tyres were shredded: knotted cords wrapped round the wheel rims. Torn by moon rocks while a black bat the size of a football field had tried to press them all to death . . . Flies buzzed in Deacon's face, attracted by his sweat.

Shriver poked about the hood, then the trunk. He ran his fingers over the steel. Crouching in the grit, he squirmed under the car.

"It's very neatly welded . . ."

Scrambling out again, he snapped a long twig off a prickly bush and stuck it up the exhaust pipe. It bent back and snapped.

"Our own gravity-drive spacecraft! And we got it back!" He dusted himself.

The heat began to make Deacon sick. Over the broken hills to the south hung massive, motionless cumulus thunderheads, stained pink by the Sun sinking down to the horizon, swelling and trembling. He leaned back against the car. The metal felt warm already. If he'd been dropped here at midday he wasn't sure he could have survived. Shriver seemed not to notice the heat. He could probably have picked up red-hot metal and not noticed till his hand burnt off. Hot breezes began whipping the dust and grit through the bushes in whirling scurries. Soon no doubt it would become freezing cold, when the sun disappeared.

Deacon felt the weight of Solomon's *Lemegeton* in his jacket. The Book of the Spirits. Only by magic could cars fly. Yet what was meant by magic? Shriver *must* realize the trap, now that the magic excursion outside ordinary consciousness had expired . . .

As Deacon clutched his jacket feebly, his field of vision narrowed down to a little cactus—a tangle of prickly pads rooted in coarse light soil. He saw it at the end of a visual tunnel. All the little tufts of bristles—the glochids from which rose each spine, needles sheathed in tissue paper. A half-moon scab bit into the edge of one pad. Beetle work. Was the cactus aware of him on some vegetable wavelength? Did it detect a web of coherent, invisible energies in its environment? *Devas*, otherwise known as devils, *alias* UFO entities—all of which were simply empty names springing from alternative frames of reference?

Was there really some more primary reality that the cactus existed in, beyond all these human frames of reference? Deacon thought he would never believe the world again, never trust that it was entirely there. The cactus didn't need to believe; it simply existed in a primary way. As this desert too existed.

Yet in this desert had landed a flying car that crushed its creosote bushes flat, smearing them with moon dust! Now that the car was inert and drained, had it simply readjusted itself, had it recaptured orthodox reality? Was that dust on its torn tyres moon dust or just desert dust?

As the sun slipped below the rough barren horizon the wind blew stronger. Deacon half shut his eyes. Spines, pads, tissue paper . . .

Michael climbed out. The Moon was visible high up in the sky, a piece of mottled eggshell hanging in the deepening blue.

Michael pointed.

"It's still there! It's still coming!"

They all saw it then: the black bat wings hanging high over the desert.

"It's only a bird," said Shriver, helplessly. However, the shape grew larger as it sank down towards them. It took on no extra details, only size and density. Such huge density, as of a rock in the sky—a sculpture in black lava of something winged, sinking gently. It looked very much smaller than when it fell upon the Moon. It was just a shred torn off the bat thing, keeping the same entire shape as before. If those were wings they did not need to beat or flutter for it to fly. They did nothing, they just *were*. As Deacon stared, he felt he was seeing some ultimate reality, some void-reality up there. Compared with which neither Michael nor the American existed. Nor the ruined, drained car.

Nor the desert. Nor he himself. He didn't exist, he thought coldly. Only that void had existence.

"We'll split up! Scatter! Head for the highway—three different ways. Meet up there. Confuse the damned thing." Shriver dragged his fingers one last time, yearningly, across the Thunderbird. His hand wished to stay attached to it forever. He tore it free and took off through the scrub, casting heartbroken anguished glances back at the Ford as he ran.

"Get yourselves out of there!" he cried; as much jealousy as concern was in his voice.

Michael fled to the north. Deacon followed, more slowly, trotting north-east.

Shriver stared back from the side of a small butte and saw the blackness sink lower. It had no distinct body or head or wings. It was all the same substance. Without detail, it was the destroyer of details.

It sank down upon the desert floor where the Thunderbird sat abandoned.

"No!" he shouted at the dark thing. "Not the car! Me—instead! I'll give you myself instead!"

A muffled thump sounded from under the black mass. Its edges lifted and fell, then the whole mass rose twenty or thirty feet up to drift slowly north-east.

Even from a distance Shriver could see how crushed the Thunderbird was now. He wept from frustration.

After a time he squared his shoulders and hiked on. The desert darkened more. He should be a few miles clear of the half million acres occupied by the Marine Corps Desert Station. If any night patrol of Marines were out practising how to defend some Middle Eastern oilfield against Bedouin guerillas, though, and they happened upon a grown man, an ex-Air Force man, weeping—he'd be so ashamed.

Oil? The UFO thing that crushed his car had looked like an oil slick as it drifted off. Mischievous power source—dirty, contaminating, choking . . .

Or was it ink? A Rorschach blot? A thing without referent, with no definition save for a subjective personal one. Whatever it looked like was in your own head. Unlike the reality of the car!

The air chilled. He heard a coyote yip sadly somewhere in the distance. Something undefined rustled and squirmed clear as he was just about to tread on it.

Half an hour later he cut on to an unpaved road running north-west through the scrub. Towards Daggett or Barstow. He trotted fifty paces down the dirt track on the count, switched to a fast walk for another fifty paces, trotted again. If he could hire a wrecking-car from one of the garages in Barstow. Or a jeep and trailer with a winch.

Then he realised that he couldn't possibly do that. The recovery would have to be official, or else it would mean nothing. Were they all going to tell the same story? Damnable the way they'd been split up!

"John!" he called into the unresponsive night. "Mike!"

No answer came.

He ran faster for a while, scared of attracting Something Else. He should be in Barstow by midnight . . .

Michael heard the muted thump but had no idea what caused it. He looked back, saw nothing and ran on, dodging bushes. These soon thinned out, growing sparser and disappearing entirely as the land dipped into a dry lake. He paused on the lip of a shallow basin a mile wide, the clay surface mazed with cracks in the partial moonlight, barren of vegetation. He was too scared to take advantage of the flat *playa*. It was too open a terrain, too exposed. He began to run round the perimeter instead. A stitch ached in his side; he slowed to a walk, glancing round nervously now and then. He noticed a figure emerge on to the lake bed away to the east of him. It walked a little way then stopped and stared back. It stood quite still.

On to the blank *playa*, from the scrub to the south, drifted the black thing, at not much greater height than the man. Michael squeezed himself down behind a tiny shrub.

The figure down on the dry lake watched the oncoming black thing, too—awaiting it, with resignation, almost with indifference.

A great umbrella, it hung over him. Umbrella-like, it closed up,

184

enfolding him. A pillar of darkness stood out on the dusky lake.

Squirming back from the shrub, Michael sprinted on, his side on fire.

Where are you, Suzie? he prayed. Be with me, let me be with you. He tried to conceive at what angle a line would enter the soil to re-emerge out on the other side of the planet in Sandstairs. The imaginary line became his compass needle. Forgive me, forgive me! He heard his shoes squeak her name, voice from a grave, noise of bereavement and desire. Love me, save me, you're my magic. He refused to think what else he'd seen.

Finally he reached the highway. Rocking with fatigue and cold, he stood flagging down a refrigerated truck. As the driver slowed with a hiss of air brakes, his legs buckled. Country music flooded from the cab.

I've got four kids
And one needs a spankin'
And one needs a huggin'
And one needs a changin'
And another's on the way—!

When the driver bent over him, after first checking with a torch sweep that no one else was hiding in the bushes, Michael looked up into his face, managed to say, "Suzie," once again and passed out.

John Deacon could trot no further; he didn't even want to. He looked back at the bushy rim of the *playa*, still clutching his jacket in his hand, one sleeve trailing on the dry salty clay, though it was chilly now and he should have put it on. The black shape drifted over the bushes. With all the time in the world, it floated towards him.

He was nothing. Not an individual, a personality, an ego; not an identity. That was all a dream and a mirage. Only this was real: the Void. He chuckled softly. At last he understood the Joke that had puzzled him so long, the irony that made itself known as consciousness approached awareness of the deep-down void.

The blackness hung over him, and he gave himself up to it. The void received him into itself, gently.

TWENTY-EIGHT

THERE WAS NOTHING to be seen, yet one still saw: featurelessness. Nothing to hear, yet one still heard: stillness. Nothing to touch, yet one still felt: perfect balance, equilibrium. The Void was pure awareness. It was aware only of its own awareness—there were no objects of thought ...

Death, he thought; I've died. This is being dead.

Instantly, in the moment that he thought 'I', a whirlpool sprang up around him: a vortex that resisted the Void, and contradicted it. This vortex separated him from his previous state, which was now uncapturable—though now he yearned for it. The vortex walled him off; it only possessed an inside surface.

It spun, and its spin generated time.

It spun, and its spin separated out all the hierarchies of existence: particle, atom, molecule; bacterium, animal, intelligence ... turn upon higher turn of organization. He sensed that this miniature universe *was* the Universe in essence: that it contained all galaxies, all worlds, all living beings, all his memories.

Its umbilicus was everywhere at once, spinning vortex out of Void, drawing it back again. Particles constantly emerged, and returned. Minds too: all minds arose from the same Void-awareness, and rejoined it ...

How long did this universe last? It was instantaneous, since its starting point and its vanishing point within the Void were the same timeless event. The white hole of emergence was the black hole of disappearance, around the turn of time. Yet within itself it enclosed aeons, tied up in this Moebius strip.

How did it sustain itself? By exclusion, by separation, by inaccessibility. By the split of subject from object, of observer

186

from observed—which brought about cause and effect, and natural laws. By the indeterminacy of fundamental events. By the inaccessibility of light-years: whereby light, which allowed observation, at the same time denied it. By the inability of mind, which fostered knowledge of the world, to know itself except partially . . .

How did it rejoin the Void? *By the very same process.* For all these inaccessibilities caused a fierce suction towards ever higher patterns of organization, towards higher comprehension. So molecules became long-chain molecules, and these became replicating cells that transmitted information . . . till mind evolved, and higher mind.

The universe, he realized, was an immense *simulation*: of itself, by itself. It was a registering of itself, a progressive observation of itself from ever higher points of view. Each higher order was inaccessible to a lower order, yet each lower order was drawn towards the higher—teased by the suction of the higher.

When the universe simulated itself perfectly, then it could cease to be . . . as it was, indeed, always doing in the no-time which the whole vacuum fluctuation of existence occupied. The ultimate knowledge of the universe would *be* the universe itself; then subject and object would be one. Yet within time, meanwhile, the suction of the unknowable was a wind howling through the world so that the world could continue to change, and life evolve . . .

The vortex spun about him like a saucer. A flying saucer. This was the image of the Whole—which could not be known, yet which must constantly intrude into the world, as a goad to bacteria—and Men. This shape was an archetype, deep in the nature of being; it was the image of the whole vortex, casting its shadow. It was free from the laws of time and logic and gravity, for in the Void that it came from there could be no 'law' . . .

Saucers and their kin did not intrude *into* the world, though, he realized. The world was actually within them.

As he realized this, the vortex firmed into a craft.

He wasn't alone in the craft. A man in green stood at the controls.

His face was made of blades of grass, and leaves of trees, and scraps of vegetables. Deacon realized that he'd seen someone like him before: in an oil painting by the eccentric Giuseppe Archimboldo, portrayer of the Four Humours and the Four Seasons in this style, hanging in Vienna's Kunsthistorisches Museum . . . Here was a simulation man, to present this knowledge of how the whole universe must simulate itself, by means of mind evolving out of the primary awareness—rooted, in turn, in the Void-awareness out of which this universe arose . . .

Here was Khidr, pilot of the vortex saucer. The Unidentified One. He who existed yet did not exist. He who was the necessary suction that compelled new organs of knowledge to come into existence, which he would then constantly evade.

Khidr wasn't any human person. Nor any alien either. Nor even any Godlike future being from further up the turns of the spiral. He was simply a membrane: between evolving knowledge, and the nature of reality; an interface between higher turns of the spiral and the turn which an evolving being currently occupied.

"Why are you a vegetable man?" Deacon asked. But he already knew the answer. Khidr turned and grinned, greenly; and said nothing.

The walls of the vortex craft now sprouted portholes. They flew, inconsistently, over deserts, forests, seas and cities—as though Deacon's re-entry point to normal cognition wasn't quite pinpointed yet. As though he had to understand a little more before he could re-enter the world consciously.

"The Gebraudi were an invention, weren't they?" he said.

The Gebraudi were miracles. Intrusions of higher-order knowledge into a lower-order system, namely the human mind, to draw it upwards. *The alien was the miracle from now on*: this was the message of the UFOs. And how Man needed the image of the alien, to help himself evolve, now that he had filled his world and there were no more 'Here Be Dragons' zones upon the map!

"What did they tell us? That the whole universe is recorded within itself. That's true. They had to seem alien, didn't they? From outside. Or else they'd have harmed the world—distorted it. They had to be crippled beings, ludicrous and under pressure

—because *we're* incomplete, and have to be. *We* can't grasp this knowledge whole. It had to be the back side of the Moon too, didn't it? For the same reason: there's the blind spot, the image of unknowability. Then they had to disappear—just as you disappear! There's no wreckage on the Moon, is there?"

So many questions—which, in fact, were all answers.

"It wasn't *you* who took us there. It was ourselves: our own need—in our shared psychic life. Shared, because all separate minds are simply transmitters, vortices, out of the same void! You aren't an angel or any such thing. *You are us*, Khidr—the psychic pattern we're all part of."

Khidr spoke then, amiably, with the same green grin. His teeth were artichoke leaves. Deacon didn't recognise the language he spoke. It might have been Persian or Arabic or Sanskrit or even some alien tongue; it didn't matter, for Khidr wasn't denying what Deacon said. The fact that there was any answer was enough; it affirmed.

Deacon grasped further. "I'd be tempted to see you as some sort of Godlike being—except that your face is made of leaves and brussels sprouts! Because *yes*, you're primary. You're an essence of things."

With grass hair, bunched sprout cheeks, translucent grape eyes, tapering tuberous chin, this being would have been a demon at any other time.

"I know why you're green! I know why Khidr is the Green Man! You represent the Primary Perception, yes—but there's more to it." Deacon remembered Michael's description of the twin halls in the 'alien' dome in Tsiolkovsky crater: the one hall, for humans, lit by yellow 'sun' light, and the blue-green hall of the Gebraudi drenched with 'alien' radiance. And he remembered, too, the seminar on ordinary perception he used to teach once, before he turned his attention to extraordinary states of mind.

"The light from our Sun only *looks* yellow. It actually has maximum intensity in the blue-green part of the spectrum, doesn't it? The majority of information comes through there. That's where our eyes are the most sensitive. That's the maximum information channel for human beings. That's why we see you as green, or dressed in green. *You* are the maximum information channel! And it's open now—within *me*."

Khidr bowed, in acknowledgement. Deacon reached out his hand and laid it on the green-clad arm. The being's hand was mango-skinned, its fingers were thick asparagus spears.

Khidr offered him the controls; he accepted them.

TWENTY-NINE

THE FAT BLOND policeman swung a chair round and bestrode it. The chair back pressed ungainly clefts into his splayed thighs.

"I'm Captain Carl Dorris." The name spilled out as one single word; the Captain had no intention of his surname being mistaken for a lady's name, jokingly or otherwise. He'd suffered enough kidding in school about his name, besides being a fat boy. When he joined the San Bernadino County Police he anticipated that would evaporate. Not so; it merely went on behind his back. Worse than being kidded, he hated the falsely innocent face.

Carl Dorris had brought in a quick-snack take-away of crisp bacon, scrambled egg and hash potatoes on a paper plate and a cup of coffee for Michael. As soon as Michael was more awake he ate hungrily.

Michael was lying in a camp bed in T-shirt and underpants under coarse grey blankets. The window—large enough, though with thin white bars—looked over railway yards towards some mountains. A diesel engine shunted to and fro, hooting.

Captain Carl Dorris rolled his tongue round the inside of his mouth between gums and lips. A boxer munching a rubber protector into place.

"You were flat out. The doctor looked you over, but all you needed was rest. You mentioned a girl's name to that truck driver."

Michael gulped the coffee. He remembered his fervent mumbling as he tramped through the scrub. "She's safe. She's in England—"

"So what happened?"

"I—we, there were three of us, we had a car accident. We crashed—"

"Uh-huh. Mr Shriver did report the accident a while after you were brought in. He's sleeping it off at the Astro Hotel. We sent a helicopter out at first light to hunt for this guy Deacon. No luck yet—we just heard it's heading back for more fuel. So I'd like to know some more about this accident of yours."

"What did Barry Shriver tell—?"

"Oh no." The Captain shook his head. "What do *you* say?"

Michael took a deep breath. "When I say we crashed I actually mean we . . . crash-landed."

"You were flying an airplane?"

"We were flying in a car."

"Sure you were. A car with wings."

"Oh, it didn't need wings!"

Captain Carl Dorris sucked his gums some more. "You've not got tracks in your arms so what is this, acid? I'm trying to be patient, do you see? I'm broadminded. Just don't mock me, boy."

"I'm not! This all happened because of . . . because of U-F-Os." Defiantly, he spelt the word.

"What about them?" The tip of the Captain's nose whitened. The chair creaked as he squeezed it between twin slabs of himself.

A larger ambulance helicopter flew in from Victorville later. Captain Carl Dorris escorted a chastened Michael and Barry Shriver, who'd appeared from his hotel on West Main Street, out to it.

"Don't worry about all this," Shriver whispered. "I've taken it to higher authority. It'll soon be out of their hands."

"Just show me where," smiled Dorris icily. "One flying Thunderbird, please."

"Aren't we going to search for John Deacon?" asked Michael.

"Well now, he might just be where your magic car is, and we've not found *that* yet."

"Maybe your other pilot didn't recognize it," said Shriver. "It did get crushed."

"Sure. You all rolled on it. You've all been to the Moon—and I'm Santa Claus! I'd figure on illegal entry or drug smuggling if you weren't already two hundred miles north of the border. Nobody could be so dumb as to be still stuck on back roads. Unless of course you *were* flying—a light plane, and couldn't even navigate. But you were an Air Force pilot once, hmm?"

The helicopter headed south-east over the service stations, motor lodges and stucco tract homes of Barstow into the desert. After a while Shriver saw the unmade road he'd come by the night before. The sky was clear blue, the desert sombre-toned.

Michael pointed. "There's the dry lake. That's where—" He swallowed, realizing some of the possible consequences if John Deacon's body was indeed found battered to death in the clay.

"Where what, exactly?"

"I saw Deacon crossing it and the black thing was after him—"

"Circle around, Tom," Dorris instructed the pilot; the Captain bounced his fingers on his knee.

Salt crystals on cracked clay twinkled faintly in the early sunlight. A tiny kit fox fled towards its den as they throbbed above it. Scurries of wind bowled tangles of weed along. Nobody was there on the *playa*, alive or dead. They flew on, following Shriver's directions, till they found the wrecked car. Nobody was there either.

"Why should anyone haul a wreck out here to dump it?" wondered the pilot.

"Take us down, Tom. We ought to find the tracks of whatever hauled it here."

"If we don't, that means it fell out of the sky?" The pilot laughed uncertainly.

They landed.

Shriver was soon prising at the broken hood. The whole car had been reduced to a compressed, rumpled oblong as though fed through the rollers of a mangle or squashed by a mechanical crusher. But it had been done right here on the spot, since crystal granules of window glass littered the soil; unless, that is, someone had brought the glass here deliberately to scatter it . . . Wheels had all snapped off their axles. Two were impacted under the chassis, two were splayed out. As the pilot was climbing down to join them, Shriver bounded back to him.

"Have you a crowbar? I must see how the engine looks."

"Mister, that engine just *isn't* any more." However, the pilot popped back inside and obliged him with a steel bar.

"What's that you're giving him, Tom?" Dorris's hand fell to his gun. Realizing, the pilot backed away from Shriver, who shouted angrily, "Dammit, I'm not wanting to hijack your helicopter! It's the *car* I want."

"Still, you do know how to fly choppers, don't you? From the Air Force."

"Like hell I do. I flew fighters. We weren't all nuts on choppers then."

"Drop the bar. Let it fall right there."

Shriver retained the crowbar, though he let it dangle uselessly between two fingers. "Captain, cover me if you like. I must see inside. I beg you."

One eye still on Shriver, Dorris stooped to lift a piece of bent metal: it was a number plate.

"Call Barstow, Tom." Dorris read off the number. "Get it fed into the computer." He tossed the plate down again. "Okay," he said. "You lever the hood open. Just don't reach inside, right? Keep your hands in sight. I'd like to see what you're so anxious to see."

Sweating, Shriver forced the crowbar in and twisted up part of the hood.

"One crushed engine?"

"Not really." Shriver grinned. "Take a look at it."

"You move away first, hmm?"

Shriver walked off.

"Not too far!" Dorris squatted down and peered under the hood.

Within, was not an engine, certainly, though what exactly it had been was hard to say. Fused, crushed glass, knobbly as malachite, was there; and a dark green glue that might have been oil; and bundles of coppery hair like mattress stuffing. Dorris reached in, teased out some glass and hair. He sniffed it, wrinkled his nose and dropped it.

"Shit, it's like a trashcan in there."

"That's an alien gravity-drive, Captain!" shouted Shriver.

The top of Dorris's nose went white. "Do you think you're funny? You tear out the real engine and stuff in all this filth! How did you get the car here? I don't see any tracks."

Tom called, "Barstow say a new Thunderbird with those plates was stolen near Cheyenne six weeks ago."

"Brand new, now look at it. What kind of sick mind?" Dorris flicked a fly off his fingers.

"If there aren't any tracks . . ." said Tom.

"Winched down from a chopper? How do I know! This isn't drugs or anything. It's some kind of publicity stunt!" .

Controlling himself, Shriver insisted, "This—was—a—space-craft—rebuilt—by—aliens! Aliens who are lying dead right now on the backside of the Moon. Right at this moment, in the ruins of their starship."

"Oh yes, we'll just fly up there and check that out. Do you think we could get up to the Moon and back for lunch, Tom? You make me sick, Shriver. Is there really any guy called Deacon? Aren't you making him up too? Which of you two jokers stole this car, anyway? Oh sorry, I forgot you were given it by aliens. What do they call themselves?"

"The Gebraudi—they're from the star Eta Cassiopeia," said Shriver, nodding in Michael's direction as though he was one of them.

"Tom, send out an APB for some aliens looking like elephants. Did you get the name? Oh dammit, I'm forgetting, they're on the backside of the Moon. Better send the APB to NASA."

"All it needs is one lunar orbiter. NASA could take films, and get real evidence—"

"Sure, a fine way to spend a hundred million tax dollars! I *was* joking, you know. How much have they spent so far proving that flying saucers don't exist?"

"NASA haven't spent a penny, just the Air Force—that's the tragedy. But astronauts have seen them! And filmed them. And Air Force pilots, and even police! It always gets played down."

"What a pity if they weren't there on the Moon. I'd have to book you two instead."

"Oh no, we didn't steal it. I was in London six weeks ago. So was Mike here!"

"Are we ever going to look for John Deacon?" asked Michael. "He's been out all night. It's getting hot again. He hasn't had anything to eat or drink since yesterday."

"You wring my heart. Don't worry, the other chopper's still out burning up fuel. Tom, I want photos of this wreck—then we're flying these two wise guys back to Barstow."

The radio came alive again; Tom ducked back inside.

"They've found him, Captain Carl! He's okay—surprisingly okay."

"Is he indeed? Well tell them to stay right where they are!"

THIRTY

DEACON ACCEPTED THE controls and piloted the UFO. It went where he willed. He wore the craft like a suit of clothes. (Where was Khidr now? Khidr was within him.)

When had this sequence of events begun? As the question shaped itself, he re-entered the ordinary world from the extraordinary side, darting down upon his own back garden in Granton, some way back in time . . .

A Sheep Dog bounded up to him. He stretched out his hand to ruffle the dog affectionately—and his hand sliced through its neck like wire through cheese.

"No!" he cried. Too late he jerked back and bobbed away.

195

Shep's whole head had been drawn in to him already, and absorbed.

How?

He realized, with a chill, that this was actually happening. It was the very event, taking place that night in the garden—but caused much later on, caused *now*, as though up until this very moment the event had been its own cause . . . Events do happen in succession, Sheikh Muradi had said, yet this isn't always the succession that men see. Impossible to pin down cause and effect within the event itself; only in an altered state could one grasp the true sequences . . .

So instead of 'how', he now demanded: *Why?*

And the Khidr within him whispered: if you intervene from a superior point of knowledge, you cannot leave the world unchanged. Were it not for heedlessness, the world would not remain in being! When the world knows itself perfectly, there is only: Void, the zero state—the state from which the whole universe of things and living beings whirlpools forth; the state where nothing is written.

He whirled away, cross-time.

He sensed a complex flow of patterns, not in space but in space-time, shifting, knotting together, untying, binding. Events existed as nodes of these dynamic patterns. The universe was freely self-determining, for all events were *thoughts*; and everything contributed thus to the general maintenance of existence—every microbe, every plant, every stone. Naturally, later events must be able to cause earlier events—or else, he saw, there would be no evolution, only random combinations; nor would there be a unified space-time. Yet if minds became aware that all events were thoughts . . .

The possessors of knowledge must be careful. They could work miracles. They could delete tumorous growths from the body, or magnify the number of loaves and fishes, or whirl a pair of shoes from Baghdad into the midst of the desert to fall upon a robber's skull and crack it. They could misshape reality, too. His control was still imperfect . . .

When you investigate something, you change the nature of what you investigate. Impossible to intervene without altering reality. Physicists knew that well enough; they called it Indeterminacy. It was proof of the living texture of events and the ability of those who saw this to become—within their limits—conscious thinkers of reality.

Yet there was a plus and minus factor at work too, he saw. When you inject higher-order knowledge, something must change within the lower-order reality or be lost to it, to compensate. The trick was to make the loss the least negative one possible—to create merely mystery, not damage. UFO intrusions all too often scared the wits out of people, maimed them, slew animals, stole flesh and blood. 'You had to pay the Devil . . .' But really, the UFO wisdom was an awareness of the universe thinking itself, causing itself, evolving itself.

Briefly he grieved for Shep. Yet Shep wasn't lost. His being had merely re-entered the Void.

Deacon imagined a Klein bottle of events embedded in four-space, space which its own shape defined; from the viewpoint of ordinary sequence it crossed back upon itself irrationally . . .

Time was simultaneous within the Void; time was tied into a knot. This was how the laws of form which allowed life and mind to arise could in turn arise out of these latter, later organized patterns. Hadn't the alien Bonaparte said as much to Michael with his talk of UFO events possessing a different, higher time sequence? One which couldn't be proved within the lower sequence of events?

Still searching for his own place in this, Deacon probed towards his earlier self. He found himself sitting at a desk with a cassette recorder, and struggled to address himself; but the task of embedding a higher viewpoint into the cause and effect sequence that was the viewpoint of Deacon-*then* . . . screeched, grated, tore through the magnetic tape of Michael's seduction and UFO flight, erasing precious evidence.

Again, he tried.

What he said to himself-*then* passed through a shape-scrambler, through a topological transformation as he stepped down from the higher pattern to the lower. The information shifted in register, tone and content:

"You — mustn't — ask — questions — about — flying —

saucer — beings. You — must — accept—" Words failed. He became a flying monster, glaring at himself through the window from outside.

He broke off, flew further along the timeline of connections, and was drawn down, still learning, on to Granton Common . . .

Clad in Khidr-green, he warped himself askew to forestall a more fearful warping of the girl whom he would contact. He took upon himself an alien image, and twisted it yet further: to safeguard the one he would meet. One shoulder hung low, the other jutted high. One arm thrust way out, the other clubbed up tight. Drifting out of the woods, he barely kept contact with the ground. A pair of swans fled, so as not to be consumed. He dared not frame words this time—did not know them—and could only make slow, languid gestures.

Suzie Meade's face twisted. She fell. She tore off her shoe and flung it at him, to ward him off . . . He snapped away, having merely frightened the wits out of her. Yet in the wider network of connections, this event disconnected Suzie from Michael; so that Michael was free to meet the Gebraudi, and so to open Deacon's mind. Suzie would recover, he saw. His precautions had been moderately successful. Michael could even recover *her*, though there would be a fee to pay . . .

Even so, Suzie's recoil from sanity split his own mind wide open for a while. He dissociated into two idiot figures dressed in Air Force blue, enquiring after her health. In this divided state, his Id sported. Sexual impulses surfaced: a lust for Suzie which he hadn't realized. Ribald seaside postcard thoughts ran through the two sides of his mind: a text of innuendos through one side, pictures of tits and buttocks through the other. So he/they insulted her—and might have assaulted her. She shut the door on them.

Yet in the wider network the event drove her to his house, on the very evening that Shep died, thrusting Michael yet further into the zone of miracles, where Deacon waited:

still binary, but more purposeful, to save Michael when younger from a fatal crash on a steep hill as he rode home— which Michael must forget, that minus in Michael's memory balancing the plus of life preserved . . .

Finally, he landed the saucer on Swale Moor, drawn down there by Michael's imminent arrival. Sexual impulses were still present; now they focused upon Michael. He had given him life, after all—by saving him. He could still only beckon and broadcast emotionally his need to convey knowledge. He was split three ways now, his emotional self resident in dumb Luvah, with binary aid from the same Tweedledum and Tweedledee mutated into slant-eyed Space People, claiming now that they were from the Pleiades rather than the Air Force: telling lies and offering assistance—at once presenting plus and minus. Here he modified the boy's life, giving and injuring at the same time—commencing a sequence that would finally lead to higher understanding. The boy forgot it—*minus*—else his life would have been twisted too far askew for his life and Deacon's ever to converge.

He flew away from him, bobbing over the ripples of the dark moor, then, in sudden sunlight, over the ripples of the sea beyond; he whirled upwards into darkness, to hide himself . . .

What of the aliens whom Michael must meet, more recently in the network of events, on that some moor? What of the Gebraudi? Deacon directed himself towards them.

They weren't from Eta Cassiopeia, he felt sure, any more than Luvah was from the Pleiades. Despite their claim to lay siege—for the most benevolent motives—to the 'hostile Unidentifieds' of Earth, they must be a UFO event themselves. Yet somehow he couldn't reach them in the event network.

But of course! They must necessarily be a *higher-order* UFO event: a second stage pattern influencing the first and lower stage, at the very time when this first stage was about to integrate itself into his own consciousness! At the very time when he became able to operate within it! They were part of a higher pattern, still inaccessible. Necessarily they had to seem separate from Earth's UFOs—walled off from them unknowably. Of course they must vanish from existence, as soon as they had fulfilled their necessity.

Who guided them? How did they arise? He didn't know. Nor, he suspected, could he know. They were a higher stage of unknowability—and it was necessary that there should be one.

As he simultaneously reached for them and acknowledged the

need for them to vanish, he found that the UFO-craft was no longer in the darkness close to Earth. It had leapt away from Earth. It was commencing a descent upon the Moon. It was pressing down, erasing. He spread his arms like wings. The elastic craft felt vast, and massive. It had already practically erased the alien base, he remembered—the memory came from a tangent of events which he hadn't yet actively explored; but it was there. Now the craft descended once again to expunge all witness of the base.

But *he* was a witness of the base! He was on the Moon, himself, in the Ford Thunderbird, staring up appalled at the Cloud of Unknowing that was descending. Again he fissioned. He was both on the Moon, and over it.

He must escape—or be erased. In the craft, he chased himself; and he was in the car that flew away . . .

How 'real' were the Moon and the alien Moonbase? If events in the 'real' world were all thoughts—processes by which the universe thought out its own reality—and if one learnt to think of these events as thoughts; if one grew aware of the universal thought processes rather than the 'events' which were their language—why then, the landscape of action would become symbolic: a 'virtual' landscape directly manifesting symbols—rather like dream imagery, yet operating not privately within one's own personal consciousness, but instead publicly and collectively, just as the Thunderbird flight to the Moon had been a shared 'virtual' experience.

So there could be false events (which were still valid), imaginary landscapes (which were nevertheless true), and imaginary beings which were actually symbolic entities, yet which interacted, apparently authentically, with human personnel . . .

When the 'viewpoint Ego' had drifted through the alien ship and up into the Biomatrix to rejoin it, hadn't Michael said he guessed that he was caught up in some higher, symbolic thought process, *using* apparent reality as its mode of thought? And been scared into accepting it as wholly real . . . for otherwise, how could he return to the world he knew?

What, then, of the fate of Helen Caprowicz, crushed to death in her car on the Moon within this symbolic reality? Holding fiercely to the image of the crushed Pontiac with that naked human arm thrust out, sandwiched between metal, Deacon enlarged his perception of the event network associated with that car, reaching behind the symbolic reality to the event-thoughts in the real world . . .

While he chased the fleeing Thunderbird, hunting after a car which sped along a highway that was at once upon the Earth and also out in space, he hunted a silver Pontiac too in the traffic stream.

He caught a glimpse of the driver's face: a woman's. Her jaw jutted. Her hair was brown and bobbed. She wore an old suede jacket. She was driving on minor roads through forested hills and mountains, past lakeside communities. *Big Moose,* pointed a road sign.

She speeded up, accelerating round a bend just as a tractor was hauling a long timber trailer out from a forest road; trimmed treetrunks blocked the whole way. She braked and skidded under them; the hood of the Pontiac jammed beneath. A restraining cable snapped. The timber load shifted. One tree, then a second, slid sidelong on to the car. Window glass shattered in a spray of ice crystals. A bare arm jerked out of the gap, jacket sleeve torn away, fingers grasping then relaxing.

(But Helen wasn't dead. Further along the event network he saw how she lay recovering in a hospital bed. Still further along, she seemed to stand wrapped up warmly atop a mound of bulldozed snow, hand in hand with a blond man who also had a long jaw, and a grin full of ice-teeth, watching in arctic darkness as a rocket flamed skywards from a launching pad, lighting up snowfields and pine forests . . .)

The image of her out-thrown arm fused with the same image seen upon an arctic backdrop of the Moon . . . and as it fused, two streams of traffic fused; and Deacon overhauled the Thunderbird trapped in a desert.

He descended on the Thunderbird—the miracle vehicle no longer needed in that form—to change its form, to crush it.

He escaped through the scrub, and the night.

Once more he hunted and found himself: a solitary figure standing on a dark and waterless lake, as though waiting to be ferried across. The craft hovered. Mind-lines joined. And the craft leapt forward from night to daylight . . .

He set the craft down neatly in the desert. The hatch opened wide . . . to an ordinary world. He was aware of a separate Khidr once more taking the controls. Leaving Khidr to his task, he leapt down into the scrub beside a cone-shaped hill. In the east the sun was already well risen.

He breathed in deeply of the sweet sagebrush air as the saucer rose and rapidly shrank from sight, not so much flying away as becoming a point source, resorbed into the world. From its spin he had picked up a great charge of energy.

He couldn't *know* entirely; so the world went on. A few ants scurried through the dirt, perhaps tasting him on the breeze. A grasshopper sprang away. He glanced at his hand; the flesh was stained faintly green, as though he'd been crushing plants for their moisture. So he stood, back in the world again, in the Mojave Desert; and the whole world was a simulation, a perfect fiction. A book that actually was blank. Nothing wrote it, but itself; and how this could be was the greatest mystery. For if he could read it properly he knew that all the words would disappear.

THIRTY-ONE

THEY SIGHTED THE other helicopter on a dry stream bed below a rutted conical hill clad in sagebrush. They landed close by it, and Deacon ducked towards them.

Shriver extended a helping hand, however Deacon needed no assistance.

"You look chipper, John! Thank God we found you. A man can die out here. Say, our car has some weird stuff under the hood."

Deacon settled himself into the spare seat. He grinned. "I feel rather like Zarathustra—glowing and strong. Because . . . *I've solved it.* Or rather it all solved itself—just as soon as I gave up resisting and became really receptive."

"Pity it's so badly crushed," Shriver went on regardless. "What the hell, we've got the remains."

"Of course it's crushed," nodded Deacon. "You won't be able to reconstruct anything."

"Won't we? Just you wait and see."

Deacon chuckled. "I *have* seen. I saw what frightened Suzie, and how Shep lost his head. Why Luvah made love to you, Michael. Why our aliens took the shape they did . . ."

"Are you saying that the Gebraudi could control how we saw them?" Michael asked, incredulously. "Why choose a ludicrous shape?"

"Why use a Ford car as a spaceship?" Deacon countered.

"Well, that was for camouflage."

"Ah, the whole affair camouflages itself, doesn't it? Right down to that old canard about Tharmon and Company refusing to reveal themselves as it was 'against their ethics' . . . Was it, just! It was against their UFO *nature*—unknowability is built in throughout. I should know; I've been back over the whole course on the inside. No, you two, I'm afraid there's no possible proof. There's only a showing forth of the UFO reality—a demonstration of it. I've had the most remarkable experience of that."

Michael licked his lips fretfully. "What Tharmon and Company said doesn't matter. We know they weren't from the stars. They were earthly UFO presences. Sort of piebald ones: part good, but part misleading. The Gebraudi said so."

Captain Dorris torqued his tongue around his mouth. A fat finger tapped a fat thigh; his nose looked leprous. "Carry on, fellows, I'm fascinated. Just what are UFOs, by the way?"

"We'll find out," Shriver cut in hastily. "First we need that Thunderbird analysed, to give us our tools. When we get that glass and bristle under a microscope —"

"It'll turn out to be plain glass and bristle," promised

Deacon. "UFO events simply aren't susceptible to cause and effect science, *ipso facto.*"

"Dammit, the Thunderbird isn't a UFO!"

"Not any more it isn't. But it *was* for a while. Small wonder you had no bother with 'hostile' UFOs when you were off on those night rides of yours, Michael. Away on your Thunderbird broomstick, eh?" Deacon smiled roguishly. "*You* were in a UFO state. Didn't someone say that it's *all* part of the same spectrum? That spectrum included the Gebraudi! UFOs really are rather aptly named: they're objects that fly away out of your grasp and become unidentified as soon as their work is done. They're unidentifiable events—which is precisely what the Gebraudi have become by now."

Shriver scowled, exasperated. "Think straight, John. Try to remember where we've all *been.* We've got a car rebuilt by alien science—as a UFO hunter!"

"Correction: we've got a car. A pile of scrap, actually. What we had before is utterly gone. It's become unidentifiable. If it's any consolation, Barry, the UFO programme is really a very positive, life-enhancing one at heart—which is why the Gebraudi went on so about their altruism . . ."

"It was poor Helen and Axel who went on so," Michael reminded Deacon quietly.

"Ah yes, they were learning their lesson too—yoked in with you in the UFO symbol-reality. Don't worry, Helen is safe. She had a serious accident, which is an awful shame. But she'll mend."

"Christ, man," cried Michael angrily, "we saw her lying crushed in that crater!"

"We saw something. An image. I saw it all somewhat differently the second time." Deacon's eyes twinkled. "I've met the UFO pilot, Barry. I hate to mention Little Green Men—but popular intuition has chosen wisely. The Arabs call the pilot Khidr, the Green Man."

"Look," snapped Shriver, "the Gebraudi had genuine equipment to pin down UFOs—gear that worked."

Deacon held up his hand. "All this UFO 'hostility' is very much bound up with sheer ignorance of the forces involved. We needn't try to overcome UFOs; we need to overcome the limitations in ourselves. They even told you as much, Michael. The real aim is to perfect yourself. That's why the goad exists. Goads sometimes *do* hurt, though."

"Yeah, like they hurt the Gebraudi!" scoffed Shriver.

Deacon shook his head. "That's all been erased. It's been delated from the simulation."

"What 'simulation'?" Shriver tossed his own head impatiently, as if shucking off an annoying fly. "*And* we need to get our hands on some of those biosensors that Mike planted —"

"They're dissolved, too."

"I'm afraid he's right there," said Michael. "With the Biomatrix on the Moon out of action, and no sympathetic vibrations coming from it, they'll . . . well, starve. Rot down."

"Everything has reverted," agreed Deacon. "There are no nice causal proofs, only demonstrations—then whoosh, away! You can never validate a system completely within the terms of that system, Barry. Kurt Gödel proved that about the most basic tool of science: simple arithmetic. This same limit applies within each hierarchy of organization of the universe. Systems are only 'proved'—they're only fully determined—by higher systems. UFOs can't yield to our science, because they're part of a higher psychic pattern."

Shriver pounced. "So you do buy what the Gebraudi told Mike about there being hierarchies?"

"A grand intuition! It was there to discover—but not to *prove.* Imagine our universe as a great vortex, Barry. This is what I saw. The universe emerges from a Void where there's no subject and object, no cause and effect, no 'law' in our sense. As soon as it fluctuates into being, the universe is immediately a mass of subjects and objects. Now it has 'laws', a ruling causality. It has observer and observed built into it right down at the level of the atomic particle. So it'll inevitably generate observers—living witnesses of its own existence, systems of knowledge of a higher and higher order of complexity. That's what these 'hierarchies' really are. The force that evolves higher organization out of lower is nothing less than this basic separation of observer from observed, of consciousness from what it's conscious of. It's this inaccessibility—the pull of it! That's the force that pulls material up the spirals of the vortex, from the Void back in to the Void."

As he spoke, Deacon's hands made empty, circling shapes in the air, weaving a basket then collapsing it. Tom, the police pilot, sniggered, as though there was something erotically suggestive in this handplay. A female torso.

"I've seen into that Void, Barry—when the black thing took me. I glimpsed it for a moment, before I remembered who I was. That Void is pure consciousness. It's pure awareness: of itself, with no other contents involved—no subject, no object."

"In other words it's God." Shriver sighed. "You saw God."

Dorris's finger tap tap tapped. His tongue munched saliva. Flies buzzed on the outside of the plexiglass. A hawk winged overhead, hung briefly then pounced on to the hillside.

"I saw the root consciousness behind reality. I don't think that the word God helps much. Any more than your scheme for hunting UFOs helps! UFOs haunt the boundaries between levels of the vortex spiral. They pull upwards, by a kind of vacuum suction—by being present, yet inaccessible. They're shortcuts across reality; they're bridges. The whole universe is a quantum fluctuation overall, so obviously it has indeterminacies built into it. They're part of this 'ignorance' dynamic. This lets non-causal data appear all the time—whenever the separate brains that transmit consciousness tap the deeper sea. That's how higher organization can draw lower organization upwards. What we need isn't batteries of UFO 'detectors' but a consciousness-science: not to *analyze* the phenomenon into causes and effects, but to *envision* it, from within! That's the way to learn. You'll never pin down a UFO with your bits of string and sealing wax."

The hawk had risen from the hillside, something small clasped in its claws; dead prey. It flew away, to feed.

Shriver grimaced. "You're suffering from exposure, John. Or shock or something."

"Do I really look it?" Deacon enquired gently.

The hand which had touched Khidr was beginning to smart

now, and stmg, as though he'd grasped a bunch of nettles with delayed action.

"I went through the whole sequence of events all over again. But I went through them from a higher viewpoint. I *was* the UFO pilot, myself —"

"Now I've heard everything," said Carl Dorris.

However, a moment later, Edwards Air Force Base was on the radio to them . . .

"I'm not sitting here in the goddam desert!" swore Dorris. " 'Project Unsightly'—whatever in hell is that? *Unsightly's* the right name for it! How many tens of thousands of tax dollars —? Jesus, no wonder the Soviets are laughing."

"Russia has its UFO problems too," said Shriver quickly. "Back in '59 UFOs were playing ducks and drakes over Sverdlovak—that's a tactical missile HQ—for twenty-four hours, dodging MIGs. What's more —"

"Mister, be quiet. You are spoiling my day."

Whenever Deacon rehearsed events now, he no longer tried to locate at what point their common experience, shared with the world at large, had become 'other'—inaccessible to rational analysis. He was beyond that point. His thoughts were ordered differently now. In a sense, he reflected, he *was* an alien. He had sucked all the alienness into himself when the phantom Eta Cassiopeians were obliterated.

"It's like a teaching mechanism, Barry," he said soothingly. "A dynamic caused by the nature of reality. Its essence is that there has to be constantly an area of reality outside our own expanding sphere of knowledge. That's the only way a universe can be."

"Pretty weird teaching device—that burns people! Scares and confuses and crushes everybody!"

Deacon glanced at his palm. The irritation had reached a tolerable plateau, though the skin looked raw and blistered.

"Say, John, what's with your hand?"

"I touched Khidr. I grasped Knowledge."

"Take a look at that hand, Captain. Burnt! Tissue damage— maybe from radiation."

207

"Crap. He did it himself. For the effect."

"It'll clear up, don't bother about it. I was in the force-field of knowledge, that's all."

"You touch the Green Man and get gangrene, eh?"

"As soon as you grasp the nettle of this knowledge, Barry —"

"You get stung!"

"*Of course.* It's a sort of compensation factor. Whenever you investigate, you alter. When the thing doing the investigating is part of the system being investigated, you damage the perfection —the wholeness of the model. The model's what we call reality. You inject some extra consciousness, a higher awareness, so something must be deleted—if you're stuck on the same level. Or else reality would be overful. You actually take up part of the programme that sustains the 'authentic world'. It bleeds out . . . some data, which sustain flesh and blood and the world; bleeds it by as much as it's enriched."

"UFO bitches!"

"When we understand better, when we really know how to enter into the simulatory being of our universe, we'll be able to manipulate it in ways that would once have seemed magical. That's where magic actually comes into it! That's the 'higher science' of the Saucer People—who are only us, of course, part of our collective psychic life."

Dorrish shoved past them to open a steel box painted with a red cross and take out a can of Coke. He tore the tab off, drank, then passed the can to Tom.

Michael gazed out at the angle the rutted cone hill made with the dry stream bed—a pointer through the Earth to somewhere else. "I think we're all mad," he shivered. "We've been mad for days. Swept up in madness. Suzie was right."

"Now you're talking, boy!" smirked Dorris.

"I . . . I'm coming out of it. Thank God it's all gone. Crashed and crushed. We made that thing ourselves. It was our own *tulpa*—a sort of witchcraft we performed collectively. We never went to the Moon. The aliens were all wrong. I don't know where we did go, or how, or what power we tapped—"

Deacon patted him on the arm with his Khidr hand. "We

went outside normal cognition, that's where. Now we've re-entered. You're right that we didn't go to the Moon in any ordinary sense—though it was still the Moon."

"Changing your story now that the Air Force is coming?" enquired Dorris.

"Not at all," laughed Shriver. "Who do you think reported this to Edwards? I did! Last night, from the Astro. Edwards is a major test centre. This isn't the sort of thing they'd pass up. Though I never knew there was a Project Unsightly! That's strange. It must be secret. 'Out of sight, out of mind.' Don't take any notice of these two, Captain. They're burnt out .They've blown their fuses."

When the Cayuse helicopter from Edwards circled overhead, frail as a dragonfly, they took off to guide it.

Both helicopters landed beside the wreck of the car. A Major Bower emerged, a great balding man in his early forties, wearing blue tinted sunglasses. His eyes were small and piggy behind them; rooting eyes. His pilot, a Lieutenant Molinelli, photographed the wreck then checked it with a geiger counter.

"Normal readings, Sir —"

Major Bower prodded one of the splayed wheels with his toe like a child giving the token touch to a patch of wet paint, to prove it wet.

"Would you please check my friend's hand?" Shriver tugged Deacon forward.

The Lieutenant complied. "That's normal too," he said. He peered at the hand without touching it. "Seems like an allergy rash of some kind. Poison ivy? Not here, I guess! Could be some plant, though."

Major Bower lit a cheroot. "Let's hear your story, gentlemen."

The Lieutenant produced a recorder.

The sun shone hotly now. Dust devils danced. Major Bower seemed unworried by the heat. Deacon too felt unaffected; cloaked in vigour. He ceased paying attention as Shriver talked. He hunted for that little prickly Opuntia cactus he had fixed his eyes on the night before. It was still there. It continued mutely to exist, to sustain its own reality. As did a stone, as did the furthest star.

Yet that wasn't quite correct, reflected Deacon.

A stone, and a star, were not really separate entities. They weren't really discrete loci of being. Particles constantly vanished and came into being out of Void within each of them. Photons from the star impacted on the stone. The cactus soaked up sunlight and breathed out oxygen for animal life, which incorporated cactus fruit and other animal life as food, and excreted mineral manure for the plants in the soil; while body cells were constantly being sloughed and new ones built. Material was constantly recycling . . .

How did one define an 'entity'? Was it a single body cell, or the whole body? Or was it the whole ecology this body was part of? Where did one draw the line? Was a stone a separate object—or the single atoms that made it up? Or the much larger rock it must have fractured from? Or the whole desert environment? When did a stone become too small to be a stone? This was surely the 'Gebraudi' message, too, with their talk of Whole Planet Life: a human being drew the line at such and such a point, yet actually it was quite arbitrary. Really, all the 'separate' entities and objects in the world were more like amplitude peaks along a continuous line of being. And so the world was dual: it was continuous—yet full of separate objects, too, from innumerable higher and lower points of view.

Nor was the consciousness that resided in all these separate points of view quite so myriad and separate as it seemed. Rather, it was all one and continuous—yet with innumerable local amplitude peaks, resonances of individual beings each possessing its own unique energy signature, its own signature of personal awareness. Consciousness was individual, for the individual beings—yet it was also continuous; and being continuous, so it partook of the original Void Awareness from which it had whirlpooled forth. So it was rooted in that deeper continuum of awareness of 'no-thing' whatever, existing before and after the universe peaked out into all its separate objects and existences.

The separating mechanism, he had already seen in his vision of the vortex. It was: point of view, observer and observed, leading inevitably to the consciousness of separate minds. The potential for separate consciousness was built into the basic subject-object, cause-effect, law-obedient nature of reality. And all these separate, 'individual' foci of awareness, the existence of all the separate entities there were, prevented the universe from realizing itself and vanishing, for as long as these existed.

Deacon went on staring at the little Opuntia cactus, his eyes transfixed by its spines, as Shriver told his tale of alien visitors who had come to heal the Earth . . .

Captain Dorris sweated heavily. Presently he fetched a glossy gun club magazine to fan himself. Michael sat down limply after a while; he huddled, hating the Major and his interrogation methods—unendurable stress by heat.

How medieval to torture the mad . . .!

"Major Bower," said Shriver, "I never heard anything about a Project Unsightly, and I should have done because I interest myself in these matters."

"So I gathered."

"What does the name mean? Does it mean that you actually know something, but it's under wraps? I was at Muroc in 1954, Major—as an airman. What I saw there —" Shriver told of Eisenhower and the landing; the Major looked increasingly amused.

"Nothing happened at Edwards in '54," the Major said, when he'd heard Shriver out. "Five saucers landed? That's a new one on me!"

" They weren't real extraterrestrial saucers, you understand?" Shriver pleaded. "They were projections from the world-mind. The real aliens explained —"

"Maybe you saw some lights in the sky in '54. I can't agree that any flying saucers —"

"Not flying saucers in the mechanical sense! But phenomena, nonetheless, that can be detected and harnessed using the alien science! All that wreckage is up on the Moon just waiting for us."

"Mr Shriver, if saucers landed at a US Air Force base over twenty years ago, wouldn't the world be a different place today? Project Unsightly? It's a low key affair. Still in a feasibility study stage, actually. We're test-running a few cases here and there across the country, to cost the exercise. I guess you could call it a political thing. Election promises, you know? The President said he'd open the files. We're concentrating on witnesses, as much as what they witnessed."

"At least that's an improvement on Blue Book! But this case is different. We've got a car here made over as a genuine spacecraft."

"A psychological approach," smiled Major Bower. "Something new. If we do decide to go ahead we certainly won't make any secret of it. But to announce it first, then maybe cut it off because it can't be done? No one would believe us. Once bitten, twice shy. There's been enough paranoia about the whole business in the past."

The Major trod on his cigar butt, grinding it out near Deacon's cactus.

The Major was lying. Shriver knew. Something was happening.

A new organization had been set up.

"We can pack the three of you into the Cayuse. It's only built for four, so you'll have to squeeze up. We'd like to interview you all some more at Edwards. Have the Base psychologist run a few tests?"

A psychiatrist. Because they were crazy, thought Michael. This new project was set up to study craziness.

"Unsightly's located at Edwards then?"

"No, we're in Colorado. Edwards passed your report on. I flew down overnight. It sounded promising enough."

"Got on the spot real quick," grinned Molinelli.

"You're at Boulder? Where the Condon Committee —?"

Major Bower shook his head. "We're outside Colorado Springs, at the Air Force Academy. You see, no secrets?"

"What about the car?"

"Oh, we'll call in a Chinook to lift this wreck out. Keep the desert tidy. I'm a great believer in ecology."

"You said the new approach was psychological! If that's so, *what do you want the car for?*"

"Part of your story, isn't it? Material evidence."

"Just one minute, Major," interrupted Captain Dorris. "This car was stolen. That's police business."

Major Bower took the Captain aside, and talked to him for a while.

"It's *help*," whispered Deacon. "Don't you see? *Karama.*"

Shriver shook his head frustratedly. He knew, and the Air Force knew. They were going to take the Thunderbird off him; and there was no other way out.

Squeezed into the Cayuse behind Major Bower and the lieutenant, they were soon flying west by north over the hot wasteland towards Four Corners desert crossroads and Edwards A.F.B.

THIRTY-TWO

THE AIR FORCE Academy Dance Band, "The Falconaires", sat out in the sunshine under the Colorado sky rehearsing *Dixie* on saxophone, trombone, harmonium, trumpet, drums. A harsh bronze eagle, wingspread on a granite plinth, stood over them. Fountains sprayed from a moat, behind, surrounding a tiny concrete apron where a small white aircraft was parked on display.

Major James Bower paused to listen for a while, nostalgically. He'd played the moody horn himself when he was in that same band years ago. As a group of cadets marched past, his gaze drifted to the aluminium spires of the Chapel, those seventeen serried wings upright against the sky; beyond, pine-stippled hills rumpled upward towards snowy Pikes Peak . . .

A legend was carved in the plinth beneath the eagle's beak.

MAN'S FLIGHT
THROUGH LIFE IS
SUSTAINED BY THE
POWER OF HIS
KNOWLEDGE

The motto had always existed for him as an item of given data rather than actual words to be read; but now he looked back to read them and wonder.

They'd talked a lot about knowledge, those three! At least the two older ones. About alien know-how scattered on the Moon . . . and occult knowledge . . . The boy had soon started to deny it all.

Patting his briefcase contentedly, he walked over to the entrance of Fairchild Hall, the academic building.

The third floor housed Behavioural Sciences. He went along to the office of the Permanent Professor and Head of Department, knocked, saluted Colonel Paul E. Coleman. Also in the room were Tenure Professor Lt. Col. Walter 'White' Sands and Associate Professor Major Leland Fischer.

Away to the east, beyond Eisenhower Golf Course, a pair of silvery high performance gliders could be seen executing tight thermal soaring, spiralling serenely up above Falcon Stadium, maintaining the notion of its perimeter high up in the air. As the two turned in the sunlight, they appeared to shift shape constantly—becoming boomerangs, then lozenges of light, then lazy aircraft again—as though one of them was losing mass to the other only to pick it up again half a turn later.

"I'm still concerned," objected Sands, "at having Unsightly connected with the Academy. Our brief is simply to provide cadets with the tools to become career officers, period. Either the Advisory Council or the Board of Visitors are going to kick up. We ought to be increasing the number of qualified minority candidates, *etcetera*."

"Several hundred faculty members are already doing advanced research, White," said Colonel Coleman. "It's expected. The academic élite of the Air Force are here—the spearhead. Besides, this will only be the public face of Unsightly. You know that."

"It's like building a new weapons system. It isn't our brief."

"But it is. This is an intellectual problem, not a simple nuts and bolts one. I'm sure we're doing the right thing. Anyhow, the Chairman of the Armed Services Committee thinks so —"

"Because he's seen a UFO himself."

"— which effectively squares the Board. And the C-in-C Europe is in favour; so there's the Council sewn up."

"It's an educational problem too," nodded Bower. "In a very real sense."

"I feel even more dubious about teaching it—even at fourth year or graduate levels!"

Bower sorted through his briefcase. "White, it'll be listed under *Beh Sci* 480 along with Psychological Warfare, and *Beh* Sci 495, 'Psychological Operations'. Believe me, it belongs. It's something in the mass mind: an image of deep discontents, hopes and fears. We have to come to terms with it a damn sight better than Blue Book ever did. It doesn't go away—so what are we, ostriches? We need some decent awareness of this in the upper echelons of the Service. What's the point in talking about Psywar and turning a blind eye to this powerful form of Psywar already going on right within ourselves? Let me tell you about this latest case; it's a real wow . . ."

". . . so the boy showed obvious neurotic symptoms—sexually maladjusted, correct? And our ex-pilot Shriver had a way-back major delusional system festering in him—war trauma, guilt, resentment and fear brought to the boil by the loss of a strong father-protector, which happened to be his own role as a pilot. He lost his whole sense of role when his Dad got killed in a car smash. You'll note how a car crops up again as salvation mechanism? The British professor Deacon seemed to be the most normally adjusted, given the *caveat* that he does work in a very fringe area of Psychology —"

"What about the car itself?" asked 'White' Sands.

"Oh, it was rubbish of course. It had been made into a sort of cargo cult object! A horsehair mattress and other muck was stuffed in the engine. Bits and pieces of this and that."

"They hardly had time to mess it around, did they?"

215

"Well, they all had major blank-outs in their 'experiences'. Which the good professor described as 'exiting from normal cognition'. Don't smile, it's a good description. Collectively, they got up to some very strange antics. I personally think the car was stolen for some joyride and they happened on it later, *in that state*. Someone had really trashed it. Cannibalised the engine, used the car as a trashcan, put it through a crusher then dumped it. Don't forget that Shriver, our UFO buff, *was* heading back on a sort of pilgrimage to Edwards, as the original locus of his delusional system. Out in Adamski's own desert! I don't think it was any coincidence they all turned up there. Finding this trashed car when they were already in a highly abnormal state of mind, the whole moonflight delusion blew up. There's no hint of anyone but their own three selves ever seeing that car in England, of course!"

"They do seem to have got from London to the Mojave pretty quickly," remarked Major Fischer. "With no documents!"

"They obviously flew to LA International then made a lucky connexion with a Greyhound bus or something. They just had time to. Or they flew to Las Vegas, to be on that side of Edwards. Nobody saw them after lunchtime of the day they 'took off'—on their own admission—even though they swear they left in the evening. That's Greenwich time. It's a tight schedule —but possible. Anyway, our Professor Deacon pulled this very same trick before—flying off to Egypt just as 'inexplicably' by jet. So Shriver was Mojave-bound, mentally. They collaborated psychically, as it were—creating a triple *folie*. Pretty weird, I grant, but not much weirder than a lot of so-called UFO events."

"You're sure they don't realize this?" pressed Fischer.

"Our base psychiatrist at Edwards wanted to question them under hypnosis, but the boy got hysterical. The Professor had a magnificent excuse involving 'void-minds' and 'jokes' to explain why it wouldn't do any good. Shriver had a fit of temperament about custody of the vehicle. Anyway, they'd only have told us what they believed."

"One thing I'll say, it beats hijacking planes into a cocked hat."

"Nice analogy, Leland. In many respects hijacking's a kind

of mental epidemic. People who'd never have behaved that way normally get triggered by hearing about other hijacks. Just as potential suicides are switched on by seeing car smashes on TV. Likewise with UFO flaps. We aren't as fully conscious and rational as we think we are! The sad truth is that most of the damn population is maladjusted one way or another. There's a deep irrationality just under the surface veneer. Psiwar? Like I say, society wages it on itself! We have to understand these irrational forces. We need to diagnose them and be able to use them. What price 'Man's Flight through Life' if an aircrew were to enter this 'UFO-conscious' state on a mission? Or, God forbid, astronauts? Obviously it's a very powerful psychic factor in a lot of people's minds. One day we might actually need to use these forces for, well, national motivation, or abroad. The Russians aren't into psychic research and UFOs just as a hobby."

"Thus the hidden face of Unsightly," nodded Colonel Coleman.

"So the Professor and the boy got repatriated?"

"Best course. Immigration saw to it. Couple of illegal aliens." Bower chuckled appreciatively. "Our professor told us he felt like an alien. He was damn well right! That man Shriver still has the bit between his teeth. Believes there's a cover-up—all the old paranoia. We tried telling him the car was junk, but would he listen? I guess there'll be a fair amount of idiot publicity. Self-defeating, needless to say: obviously nobody *drives* to the Moon. Speaking for Unsightly, though, I await developments with interest."

In the thermal over Falcon Stadium, the twin gliders exchanged shape once more as they spiralled. They swelled and shrank, swelled again and shrank again. Reaching the top of the heat funnel at last, they shared mass equally and floated off westwards over the Douglas Valley housing area in the direction of the mountains . . .

PART FIVE

THIRTY-THREE

SUZIE WAITED BEYOND the ticket barrier, her hair a crackling flame. She wore jeans, a black pinstripe jacket with frilly-fronted white blouse, and a green scarf knotted round her throat. She smiled, she waved. She skipped up and down. Michael picked his way through the mass of holidaymakers hauling suitcases and children along. The train driver sat high in his diesel cab watching with blank detachment. Sunlight filtered from a glass canopy through fumes.

They kissed quickly. Suzie held both his hands, squeezed them tightly, then drew him away through the black stone arch out into the biting freshness of sea air, which wasn't so much cold this June day as incisively, almost surgically cleansing.

"Look, we have come through!" she laughed. "You made it too, Mike. I'm so happy!"

"Yes, I came through." Not, he thought, John or Barry.

Gulls mewed overhead and swooped down the blue slate roofs of boarding houses. Lace-curtained windows, steps and stonework shone with distemper, ornamental steetlamps had been freshly painted white and blue. The world was new, refreshed. He even started to admire a stepladder on a window cleaner's barrow, till he realized that he'd seen barrows and stepladders before.

In a small park, among begonia beds, boys crouched round the cobbled rim of a pond trapping sticklebacks in nets on bamboo canes. The sun shone through the curved glass of their jamjars to a point of focus, sending the tiny fish clustering to the surface gulping air. He saw it all magnified; an enlarged reality. Each fish, each flower petal.

"It *was* madness," he agreed. "A sort of shared psychosis spreading its suckers like an octopus, pulling us all in. It's gone now. It's all over." For us two at any rate. "I've been reading a lot of Industrial Psychology lately."

"Yes, you wrote."

"I'd like a solid down-to-earth job. If I can get any sort of degree after all this."

"I'm not worrying about any of that right now. I might retake the year from next October." She grinned. "Or I mightn't. Just now I'm quite simply busy being happy. Enjoying health. My God, not being haunted with sickly nightmares! It's something I can feel like an actual physical object, this happiness—the business of being sane and properly alive! I can feel it as clearly as I feel this pavement under my feet. Do you feel the pavement with every step you take?"

The terrace, descending, met the Esplanade arcing its way around the wide sands from Bean Head to the south (with its chalk stump of a lighthouse and rolling grassy dunes—steps of sand from which Sandstairs took its name) northward to the old-time fishing village of Liddle Bay, mainly a caravan site nowadays. Dominating the sweep of promenade was a stranded whale of a palace, a grounded zeppelin sprayed with cement, its ground floor sheltering amusement arcades, souvenir shops, cafés, and its belly housing an ice-rink and bowling alley. From each end of this mock palace rose belfries without any bells, suggesting a seaside cathedral. The open skating rink behind had been lapped by drifting sands, which a small bulldozer was spreading back across the beach. A tractor dragged a litter scoop along, sieving out yesterday's broken glass and other droppings.

Real. Real.

"You're better off out of College at the moment," Michael said. "It's pretty embarrassing. Reporters have been turning up, even a few Americans and French—and there was a Japanese bloke. Bloody Shriver! And UFO nuts too. Some TV mob wanted to do a nice little documentary reconstruction. That's why I pushed off this weekend. Well, one reason. A minor one. The main one being . . ." He smiled at her.

Two rheumy-eyed pensioners watched them abstractedly from inside a bus shelter as they crossed the Esplanade. Next to the shelter, the blood-globule of a wartime German mine was painted

222

bright red, set on a plinth for children to rattle pennies into as they clung to the black detonator spikes.

Real.

White railings were bobbly with salt rust under their coat of fresh paint. Grassy banks dropped down to the beach below them. A wedge of black rocks emerged from the sands; the rocks ran out to sea in long slabs supporting a sewer pipe buried in a concrete pathway. Glassy rolling pins of waves rippled in, parting like a head of hair along this walkway, tumbling into cracks and traps among the rocks, shattering into soda spray, leaving only a stain and a gleam behind.

He stared out to sea, where the flux of water perpetually and indefinably shifted its contours without resolving on any definite final form. A sense of boundless possibilities opening out in all directions was the sea's gift; so people came to it. Yet it had no will, no object-consciousness, to settle for one possibility rather than another; it was pure potentiality—a whole sea full of it. The sea seemed to be nothing but muscle; muscle at rest, muscle at play, rippling and rolling. It gleamed like a wrestler freshly oiled. Pure muscle without a bone in its whole body, yet stronger than if bones constrained it. He watched that plane of muscle with its fretted edge grow thinner as it flowed up the beach, fatter as it slid back again. People, incredible to contemplate, were standing up to their waists in this muscle, even ducking themselves head over heels in it, heedless of the infinite slab of idiot tissue it was.

"A nervous breakdown," he murmured. "Somehow it existed out there, not just in my own head. Collectively for all of us. It was a collapse of rational connections, of the links between events—between cause and effect. Links between people too: my parents, you and me. That was the worst part. Sanity—the texture of reality—got frayed. I'd say it was like crowd hysteria, a kind of collective irrational vision—Nazism on a minor scale —in this little bubble of our lives . . ."

The sight of the sea calmed him, and his eyes wandered to the horizon, settling on the pure curving line there: visible proof of the shaping and definition of the world, a rationality that bound the ever-inchoate muscles of the sea. A smoke stack from some ship hidden below the horizon drifted very slowly south.

Suzie leaned across the railing, her jacket hanging open. Under the thin fabric of her blouse, hidden till now by the frills, he noticed two firm threads. Brushing his fingers under her scarf, he drew up a small silver pendant cross.

"I thought you didn't —?"

"I saw a devil," she grinned, unconcerned, "so maybe there's a God, who knows? It's only an amulet, Mike, a lucky charm. I wear it to please my mother. She still thinks a bit superstitiously about nervous . . . upsets."

He let the chain slide back again.

"It doesn't mean much to me compared with the solidness of this pavement or this rail!" Her knuckles tightened on the bobbly metal; a scrap of paint flaked off against her fingernail, exposing some underlying rust. "See, this is real . . . Lovely, good and solid. The cross is just Sunday School gimcrack—an electroplated childhood mood. Something from before, from long ago. I'd actually prefer there wasn't a God, Mike. Just the world, no more. It's enough. Don't worry, I shan't become a nun! 'All things bright and beautiful'," she sang, " 'just exist, that's all.' Look down there."

A dog was racing circles round a man, leaping up at the leash he flicked, whip-like, at it. A dog—or was it a lion? With its white mane, leonine flanks, wasp waist, tight naked little bottom? Its master had shaved it from the waist downwards, to grow a lion's mane round its chest and neck. Waist, thighs and bottom shone so smoothly in the sun; it might have been shaved this very morning by the lion tamer. The man cracked his whip, sending his white thin-hipped lion racing round him, leaping, snarling. In love with that white lion, he caught it a stinging flick on its naked flank so that it scampered into the bright ripple of incoming tide, stamping up a spray of electricity. Leaping light, electric sparks, white muscled buttocks.

The man threw out his chest, laughed and laughed with the giant poodle.

"And of *their* existence," she said firmly, "there's no doubt." Suzie kicked the lowest rail emphatically with her shoe; and Michael winced, recalling something else . . . an incident outside of time, outside of causes. Involving one Helen Caprowicz who had maybe died in a car crash somewhere in upstate New York—whose life and death he'd dreamt, collectively, out in the open. The sea drank up the memory. It was only an improbable event, one that had only tended to exist and had now become quite improbable.

"When they stop existing they become lovely soil and grass and other solid things," she added.

The lion tamer swung up his left arm to look at his wrist watch. He whistled for the dog, turned and trudged from the sea towards a flight of stone stairs. As he left hard wet sand behind and waded through the softer hinterland his footsteps grew more laboured, his bearing more sluggish. He sat at the base of the steps to empty his shoes. By now he'd become demoralised, as if the joy and energy generated a few moments earlier had drained away through the soles of his feet. The white lion wasn't affected by the journey through softer sand; it still capered, kicking up sand in the same electric way it had kicked up spray. Yet now that its owner had capitulated, it was plainly just an overgrown poodle with bare shivering flanks and a shaggy grotesque mane . . .

"Let's visit the funfair," she suggested.

So they fed fruit machines in the bowls of the white zeppelin. They paid a Laughing Sailor doll locked up in a glass case to rock from side to side guffawing at them. Clutching the red firing button on a periscope they fired orange torpedo tracks through green gloom at merchantmen hauling from island shelter to island shelter. The orange tracks fore-shortened away, with a ratchetty putter, and the background sky lit with a red clanging volcano of pretended destruction. They steered a crane over a turning treasure island of trinkets, rings and dried-up cigarettes, trying to snare the single banknote pinned to a wooden cube; they grabbed up a cigarette instead. Although it was stale and the tobacco tending to fall out of the end, they shared it, taking a few puffs each.

They dared the House That Jack Built. Wooden floors bucked and heaved underfoot as mechanical muscles flexed and unflexed beneath the planks, imitating the swell of the sea. They kept their balance. A narrow corridor tried to pull them apart, one side of the floor jerking ahead while the other side jerked back. They held together. Another floor slewed sideways under the wooden walls like a scythe; only a strip of dirtier wood down the centre was safe. They survived, unreaped. They laughed at themselves in distorting mirrors: blown up into balloons, pinched in at the midriff like dumb-bells. They turned into Siamese twins. It didn't matter; the shape distortions, like the treacheries of the floors, were simple deceptions, trivial snares, creaky old practical jokes. With a siren wail, a draught whipped up their legs. Suzie gasped and giggled but she was wearing no skirt to be whirled in the air around her waist, revealing old time nylons and suspenders; the funfair's repertoire of tricks was out of date.

Finally a moving belt carried them down and out through rotating drums which banged together, bounced apart then bounded back again. It was like entering a car-wash. With upright rollers for . . . *crushing cars*! Michael hesitated only briefly before bunching his fists before him and riding down the belt, bursting the spinning drums apart—which weren't quite as light as a feather, since he slightly sprained his wrist on them. He laughed as loudly as the sailor in his glass case. Look, we have come through.

They emerged from the zeppelin; now it was hot. The beach was getting crowded. Territories were being defined and consolidated with deckchairs, sand castles, transistor radios and beachballs.

They sat outside a low white stucco hotel, built in Art Deco flats and curves, and drank pints of John Smith's bitter at an iron table.

They walked on. They ate fried haddocks, wrapped in last week's newspaper.

They caught a bus to Bean Head and walked on beyond, between grass-laced dunes and sea; the sands were deserted this far from town. The tide line was spotted with cork, worm-holed wood, sea coal, dried bladder wrack, knobs of green glass. They beachcombed; he found a razor shell, took the comb from his pocket and slid it into the horny case, then slipped the shell and comb into his pocket. A warm breeze from off the land teased milk teeth from the waves. Oyster catchers sprinted and scattered into the wind.

A line of tilted concrete blocks straddled the beach from the dunes right out into the water, to foil advancing Panzer tanks which never came.

The real world.

"I suppose in a sense we all got something out of it. Barry Shriver found his proper niche as one-man ginger group to nag NASA to visit the backside of the Moon—even if he didn't get the appropriate junk to haul round the lecture halls . . . So now he can spend the rest of his life accusing them of suppressing evidence. Bloody Deacon got 'illuminated'—now I suppose he's off on some secret pilgrimage. And you got an amulet to wear. Which is more than I could winch up from treasure island back there!"

"Oh no, Mike, don't you see, I got the whole world given me —more tangibly than I ever gripped it since I was a kid! This world had grown fuzzy without me realizing it. It was like a bit of muzak I'd been humming without paying attention to. Maybe I needed a shock . . . the absurdity of what happens when you don't hold on to everything that's really there. That leaching away was turning me into a sort of merry automaton—like a musician on automatic pilot because he's bored with the piece and the conductor. I swear from now on I shall play every single note! My own horror slapped me in the face, and made me *be* again. I gained everything there is. I regained it. The sharpness of things. The scrupulousness." She whistled a tune: it was the Queen of the Night's aria from *The Magic Flute*. Her pursed lips reached and achieved the highest notes of all. A cross wind was chopping the rollers up into ignominious fluffy things now that scampered and scrapped childishly. All the deep undulatory rhythm was hidden under a coat of icing—neutralised, for a day of play.

"Can there really be such a thing as a contagious nervous breakdown? A whole group of people failing in their duty to

227

reality?" she asked. "There must be. And I was vulnerable, oh yes! I wasn't really plugged in to the world, you see? My points weren't making contact. What did you get out of it, Mike? Apart from . . ." Briefly her confidence sagged. She looked haunted and bewildered, unable to accommodate the datum or neutralise it. "Apart from a trip to America," she said quickly. "What did you get?" A challenge, now; a demand.

Michael looked at Suzie and he thought: *Why, you of course.* He said nothing aloud, but she laughed anyway.

"That's really corny!" (He stroked her hair.) "We should make love, Mike. There's not a soul about. We should make contact again . . . Get plugged in." She winked lewdly.

"Come on," she ordered. So they climbed to a hollow in the dunes, a cup of soft sand lipped by marram and fern grass, veined with purple cranesbill. From that dune crater they could just spy the main mass of the sea if they craned their necks, though sands and separate waves were hidden. He shed his anorak, she her jacket. They spread them out.

They were in perfect key this time.

None of the old problem. Nothing premature. Michael made love with an almost mechanical perfection.

In the midst of their love he raised his head briefly and stared out to sea through the grass. A ball of golden light bobbed about above the waves far out. But the Sun was in the west, not in the east. That ball of light was neither the Sun nor the Sun's reflection . . .

Looking away, he buried his face in her red hair; inhaling, he possessed her—who now possessed herself.

It was only an afterimage of madness. An aftersensation, not on the retina but in the mind's eye . . .

Inside Suzie, then, he died the little death. When he looked again later, the ball of light had vanished. It wouldn't come back, he was sure.

They got dressed, hiked back along the sands to Bean Head and caught the bus into Sandstairs again, where the streets were packed with holidaymakers trooping homeward.

THIRTY-FOUR

ABSENTLY, MARY DEACON unlocked the glass-fronted cabinet and removed one of the fragile Goss Ware curios: a miniature china cruet bearing the town crest of Caernarvon. She held it quizzically between thumb and forefinger, then let it fall. It bounced, unbroken, on the carpet. So she trod on it; it crushed easily.

"Please don't." John's voice caressed, but from a great distance, from another world. "If you'd been where I've been—"

"Oh, I know that *I've* only ever been on ordinary holidays!" She removed a tiny jug in the shape of a harp: a Victorian souvenir of Aberystwyth. "Can the tourists on the Moon buy these?" she asked tartly, and dropped the harp. Hitting the broken cruet, it cracked in half, emitting the only note it ever had or would. "They're *mine*, so I'll do what I like with them! Oh, they only cost a few pounds each. They can't be more than a hundred years old. What's a hundred years to sweep away? Or love? Or a family? Or a career? Where's *my* souvenir?"

"Career?" Deacon frowned. "The Vice-Chancellor only said he wanted to *speak* to me."

"He'll ask you to resign, quite rightly too."

"This time I didn't give any silly interviews—"

"Friend Shriver did. And what about next time, John?"

He shrugged. "I could use some free time. I've got a lot to think about. I might have to write a book."

"To guarantee you never get a decent post again? If you must burst out, why couldn't you have had some sordid little affair with a secretary? So much simpler."

"Something *is* bursting inside me."

"Like a rotten appendix?" Discriminatingly Mary selected a tiny bowl.

229

"Please stop doing that."

"Oh, I love doing it. The name of the game is wanton destruction."

No doubt she would carry on breaking her curios in the same restrainedly discriminating manner for as long as he stayed in the same room as her. Killing her hostages one by one. Her own hostages. Wounding herself exemplarily, as Bonaparte (or whatever its name had been) had nearly wounded itself to death on the Moon—in an alternative reality which had now readjusted itself, renormalised. The false infinity was gone; the real world had swept back tidally. Except that . . . the glimpse of infinite underlying shores stayed with him now forever.

He walked through the house, out of the kitchen door into the garden, and stared up past the great horse chestnut tree overlapping from the neighbouring garden, its flower candles deliquescing into decayed pink confetti on the lawn. The sky was flocky with cumulus; a light plane buzzed overhead.

Shutting one eye, he watched a little floater in the vitreous humour of the other eye traverse that sky-blue screen like an aerial jellyfish . . .

An impairment in his vision.

The universe must envision itself, he reflected, if it is to erase itself and become Void again. It must model itself, through the agency of life—whose nature was therefore metaphorical: all theories, belief systems and experiences tending towards that envisioning, but only in parable form, built out of the things of this world. Life was a vehicle for approaching the Void-Awareness which was the true tenor of existence; which was the meaning behind meaning—beyond definition, or object and subject, or effect and cause. Life was the literal meaning of the world, for just as long as the true meaning evaded life. In the meantime, therefore, one lived the metaphor of one's life. One sustained the world. That was the task.

How should he proceed? By heedlessness? So that the world could go on?

Ah, but he had grown heedful.

He stared up at the sky, hunting for his own self regarding

230

him through some extraordinary entry point—where he had once already been. He did not find himself. That floater in his eye suddenly seemed like a necessary imperfection to full vision, which let life go on; a blind spot which must be there.

Maybe heedlessness was best, after all.

He went back into the house, to Mary in the lounge.

"Maybe we could try something else entirely?" he suggested. "Maybe we could run a market garden, or manage a pub?"

His wife recoiled, as though slapped.

"I hardly think so! That's even stupider and crueller."

"I can't go on doing the same thing. It's all changed, Mary."

"At least you can remember my name."

Memory: the tag of past time in the mind . . . Which could sometimes come unstuck. Which had done so when he looped back to Shep's death and Suzie's torment and Michael's initiation—becoming alien, capable of being anyone or anything at all while the 'Khidr mode' lasted. He had really seemed to dart about through time, then, being someone other than himself—yet retaining a sense of himself, even so.

He recollected the UFO flight carefully again. He'd been aware of who he was; yet he had fissioned—split apart—and had been hunting for himself. When he caught up with himself, the flight ended, and he was back in the ordinary desert.

So, in his flight, he had evaded not only the time-tag but also the ego-tag that must be time-bound to the present, glueing attention to the ongoing world. Yet he had done so without real loss of identity. Other connections *could* be made within the network of existence. One could travel through space-time. Yet ego is the loading stabilizer—the baseline. Ego constantly pulls one back. Roof brain chatter glues one to the present moment: the clichés of existence. Chatter under a roof . . . What other way of living is there?

"I think I'll walk over and talk to the Vice-Chancellor at home," he decided.

"What, *now?*"

"No time like the present," he smiled, knowing how untrue this cliché was. "I must get out, Mary. I need to take a walk and think."

She shrugged. "Go ahead. You don't have to ask my permission. You're a grown-up."

The stranger appeared from behind the pillar box as Deacon neared the corner. Deacon wasn't paying must attention to the street, and hadn't noticed him till then. The man wore a dark suit, dark spectacles, a tie with an emerald box hedge pattern. He held a map. A street plan. His face was suntanned, sharp and dark. Somebody from abroad hunting for a flat.

"Mr Deacon?"

How did he know his name? Deacon stared at him.

"We've met before, John."

"Have we? Where?"

The man consulted his map. "I was looking for you."

"You won't find me on a map!"

"Ah, this is a special map, John. An extraordinary one." No car turned into the street and nobody walked along it. Not even a dog or cat prowled by. No birds were on the wing. Time might have stopped, or slowed to a snail's pace.

Deacon peered at the map. It was the street plan of a strange city with no obvious place names on it, nor scale to it nor key to the symbols used. A maze of a city. Was this Cairo, or Isfahan, or Akhetaton? Or some city on an alien world? Or a city not yet built? Or an invisible city which existed and always had existed just beyond some borderline?

"I would introduce myself," the man murmured. "But really, I have no name, though I'm known by many names . .."

A man free of false ego? Someone who could travel the whole manifold network of consciousness events? Just as Deacon yearned to . . . The city plan seemed to contain within itself the complete circuitry of the *Lemegeton* of King Solomon, all its channels and thoroughfares properly linked together, with whole suburbs of permutations and interlinkages. This was a city that he would dearly love to inhabit. It seemed infinitely detailed. The more that he gazed at it, the more there was to see. He read its mandala palaces, its pentacle plazas, its cabbalistic ziggurats, its courts of symmetry which were at once places, scripts, and ideas: locations that dissolved into ideas more substantial than

232

brick or tile, into self-generating patterns which spun the city forth from its own idea of itself. He read its water gardens of many depths. He read its mutating mazes: for the city was alive, and thoughtful, constantly evolving. The city was the higher patterning awareness.

At last he understood the full significance of that little book of magic, the *Lemegeton*, the 'little key'. It contained many symbols of power—and symbols, as Tom Havelock had suggested at that meeting of the Group in February, possessed an existence of their own beyond any individual mind that experienced them. This had to be so—for the higher order systems in the universe, which caused lower order systems to arise, evolve towards them, and finally become them, were powerful symbol-entities, symbol systems superior to the 'event-thoughts' that formed the web of ordinary consensus events in which Humanity still dwelt.

Yet the disconnected sketches of 'keys' to these symbol-forces, as presented by the *Lemegeton*, were like so many different components of a dismantled engine being used, by all too human sorcerers, not together to power a vehicle, but separately as so many blunt instruments to kill or maim, or find buried treasure, or compel success in love: as so many tools to sustain human Ego.

Just so had Deacon first launched himself into UFO-consciousness research: to see his name on startling research papers, to attract Air Force dollars from America, to win power over the UFO force. He remembered with a wry amusement, now, his childish euphoria at these prospects—and that grotesque press conference when he returned from Egypt. When he'd returned to Granton this last time, though, there had been none of that. It had been burnt out of him. He had surrendered it—along with himself—to the force that took him into its heart in the Mojave Desert.

The little book contained a whole array of little partial keys; and side by side was a list of the lusts, aggressions, ambitions and false desires, covetings and appetites they catered for. He had become nakedly aware of these on board Khidr's UFO craft as he tried to navigate towards the truth at the same time as he desired Suzie and assaulted her, seduced Michael, and killed

Shep with casual, misdirected power. But that was gone now, burnt out, he was sure . . . and the Khidr force had even corrected his excesses in the event network—for he was very nearly *there*—bringing about, instead, awakenings . . .

At long last he felt in control, of himself.

"Where is this place?" he asked, touching the map.

"Right here, John," smiled the stranger. "Right now! You can enter it anywhere. Only, you can't return again—except extraordinarily."

The map was a one-way membrane, leading to another state.

"You can't afford to modify reality overmuch, John. Or you harm the world before its time. The miracle must always be from outside, from somewhere alien. From this alien city, here."

The stranger laid a finger on the map, at a point where Deacon now recognized the UFO field diagram (which supposedly invoked the monster Forneus, who could teach the operator all arts and sciences) integrated at long last into the over-pattern.

"You too can lose your name now, if you wish." The stranger took him by the arm.

"I wish it," said the one who had been called John Deacon.

The map stretched vastly now, becoming in reality what it had only hitherto been the emblem of. As it became fully real to him, he stepped inside it with the stranger—who was no longer strange at all . . .

Briefly, a sea appears. An empty sea. A sea of Void. It rests in perfect balance. Nothing disturbs it. It contains nothing but its own self. It has no separate parts, no dimensions to define such parts, nor time, nor space to locate them. Every point in it is the same point; empty, it is infinitely dense . . .

He recognizes that sea—and just as he recognizes it:

instantly, a world of time and space projects from it—all the peaks and valleys of existence—as though an infinite Pacific has been drained this very moment.

Life whirlpools out, to know this object-world: mind-islands afloat in a common sea of awareness, all unaware at first of the fluid which is their mutual medium, yet linked in a pattern of

consciousness, in a fluid city with many pathways, many build-
ings, many architectures. This city.

An infinitely branching U-tube links all consciousness. And it
separates it, too, cupping consciousness in separate transmitters:
here, there, there . . .

Every amoeba, every fly, every cat and human being, every
alien being wherever, is an arm of this same multi-branching
tube, 'cutting out' in its separateness all the separate items of the
world. All kinds of linkages are possible to one who knows, across
space-time . . .

The city stands around him, alive, thinking, unfolding. Buildings, avenues, mazes of mind, with doorways yielding into other
lives, other existences.

Free now from ego-binding, yet still aware of a 'self', he can
phase into any other life; become a dinosaur, an insect, a dervish.
Which is one way: the way of the untutored who die into the
void sea and struggle clear, grasping for another time-bound life.
The way of karma. Choosing another way, he can soar far
through the city of mind to where alien minds elsewhere in the
universe, more aware minds, will welcome him. For there exists
a higher consciousness level, he knows now; there are beings on
alien planets circling alien suns who are also, in their minds, inhabitants of this same city, of its palaces and mazes. The city extends itself as they think fit: they who shape the Pattern they
have come to inhabit.

Surely such beings as the Gebraudi must actually exist: on
another world elsewhere, elsewhen, orbiting some alien sun. For
the symbolic visions that Michael experienced in the alien Moonbase, and the symbolic alien presences he met there, surely came
economically from elsewhere in the network of mind which
Deacon had only just begun to tread. Surely the Gebraudi—
living creatures somewhere in space and time, in constant touch
with the higher patterns—must be aware of this city. Down
through the infinite branches of the U-tube, and up again, surely
they can be found. He prepares to soar. To dive.

His companion—who has freed himself many years ago, to
join this network—quickly takes his arm.

"You're still impetuous. Don't be too hasty. Don't enter the mind-space of other branches yet," warns his companion. "It can harm your own separate self, and theirs. You might lose yourself in another's existence. First, learn control. First, learn your duty to your world. You're part of what is unknowable to the world, now. Part of the guiding suction. We have to help the world evolve, isn't that so? You have world enough and time. There are doors and windows to everywhere. When you are ready, re-enter. But remember: you are unknowable. You are an enigma now. You offer no proof, you can only offer clues."

And he nods. He nods. It is so.

So they set out together, at an easy pace, to explore the nearer sector of the city which lies at the centre of the world, and of every world.

John didn't return home.

He became a missing person. Yet Mary was sure he was alive somewhere in the world. Hiding under an alias. Curiously, she bore no regrets. Nor did she resent his childish defection, his abandonment. Occasionally she dreamt of him; when she did so he seemed more intensely present than ever he had previously. Waking did not, strangely, produce a sense of emptiness.

His defection solved several matters. Celia seemed bitterly glad, swiming back again to shore, homeward from the waves she had flirted with, as though she had only wanted the excuse to return. Rob involved himself deeply in his own hobbies, amateur botany, geology. As autumn came round again, he even persuaded his mother to cook some of that year's crop of parasol mushrooms.

Which, in fact, tasted quite delicious.

THIRTY-FIVE

NOW THAT HE'D graduated and been posted to Tanta in the Delta, Salim visited the Cairo headquarters of the Fihi'iya Order less often; however, a small *zawiya*—a lodge of the Order —existed in Tanta too. He suspected he may have been assisted to his post in Tanta, rather than some other town, to help reinforce the Order there.

One weekend in October he came back to Cairo to visit his parents. In the evening he set out for Gamaliya. His father only grumbled mildly, since Salim now had a proper job. On impulse Salim quit his bus in al-Azhar Street, to walk south through the old inner city towards Bab Zuweyla.

That gate of execution, where the last sultan had been crucified, towered darkly over evening crowds, market stalls and tardy taxis, its tenuous minarets at odds with the burly towers beneath. He saw an old woman thrust a scrap of cloth in between the wood and nails of the gate—begging the sympathy of the saint al-Mutawalli who flew from here clear to Baghdad by the power of thought in the days after the gate had ceased to be a place of death and become one of life. A few other rags and ribbons and even some pieces of paper with petitions scribbled on them clung to the ancient wood.

An old white Mercedes drew up. Salim's heart quickened as he recognized the driver, and in the rear the Sheikh himself, speaking to someone.

Surely it was that Englishman, Dr Deacon? He who had been part of the miracle . . . God be praised, thought Salim, recognizing him. He wondered why the Englishman had returned to Cairo. Yet something made him hestitate about intruding. As he watched, Deacon got out of the Sheikh's car. For a moment the

Englishman gazed across the roof of the Mercedes, and met Salim's eyes. His expression looked very different from that of bewilderment, and even anger, which Salim remembered on his earlier visit; it was one of kindly amusement, now. It was a look that Salim remembered well: the glance of the dervish-robed stranger in the courtyard.

Salim waved, but a truck loaded with sacks of potatoes came in between, blocking his view. When it passed, the Englishman had gone.

Sheikh Muradi sat gazing up at the old gateway while humanity thronged past the stationary car in their midst. A taxi hooted, flicked its headlights up, then detoured. And still the Sheikh sat watching, as though the gateway was a gate of dreams.

Sheikh Muradi sat gazing up at the old gateway while

"Sidi—"

The Sheikh blinked. For a moment he seemed not to know who addressed him.

"Ah, Salim—it's you!" Muradi exclaimed. "Thank you. Thank you for helping me to be heedless!" It was too kindly said to be a real rebuke for breaking his train of thought. Muradi opened the rear door and shifted over, offering Salim a lift along into Gamaliya.

As Salim slammed the door, he glanced up at the looming gateway; and as he looked, he saw a bright star flick out of position in its constellation and fly away across the night sky. A fighter plane, no doubt, on patrol.

"Tell me how our brothers are in Tanta!"

"They're all well. The work goes well . . . Master—I saw Dr Deacon just now, sitting where you are sitting. You were speaking to him. How does he come to be in Cairo? Is this like last time?"

"I'm glad you saw him. This time, Salim, he came in full knowledge."

"He saw me too, standing across the street. I thought he looked . . . like the one we met in the courtyard. He had the same expression."

"Ah, but did you see how he *went*?"

238

Salim shook his head. "No. A truck got in the way. He was gone by the time it passed."

The Sheikh squinted up out of the bright tunnel of the street, at the dark speckled sky. "You really didn't see?"

Salim frowned. "How could I? I suppose he went through Bab Zuweyla."

"And no one else saw, either. It isn't time yet for you, Salim. So the world goes on." The Sheikh settled back against the cream upholstery. "Do tell me about the engineering work!"

So Salim told him: about a bridge he'd helped erect across one of the many streams of the Nile delta. It had been a fine bridge. He'd brought a photograph home to show his father; and his father had been proud.

Somewhere else,
Khidr smiled.

DEMCO